SEASON
OF
BETRAYAL

SEASON
OF
BETRAYAL

ROSALYN ZOGRAFOS

TATE PUBLISHING
AND ENTERPRISES, LLC

Published by Tate Publishing & Enterprises, LLC
127 E. Trade Center Terrace | Mustang, Oklahoma 73064 USA
1.888.361.9473 | www.tatepublishing.com

Tate Publishing is committed to excellence in the publishing industry. The company reflects the philosophy established by the founders, based on Psalm 68:11,
"The Lord gave the word and great was the company of those who published it."

Book design copyright © 2011 by Tate Publishing, LLC. All rights reserved.
Cover design by Kate Stearman
Interior design by Sarah Kirchen

Published in the United States of America
ISBN: 978-1-61346-842-5
1. Fiction / Christian / General
2. Fiction / Contemporary Women
12.05.02

CHAPTER I

It was a hot, humid August night. The sound of beating music rang through the air, as did the flashing of lights from a sky filled with fireworks.

"Valerie, I am grateful for you. You did such a wonderful job pulling this birthday party together for me. Thank you," Tim whispered in her ear.

"Tim, I did it because I love you. I wanted your thirtieth birthday to be something you will always remember," Valerie said.

"I love you too. I promise I will never forget this party. How could I?" He kissed her on the left side of the face as more fireworks were set off.

"Wow! That was pretty," Valerie said.

"If you like that, you will like what I have planned for your birthday. One of my coworkers at Ford said he could hook me up. You

will have to wait and see what it is." He turned to look at a man who worked in the cubical next to him at Ford.

"Tim, we need you inside," Carl said, a man about forty, single and heavy set.

"I will be right there. Looks like my co-workers have something for me. Crazy engineers." Tim kissed Valerie and walked into the house.

"Hey, girl. I wondered where you went to," Carmen said, close friend of Valerie's from Church, they had been hanging out for three years or so.

"Hi. Are you having a good time?"

"This is the best party ever. I love the comedian you hired. It was nice of you to invite Tim's guys from work." Carmen looked at Tim as he walked inside and not at Valerie. Valerie saw the movement of Carmen's eyes but did not question her.

"Is the kitchen all cleaned up now?" Valerie asked.

She has never looked at Tim like that.

"Almost. I had two kids finish the job. How did you get the quality of fireworks for the party?" Carmen asked.

"I did an interview with a fireworks wholesaler recently. He felt I had bent over to help him, so he made a deal on fireworks for me. He gave me a wholesale price, lucky me."

"Valerie, I don't know how you do it. Everyone loves you. Nobody ever loves me, no one has ever given me a break." Carmen hung her head low.

"Carmen, I just believe in treating people the way I want to be treated. I didn't do anything special for the man. I just gave an honest story, which the other papers didn't do." What is going on with Carmen? First her eying Tim and now the comments.

"That is what you always say. You didn't do anything special. I don't see anyone bending over to help me. Even my bosses ride me hard," Carmen whined.

"Hey, girls. What is all the commotion about?" Tim asked.

Carmen sternly looked at Valerie. Silence filled the air.

"When the fireworks are over, they want me back inside for a surprise. I have a few things I need to do beforehand, so I will see you girls inside in a little bit." He kissed Valerie on the lips and walked away.

"Like I said, everyone loves you," Carmen snapped and walked away too.

I wonder what her problem is. I have never seen Carmen act out like this. Maybe she is just jealous about the party. Or is it the closeness Tim and I have recently? Tim had brought up his plans to ask me for my hand in marriage, and I told Carmen about that two nights ago.

The phone rang cutting Valerie off from her thoughts.

"Are you Valerie Sharpe?" a male voice asked with trepidation.

"I am." *Oh no, this can't be good, the voice is very serious.*

"I am calling from Mercy Hospital. You have been listed as an emergency contact. There has been a car accident involving your parents. I need you to come to the hospital as soon as you can."

"I will be right there," Valerie said, as she gasped for air. Panic flowed into her heart. *I never dreamed something could or might happen to my parents.*

"Come to the emergency room entrance. Someone will know where to send you once you get there. Have a safe trip." The man hung up.

Valerie was stunned for a few seconds. She was not sure what to do next. *Should I take the time to go home and get fresh clothes? I hope they will be okay. This can't be good.*

She took a deep breath, held it for four seconds, and slowly let it out. *On my way to the apartment for fresh clothes, I'll call my boss, Shelly, a mid-forties woman. Shelly took calls twenty four hours a day.*

Shelly had taken over when Bob, the man who hired her retired, and gave her a heads-up. The new guy they hired last month would jump at the chance for the hot interview. He was fresh out of college but good.

I'll would call the real estate agent in the morning and have him put the closing on hold until I come back.

She grabbed the blanket and her can of pop and walked into the kitchen. She took one last look at the crowd, over fifty people had shown up for Tim's party.

"Guys, it looks like you did a great job cleaning the kitchen. Thanks. Go ahead and put the food in the fridge, I won't be taking it home as planned." Valerie said.

"Thanks," Kimberly said, college student from church. She was new to the church and the group.

Valerie dialed Tim's cell after she hunted for him and Carmen but could not find them. *It is strange Carmen's car was there but Tim's was no longer parked in the garage. What would he have gone out for? She had covered every base*

"Tim, I have an emergency. I have to go to back to the country tonight. My parents were in a car accident I'll call you in an hour," Valerie left on his cell phone voicemail. In an hour most of the guests would have left, it would be past midnight. She would be on the road with still time to talk before arriving at the hospital.

Quickly he called back. "Are they okay?" Tim asked.

"I will find out when I get there. I have put the leftovers in the fridge. Take them Sunday for the singles meeting. I don't know how fast I will be back. I doubt I will be back for Sunday's service. I love you."

"Valerie, I love you too. It will all be okay. Thanks for the wonderful party, and thanks for inviting the engineers I work with. Drive safe. Okay?" He hung up before she could say anything else.

Valerie shut the case to the phone and walked to her car. *That was weird, he sounded preoccupied, but maybe the party was the reason.* Carl, Tim's co-worker from Ford Engineering, was resting on her Volvo front quarter panel.

"I love your car. How long have you had this car?" Carl asked.

"I bought it right after collage. At the time, I felt I deserved a reward. Now it's comfortable and economical," Valerie said. *I wish you of all people would stay away from my car. Can't you see I am dating your friend Tim?*

She stopped short of the trunk. She popped the trunk lid open with her remote.

Well, at least it was clean since I'd been carrying goods around for this party for weeks. The only bad thing is I took my travel bag out of the trunk. I wish I could just go to the hospital. A sixty-minute drive is not my idea of fun at eleven o'clock on a Friday night.

She pushed the lid back down and opened the driver's door with the remote control.

"Why are you leaving so early?" Carl winked and smiled at Valerie.

"I have a family emergency," Valerie answered. *I don't need to explain to him. He kinda gives me the creeps. This was the second time she had met Carl, both times he had tried to find her alone for a few minutes. It wasn't so much of what he said but the looks he gave her.*

"Don't drive too fast," Carl said.

The drive was only two miles but seemed like fifty. Thoughts ran wild in Valerie's head. Something fishy was going on with Carmen. Sitting at the stop light Valerie looked in her rear view mirror. Her porcelain face looked washed out and without life. She was white as a ghost. At least the party was almost over for the most part. It started with dinner being served at six, that was five hours ago.

Valerie grabbed what she would need for a few days from her apartment. Working as a journalist, she knew she had to be prepared for the worst. She took casual clothes and a suit just in case. She had a travel bag packed for emergency trips, so she grabbed it. She never knew where her job would take her at the last minute. She normally carried clothes and the travel bag in her trunk; however, she had no room with the party products in the last few days.

She had an hour plus drive. She plugged in her mp3 player and listened to a new teaching series on wilderness living.

As Valerie approached the hospital, her cell phone rang. She saw that it was Carmen.

"Hey, Carmen. I was going to call you in the morning."

"Tim said you had an emergency and left. Are you okay?"

"Thanks for asking. I'll find out shortly what the deal is. Can I call you in the morning? I am headed into the emergency room now."

"Sure," Carmen said.

"Oh, I almost forgot. Can you take care of my cat until I get back?"

Carmen hung up, not responding to the question.

Stunned by Carmen's response, Valerie put the phone back in her purse after shutting it off. *I have a problem to resolve in the morning. First things first. I wasn't sure before, but something is wrong. I can't believe it, all in one night. I wanted to ask her where she and Tim took off to.* Anger was normally not a part of Valerie, but she sure was feeling plenty of it tonight.

I wonder what her problem is.

She ran into the emergency doors. A receptionist was sitting behind the long, winding desk.

"I'm Valerie Sharpe," She said almost out of breathe.

"Valerie, hi. I'm Karen. If you wait a minute, I'll get the doctor."

"Are my parents going to be okay?"

"I'll let the doctor talk to you." Karen put her finger in the air to silence any more questions. She dialed a number but did not talk.

Within a few minutes, a young doctor entered the emergency room. He was tall with sandy brown hair. His deep blue eyes were soothing.

"Ms. Sharpe, I am Dr. Jonathon Thomas. Please have a seat." He motioned to the chairs by the wall. "I am sorry to tell you this, but your mother did not make it. Your father is in critical condition. He has a punctured lung, a broken leg, and a concussion. He's currently in a coma. I am sorry for your loss."

"Thank you. Can you tell me what happened?" Valerie asked swallowing hard. She had a feeling things weren't good a few days ago. All kinds of emotions swirled through her head.

"The police say that a teenager ran a red light and hit them broadside. Your mother was dead at the scene."

"Do you know if she suffered?" Valerie grabbed the doctors hand holding it tightly.

"It looks like she died on impact. Right now, we don't know how much your father remembers or if he ever will remember. He was in a comma when he arrived here."

"Can I go see him?"

"Sure. I am going to have you put on a face mask and gloves. We have him in the critical care unit now."

ROSALYN ZOGRAFOS

CHAPTER 2

It had been a long night of much waiting, not knowing what would happen. Anxiety filled Valerie, but they had moved Jacob to a critical care step-down unit. He was at least stable. They set his broken leg and put a breathing tube in. He was on oxygen and a feeding tube. Jacob's face was badly bruised. He had some cuts that had to be stitched together on his left leg and left arm.

The doctor said, "go home and get some sleep," that morning.

I'll take him up on that, at least get a shower and change my clothes. I smell of smoke from the fire the night before. New sandals hurt my feet.

As she walked out the hospital doors, she turned her phone on. There were no new messages, but she had three calls she needed to make: Shelly her boss, Carmen, and her real estate agent. Shelly would call her back in a few minutes, the agent was fine with her

news; however, she could not locate Carmen. She even tried the printing company she worked for. They said she had called in sick. So Valerie dialed Tim's number, hoping he could take care of the cat. He did not answer either. *Right now I want to talk to a friendly voice that understands. My head is spinning.*

The hospital was only a few miles from the farm. Driving down the long country road, Valerie started thinking about what she would need to do with the farm. The soybeans were about to be harvested. The animals needed to be fed. They had to be starving. A local restaurant bought the milk from her parent's six cows. They also bought organic eggs from her father. It had been a few years since Valerie was around to know the details. She might have to go through their records to find out where to deliver to.

She pulled up to the wide, circle driveway and pulled her Volvo in close to the house. She grabbed her bags and entered by the way of the kitchen. There were four messages on the answer machine. One was from her aunt, one was from the Green Pea restaurant, one was a sales call, and the other was the neighbor calling to find out if he should feed the animals, noticing lack of movement at the house. Valerie dialed the neighbor first and asked him to feed the livestock. They agreed on a weekly price. She called the Green Pea and found out that she could wait until later in the day to deliver the dairy products. Trying Tim again the phone went to voicemail, she asked him to call her ASAP. She finally dialed her aunt, expecting the call to take more time.

"Aunt Rose, I don't know if you have heard yet, There was a bad accident, Mom is dead and Dad is in critical condition." Valerie hung her head low in shame. *Walking away from her roots when she left for college was wrong and she now knew it. She hadn't even called home for three months. The guilt and shame of wrong priorities hit Valerie in the face. I know I am not feeling the full impact of all that has happened, between the party and my parents.*

"Valerie, what happened?" Excitement rang from Rose's voice.

"They were driving home from a Bible study last night. I guess a young driver had been drinking and ran a stop sign. The Blazer hit them on the front corner panel, spinning the car around. The car hit the driver's door on the telephone pole. The broken glass came in and cut Dad pretty badly. The car must have been going over eighty miles per hour. You know Dad. He must have been driving his normal forty miles per hour," Valerie said, as she grabbed a Kleenex and wiped her nose and eyes. *She felt numb, almost like she were in a bubble with all this going on outside the bubble.*

"Okay. What can I do for you? Do you want me to contact the funeral home?"

"That would be great. You already know them from your husband dying. You know what Mom would like. I never expected her to die before she hit fifty. I can't believe it."

"Now, Valerie, you have been well-trained to handle trauma. Take a deep breath. Now let it out slowly." Rose was her mother's younger sister, a vibrant loving woman, fifty-five years old.

"Thanks, Aunt Rose. I will call you later tonight. I am going to shower, take a short nap, and go back to Mercy hospital."

"I will have the ladies at church pray for you and Jacob. Call me if you need me," Rose said.

"I will." Valerie hung up and looked in the fridge for something to eat. She shut the fridge door. How could she eat with the problems at bay? Her cell phone rang.

"Hello. This is Valerie."

"Valerie, this is Dr. Thomas. I called to let you know that we have stabilized your dad. His heart rate has returned to a normal beat. His breathing is almost stable, so we can take him off the machines soon. He looks like he will make it. I hope I did not disturb your sleep."

"No. I had calls I had to make. Thank you for calling."

"Have a great day." Dr. Thomas hung up.

Well maybe I won't lose Dad too. I have always shown bright in the star light, so why do I feel like such a failure right now? The ones I have put first are nowhere around. The ones I loved I put aside for what? Dad, I need you to pull through. I could really use one of your hugs right now. I feel completely lost.

Valerie still had not heard from Tim or Carmen, so she dialed both cell phone numbers only to get voice mail. So she tried another woman she had a few lunches with from the church group.

"Ceil, this is Valerie. Did I call at a good time?" Valerie questioned hesitantly.

"Why, sure. What can I do for ya?" Ceil was almost fifty a little on the heavy side but a nice lady.

"Ceil, my parents were in an accident last night. My mother died, my father is unconscious, and I have been trying to get a hold of both Tim and Carmen. I can't get either to answer, which is weird." Valerie paced the floor. She didn't want to admit to anyone what she sensed or what Carmen's responses had been last night.

"When I left last night, they were the only two left. Carmen was hanging all over Tim as if she was trying to trap him or something. I am really sorry about your kin. I will put a prayer request in at the group meeting Sunday. Is there anything I can do for you?"

"If I can't get Carmen or Tim to respond, I might need you to feed my cat. I will pay you," Valerie said softly, feeling guilty for asking someone she hardly knew.

"I am in transition right now. I gave my apartment up for a foreclosed home I had a deal on. Now it looks like I am not getting the home. I will pay you to stay at your apartment for a couple of months. It would be a win-win situation. I need to be out in a week and have no idea where to go. Do you have any interest?"

"Let me think about it for a day. I have already given Tim and Carmen keys. I don't have any spare keys around." *That might just work out, I may not have a choice in the matter.*

"Listen, Val. I can go to the print shop and get the key from Carmen if you want me to. Just call me. I have to run. My boss is motioning me to come in his office." She worked as a secretary at a vet clinic. Saturday mornings were normally busy.

Valerie was stunned by the words she just heard. *It can't be true. Carmen is not a flirt, and Tim is trustworthy. Or is he? Valerie questioned. What has Tim really shared with me? What has he really done for me? Most of their nice dates had been provided by her perks as a* journalist from the Columbus Dispatch. Tim had been elusive at times. We went to his department Christmas party and hers; both of those events were provided by our employers. In June we had gone with the church group camping, but we each bought our own tickets.

Valerie tried to relax and take a nap. She could not relax. It was now mid-morning. She paced the bedroom floor. *Should I keep calling Tim or Carmen?*

She tried one more time to get some rest. Her thoughts kept returning to last night. Flashbacks of small bits flowed together, the fun and laughter, the fireworks, Carmen looking at Tim, the phone call that ended her time at the party she had hosted. Pieces of the drive back home came up. She could not silence her mind.

"Mom, I am so sorry. And now I can't bring you back. I can't take back all the neglect I have shown you." Valerie sobbed. "I can't take back not returning the call you made to me last week."

She pulled her journal out. It had been a long time since she had jotted down thoughts and feelings. She knew how to plow through anything but this.

August 3, 2009

The longest and hardest night of my life. I am so torn up by guilt. My parents were coming from a bible study and a drunk driver hit them. What justice is there in that? Last year Bill died serving our country. What did I do? Nothing.

If that isn't bad enough, Tim and Carmen are getting chummy. I thought I could trust them. How far did they go. Is it true they were together? The evidence looks pretty strong they were. Tim and I have always talked a few times a day. Now he won't even take my calls. I am so hurt by what I thought was my true friends.

I don't know how to help my dad. I know so little about what has been going on here at *the farm. Right now I feel like a failure. I feel like I have made so many bad choices by putting my career first.*

Why did I hate this life so much that I walked away from the only security I really had to start with? What was so special about Columbus, Ohio, anyway? How could I hate a life so bad to abandon my parents?

Valerie set the pen down. Somehow she would have to work through the negative emotions flooding her mind.

Even if her dad came out of the coma, he could not go back to work with a broken leg and the other injuries. She would need to either hire help to take care of him or get the house ready for him to get around. From her experience, an accident of that velocity took months to recover from. Her father might never totally recover. In her thought process, the cell phone rang. It was her boss, Shelly returning the call.

"Valerie, will you be back in a day or two ? I have a lead story I want you to run with."

"Shelly, I should request a family leave. I am going to be stuck here for a while. My mother died in the accident, and Dad's not doing well. Since Bill died last year in Iraq, I am the only one to take care of things."

"I'm so sorry for your loss. This has to be really hard for you. Do me and yourself a favor, don't worry about anybody but you today. You are great at taking care of what is at hand but neglecting yourself."

"You are right. I will try to do that"

" I will put the request in for you. You will be paid for three months. After that, you have to make a decision to quit or come back to work. Let me know if I can do anything else for you."

"I guess that is fair. Thanks, Shelly. I will miss all of you guys." Valerie felt relief flow over her. *That gives me three months, that was more generous than I thought the paper would be. Family leave paid 75% of the wages, I should be OK. I hope dad is doing well by then.*

ROSALYN ZOGRAFOS

"Call me with the funeral details. I want to be there, and the company will send flowers. Valerie, take care of yourself. You hear?"

"I am trying. I have dealt with everyone else's trauma but never my own."

"What about when your brother Bill died?" Shelly asked.

"We were never close. He was ten years my senior. It wasn't a big deal at that time. Once I started my career, I never looked back. I feel bad. I left my mom in the dust. Now she is gone. I can't change it. I won't fail my dad this time."

"Val, you are a good kid. I've always liked you. You have always been focused and driven. You are one of my best journalists I have ever worked with, Bob hired the right gal five years ago."

"What has that gotten me? What should mean the most to me is now gone. My two best friends are like vapor. When I need to count on them, they are gone."

"Val, you got used. You had the in on many things. You were cool to be around. Think about it—free tickets to all the games, shows and entertainment in town. You gave many a free ride. You are an easy going gal. Now it is time to take care of Val."

"Thanks. I'm not sure I know how to do that."

"I think your new situation is going to force you into doing it, like it or not. I am much older than you. Trust me on this one. The end will prove to be good. Right now, you have emotions going all over the board—and rightly so. The source you need to tap into is God. Let him be your shelter in time of need. Let him have the guilt and shame or it will totally destroy your life. Call me with the details. I have to take a call." Without any delay, she was gone.

Valerie was twenty-six years old when Jim, her brother, died. Bill never made a commitment to God. Val didn't know where he would spend eternity. She knew her mother lived a right life. She was a gentle, loving woman. It was the gentleness Valerie had walked away from—not because she was offended but because her mother never pushed her way. She never manipulated situations or people. Valerie had gone off to school made friends and hated the quiet life on the farm, so she never returned. She came home a few times for holidays, but that had stopped in the last two years. She was home for Jim's funeral and then went back to the city. She loved life in Columbus—the concerts, the art shows, and the church activities. Living out in the middle of nowhere had been boring as a child. The one good thing it taught her to work hard. As a child, she was up at 5:30 a.m. to feed the animals, and she had to feed them after school each day. In the summer, she bailed hay, which was a hot and sticky job. She remembered the fun she had when Bill would toss her from the loft into a pile of hay. She must have been four or five years old then. Bill had her mother's nature; he was quite and gentle. He was the compliant child. He did whatever they asked him to. He would never have ended up enlisting and leaving the farm, had it not been for a huge offer to pay him double for one year of service. He was a talented equipment mechanic. They offered him nine thousand dollars a month to repair equipment. A bomb was dropped in the building he worked in, killing him and three other men.

How could I be so insensitive to those who have been the closest to me? I wish I would have called mom and come home more often. I hope she knew I loved her......

The cell phone rang; Valerie was awakened by the loud music. It was Ceil.

"I have your key. I ran into Carmen at the grocery store. I told her you were trying to call her and Tim. I don't want to upset you any more than you already are. She gladly handed the key to me and said good luck. She walked away with no more comments."

"That is strange. None of this with Tim or Carmen makes any sense to me. Well, anyway, do you know where I live?"

"No."

"I am at 135 Water street. It is off 23 North." Valerie wiped her sleepy eyes. She must have fallen asleep.

"I have a GPS. I think I can find it. So what is the apart-ment number?"

"Oh yeah. That would be helpful. Sorry. I am out of it. I am on the third floor, apartment three. The cat food is under the sink. I think the trash is full. If you could take it out, I would appreciate it. Eat whatever you want, and toss anything you can't eat. I will talk to you in the morning. Hey, thanks for waking me up. I need to get back to the hospital to see Dad."

"I will call you at eight if that is good," Ceil asked?

"That works for me. If I am in the hospital, the phone will be shut off. So leave a message and I will call you back. Thanks, Ceil. I owe you one"

"I think it is me who owes you. Good night."

"Good night." Valerie stood up a little too fast and found that she had poor balance. She sat back down on the bed and steadied her body. *At least something is working out for me. Ceil is old enough to be my mother. She had been through her own string of hardships. Her husband had a heart attack and died a few years ago, they were unprepared for the loss of his income. She had to sell their home and go back to work full time. One thing I know for sure about Ceil is her passion for God.*

CHAPTER 3

It had been a week since her mom's funeral. Valerie had not heard from Carmen or Tim. At this point she had given up on either of them returning her calls. Ceil had just left her parents' house with her mail and more clothes. They sat and talked for hours on the back deck of the farm house until it was very late. The crickets were chirping soothing the country air. It was Saturday night, and Valerie wanted to go to where the accident had occurred ten days ago. The sheriff's report made no sense to her. She wanted to see with her own eyes what it might have looked like that night, from the other driver's viewpoint. As she neared the road where Ridgewood intercepted, she saw the road take a curve to the left for a short distance. There was no way the driver could see if another car was at the intersection if he was driving too fast. There were plenty of signs to mark the intersection though. Marks crossed the

road into the brim. Debris from the accident was still on the road. The place of impact was very clear. In the morning, Valerie would go look at the totaled cars. She was told they were both at Bernie's, a local storage yard. The place was charging sixty-five dollars a day for storage. The insurance company had not closed the case. The sheriff's report made it clear that Tom Biden was the one at fault. The deputy told her that it was normal procedure when a death occurred to keep the file open longer and investigate everything. Valerie, disheartened, drove her Volvo back home. She started feeling dizzy again. She made up her mind to call the doctor on Monday. Dizziness had been going on for almost two weeks. She made it home safely, parking the car out by the garage. She didn't want to advertise her car in the driveway, although she doubted anything would happen out there in the country.

Valerie wanted her mother's comfort. She put on her mother's nightgown and slipped into her bed. The dainty scent drew tears. She couldn't imagine life without her mom. Her mother was a simple woman. She didn't wear much jewelry or fashion clothing. Her only makeup was powder. On a special occasion, she used a light pink lipstick. She sewed most of her dresses, but on weekdays, she wore jeans and t-shirts on the farm. They could take the wear of a dirty environment. Sweet sleep swept over Valerie. She slept for eight hours and was awakened by the rooster across the street. It was her day to feed the animals. She had no clean clothes to put on, so she dressed in a pair of her mom's jeans and a yellow t-shirt. She would need to do some laundry. She wanted to find a church to worship at. She hated the Methodist church she had gone to as a kid. It was boring, and the people were cold. She missed her mega church in Columbus. It was full of life and excitement. They had activities five days a week. With her career, she was not around for most of the church activities but always had something to do when she wanted to. Mondays and Thursdays nothing was scheduled normally at church. Those were nights she and Tim usually went out to dinner and a movie, or she cleaned her apartment and did laundry.

After feeding the animals, she sat down and started writing thank-you cards. Several from work had attended the services. A few had come from her church. Her aunts and uncles were all there—all three of them. She had five cousins attend, and plenty of locals. Her parents were well respected in the small community. Everyone knew each other and their business. The Methodist church had put on a nice little luncheon. It was similar to ones her mother had done for many.

Aunt Rose pulled into the driveway in her Ford Explorer. Unlike Valerie's mother, Aunt Rose was spunky. She was full of life and energy. She came bouncing into the kitchen.

"It is time to get you out of here. Go put on a dress. We are going to church. A new one has come to town. You are going to go with me. I won't take no for an answer. I promise you will love the people. They are warm and friendly." Rose took her by the arm and pulled her up.

"Aunt Rose, why didn't you call me? You know I hate surprise visits. It makes me feel controlled."

"I figured you might say no. You are depressed and need to meet new people. You will be here for a while. It is time to have a support system. Grief will kill you if you let it. We can't have that, now can we?"

"Okay. I will put on the outfit I wore to the funeral."

"Val, do you have anything else with you?"

"I will have to look at what Ceil brought me last night. I should have more church clothes."

"That was kind of her."

Aunt Rose followed her to the bedroom, where the clothes were hanging. She barged her way in and sorted through the clothes.

"Here. This one. It is nice and summery. It is bright and will cheer you up. The soft silk will bring you comfort. The dark suit you had on is depressing. Here, put this on." She pulled through the box on the floor and found sandals to match, handing them to Val.

"Aunt Rose, can you tell me more about my mom?'

"What do you want to know, honey?"

"Did she get upset when Bill died?"

"That tore her up something fierce. She became bitter after his death. She wrote letters to the government, which made her more upset. Your mom has not been the same since. Did you know she was diagnosed with liver cancer a few days before the accident?"

"What? Get out of here. She had cancer? She never told me." Valerie slipped the dress on. *Not surprised, her mother had called her a few days before the accident and she failed to return the call.*

"She felt you would get upset. She had not made up her mind if she was going to have surgery or not. Your mom was depressed, like you are now."

"I understand why you want to get me out now. I wish I would have been supportive to her. I lived my own life without any regard to her feelings for too many years."

"It is not too late for your dad. You know he is a good man. He loves you very much. He let you go so you could live your life. He too wasn't happy that you took off and never came back."

"Aunt Rose, do you think he will flip when he comes to and finds his wife dead?"

"Val, he is a solid man. He is stable. He's handled Bill's death pretty well. He mourned and let God have the pain. He dealt with it better than your mom did. She held it inside, let it eat away at her. That is why she had cancer. She allowed hate and unforgiveness to rot her body."

"What makes you say that? The two might not be connected in any way," Valerie said impudently. *How dare you! Cancer and unforgiveness, never.*

"I will show you the study I did on disease. It will bring a new awareness to you. Let's go before we are late. We can read later."

"Who is driving?" Valerie asked walking out to where the two vehicles were parked.

"I will. This is my treat. I have a new place to take you out for lunch when the service is done. The lady opened this summer. Get in."

"Sounds great!" Valerie got in the Explorer, buckling her seat belt.

"I think you will like the service. The leaders are a young couple from out of state. They have joined with a few churches in the area to help them. The group is young. They are all close to your age. The music is hip. The services are an hour." Rose drove out of the driveway, making a left.

"I didn't think there were any churches around here with many young people. I would love to meet some down-to-earth young adults. I could use some real friends, not users." *It was painful to even think about all the events that had happened. The pain of betrayal only added to the pain of the loss of her mother.*

"Val, I thought you had some great friends?"

"When tragedy hits, you find out who your true friends are. I thought they were my friends. Aunt Rose, I had a coworker check into a rumor I had been given about my boyfriend and my best friend. I found out they are together now." Valerie stared out the SUV's window. "I am so hurt by the betrayal. Neither called me since the night I got the call about the accident. They won't take my calls, so I stopped calling."

"How long did you date this guy?" Aunt Rose made a sharp left turn causing Valerie to slide in her seat.

"We have been dating for ten months now." *Maybe I knew a few months ago that it wouldn't work. I did get sucked in when Tim brought up getting engaged in the future.*

"Where did you meet? Valerie, I asked you: Where did you meet?"

"I am sorry. I was going off in my own thoughts, I met him at my church. We have fifty singles. We were at a lunch after service last summer. We started talking, and a few months later, we started dating. It started out very slow. Now that I have been away, I see he wasn't really in love with me but was lonely. If he moved on so fast to another woman, he wasn't worth me being with the rest of my life. But it does hurt. I trusted him with my life. I would never have done such a nice party for his birthday if I didn't think we had a future."

"That is wise on your part. I am sorry for the hurt you are experiencing. I can hear the pain in your voice and see it on your face."

"It is painful. I sometimes wonder if it is not more painful than Mom dying. Mom didn't betray me. Carmen stole my boyfriend the same night I left town. The word on the street is they spent the night together. Tim and I had agreed that purity was important for God to bless our union," Valerie burst into tears.

"Has Carmen ever done anything like that with other men?"

"She was married for a couple years and then got a divorce. She said he was controlling and abusive. She has been single for three years now. I have not known her to date anyone since. I didn't know her when she was married. We started hanging out a couple years ago. She and I have spent a lot of time together. We have even gone to Florida together a couple times. Of course, they were trips I won from the Dispatch."

"Sounds like that was all it was—hanging out. When you get to be my age, you know that true friends are few and hard to come by. You will have many acquaintances but not friends in your life. The friends are worth gold. A friend doesn't mind if you wake them up in the middle of the night for an emergency; they are always there for you."

"Aunt Rose, have you ever been betrayed like that before?"

"When I was in high school, I had a classmate who tried to take my boyfriends. She took two from me. I don't know why she picked on me. She would seduce them and let them go. Val, I doubt that Carmen wants Tim. I would guess she will let him go in a short time. She was jealous of you. She did what it took to bring destruction to you. You can't let her steal your joy. Let God have it, and pray for God to bless her. God will bless you and bring you a man who can't be tricked. If Tim could be drawn away so easily, he is not worth your time."

"I know that to be the truth, but how do I let it all go?" Valerie took the box of Kleenex aunt Rose handed her, wiping her face and eyes. She put the box back on the floor behind the seat.

"You will have to ask God for his help. Only God can help you release things like that. Here we are."

"They meet in a school building?"

Aunt Rose put a pink lipstick on looking in the mirror to see if she looked presentable then turned to look at Valerie. "They will build a building sometime in the future."

"I am not unhappy, just surprised. I like the feeling of meeting in a school. It is less religious and opens up for neutral worship. Buildings can get in the way. I hate it when all they do is pester you for more money for this and that every year. 'We need a new gym. Give all your money to us.' To me, it seems like it turns ministry into a business, not worshiping God."

"Wow, Val. Is that why you never came back home?"

"No. It was selfishness. I guess that is why I have allowed people like me to be my friends. I was looking for a good time. My motive wasn't to secure true friendships."

"You always had a giving heart. I wouldn't say it's selfishness."

"The sanguine in me has to have fun. I was drawn to being around people my own age. I just wish I would have seen the immaturity it bred."

"Don't you think you are being a little hard on yourself?"

"Aunt Rose. right now I am so angry with myself. I have so many regrets." Valerie struggled to hold the tears back again.

The two walked in the side doors of the school. Three adults were there to greet them.

"Nice to have you worship with us." A man about forty years old handed her a gift bag filled with chocolates, a pen, and a mug. She saw that it had a sheet to fill out for visitors.

"Thank you."

"Do you live around here? I don't remember meeting you before," the short fat man said.

"My parents live here. This is my Aunt Rose."

"Hi. I am Mason. It's nice to have you. Hope you enjoy the service. I hope you come back soon.

"Thanks, Mason," Rose said, grabbing Valerie's arm.

"I bet there are several nice young people your age that you can become friends with soon."

"I hope so. This time I will be more selective of who I let in."

The two walked in and found open seats in the middle of the left side. Pamphlets lined each seat. The stage was set up with drums and two guitars. The band was playing "All Because of Jesus" by Free. After they sat down, the lights were turned down. The screen displayed the music to "Let it Fade" by Jeremy Camp. Several were singing on stage. A young man about thirty years of age stepped up to the mic and introduced himself as Damian Wade, head pastor. He briefly told the story of the new church that had been planted in the backwoods of Ohio. He introduced his worship leader who started them off with singing a song. Damian returned to the mic and announced the offering, before having the congregation stand, and read from Ephesians 6 on obeying your parents. As he was speaking, God arrested Valerie's heart, convicting her of her behavior toward both her parents. She knew that she was like the prodigal son that had returned. She had put her career and friends way above a place she should have. At that moment, she was thankful for Tim and Carmen getting together, for she knew deep in her heart that if she married Tim, her life would have stayed were it was. Her values had been shifting since she had come home less than two weeks before. The pastor closed in prayer and said that if anyone wanted prayer to come down to the front after the service. Valerie wanted to get her heart right with God before she left. She motioned to her aunt that she was going down for prayer and would be back.

CHAPTER 4

It was mid September. It had been raining for seven days. Some of the crop hadn't been harvested in time and underwater. The insurance company was bucking paying out on the accident. Valerie found her parents had taken a loan to be paid back in the next few weeks. She used her paychecks to pay all the bills she could, but money was getting tight. She sublet the apartment to Ceil since her dad was not improving and was still in a coma.

Valerie made an appointment to see the pastor at the Seeker Church. She needed quick advice. In the weeks she had been home, she had grown to see life from a new vantage point. She surrendered her life that day at church. She spent much of her time at the hospital, reading the Bible. She was letting go of her will to control her life, which was difficult.

She arrived a few minutes early, so she prayed before the appointment. She got the feeling that she was wasting her time. She hoped she was wrong. She never was gifted spiritually before, but she had a gut feeling that things were not what they appeared at that church.

"Valerie, I need to grab a bag from my car. I will be right in. You can take a seat in my office if you'd like."

"I will wait out here if that is okay."

"Sure. Please yourself." Damian turned and walked back to his Escalade.

He had a way of escaping the answer to many questions. Valerie hoped he would be open and honest with her.

Damian walked to her car door. "I am ready now."

"Thank you for seeing me," Valerie said, looking into his light blue eyes.

"You sounded upset. I don't know what I can do for you," he said almost as if asking her a question.

"Pastor, I haven't told many this, but my parents had a fatal car accident almost six weeks ago. My mother died on the scene, and my father is still in the hospital in a coma. I need to know how to proceed. I am having trouble with the insurance company. My parents got a bill from the IRS, I don't know what to do with. I have six weeks before I have to be back to work." Sobbing and pulling a Kleenex from her purse, Valerie wiped her eyes.

"I am not trained in legal matters. If I were you, I would talk to an attorney. One of our men here is an accountant. I'll get you his card. Maybe he can help with financial matters. He volunteers for us doing our paperwork. I would get some counseling for the emotional trauma. Is there anything else I can do for you?"

Valerie was shocked. She never expected it to be like a fast food place, in and out in a couple of minutes. *At least I have a number I can call. Hmm, it is Mason, the older heavy set guy I met at the front door my first day.*

"Right now, I don't know if I am coming or going."

"I am really not trained for counseling. I wish I had some way to respond to you that would be helpful. I am sorry for your losses. I have a luncheon with my wife. I hope you have a great day."

Damian stood up, walking her to the door.

Valerie shook his hand and walked out. She touched the door to her Volvo, anger boiling up with tears following. *We could have done that on the phone.* She started her car, putting it in reverse. *The man couldn't give me but five minutes. What is a church for? I could rip that man's head off right now. The first time I ask a pastor for help, and I get pushed aside. He could have at least prayed for me. My intuition was accurate, this was a waste of my time.*

As she was backing up, she heard in her spirit, "My daughter, I am enough. Come to me for help." *For me to get over this anger I will need to come to you, but I don't know how.*

She understood the feeling she'd had earlier. God was starting to speak to her. Being in the country with no one around but nurses and doctors at the hospital, she had more time to be still. She was good at listening in interviews but had never taken the time to listen to God. She had a choice to make—to go home or the hospital. She quickly decided to go home and spend it with God. That morning, she quietly listened for God's voice, knowing she needed to apply for a power of attorney and maybe a guardianship. She called the court to find out the procedure. It was pretty simple. She needed to pick up the paperwork at the court and have the doctor sign it and say that her father was in a coma. They recommended that she do a guardianship. They asked for forty dollars to process the paperwork They told her that once she turned it back in, the judge needed to sign it. The paperwork was then mailed back to her. By the end of the week, she would be able to address the issues.

Before leaving she quickly wrote in her journal:

September 8

Lord, somewhere I overheard the saying that anger and fear lead to sin. I know I am feeling both anger and fear. I do not want to sin, nor do I want to come under judgment because I judged one of your own. Help me, God, to really work through all the dysfunctional thoughts and behavior I have allowed. Today I could have hurt that man at the church. I know that is not right.

I am stricken with guilt and shame. To the point I don't want to look anyone in the eye. That is not my nature. I feel useless here.

I am so angry at Tim and Carmen. God, it feels like all the layers together are making each piece hurt even more. How can I miss Tim but hate him at the same time?

Valerie set the journal on the bed, grabbing her purse. She felt calmer now she had gotten the horrible feelings down on paper.

Driving to the courthouse, she picked up the paperwork she would need and went off to see the doctor. *My timing should be good. The doctor does his afternoon rounds from three to five.*

She had to take a detour, for the country road north of the farm was flooded, so she went south, taking Pikeway back around to connect back to Route 23. It didn't take any more time than going the other way.

When she got to the hospital parking lot, she found a parking spot up by the entrance doors. She pulled in, shut the car off, and saw the older man from church coming out the doors.

I forgot his name. It started with a M. Was it Matt or Mark or… yes, it was Mason.

"Hi, Mason."

"Hey, Valerie. I never expected to see you here. What are you coming here for?"

ROSALYN ZOGRAFOS

"My dad's here. What about you?" Valerie asked.

"A friend was hurt last night. He is going to be fine. They kept him overnight. They found a heart condition they are treating. I came to pick him up, but the doctor said that he needed to stay another night," Mason said, intently watching her.

Valerie saw his eyes steadfast on hers. "Mason, see you around."

I hope I am reading something in to his looking at me, he's way too old.

Valerie proceeded to enter the hospital. She stopped abruptly to think about where she should start. She looked left then right seeing Dr. Thomas walking toward her.

"Doctor, you are just the man I need to talk to," Valerie said with excitement.

"Good. I need to talk to you too."

"I have the paperwork for the courts to get a guardianship for my dad." Valerie handed him the documents.

"That's good. Your dad awakened this afternoon. I told the nurses to call you. He is partially aware of what is around him but not totally there yet. He will need extensive rehabilitation and therapy before he will be back to normal again." He gave her thumbs up.

The doctor signed the guardian paperwork handing it back to Valerie.

"Thanks, Doctor."

"Valerie, do you feel like a coffee? I could use a break. That was my next stop."

"Sure."

"The cafeteria is on the bottom floor. Follow me and we can get right in. It is what doctors call our secret passageway." Swiping his card across a reader, an elevator a few feet from where they were opened up. "You first." He stood aside and let her enter the elevator. He stepped in behind her and pushed the correct button for the cafeteria. "Valerie, I'm impressed with how well you have handled your dad's illness. Most young adults would have fallen apart by now."

"You do what you have to do. I'm a journalist, trained to handle difficult times. Sometimes we are on location for days without sleep. A coworker of mine worked in New York at the time of 9/11. She worked three days straight without sleep."

"That's not healthy for anyone."

"Doctor, didn't you pull some all-nighters in your days?"

"I guess I did, but I don't do that anymore. I try to treat my body better than that.

"So my dad should be up and running in a few weeks?" Valerie said changing the subject.

"Valerie, don't get too hasty. Your dad just woke up an hour ago. He's not fully aware of what is going on around him."

"Doctor, will he know me?"

"I doubt it. He doesn't know who he is right now. We will be running tests on him in the morning. I do not want you to have your hopes too high the first time you see him. Now, Valerie, I do think he will recover. It is normal for some who have been in comas to not know who they are at first. I know you have the patience to deal with this gently."

"Should I be spending more time at the hospital now?"

"I think for the first few days, that would be a good idea. Tell your dad things you remember to jar his memory. I would not suggest that you bring your mother or the accident up yet."

"And to think I thought you brought me down here for coffee to get a date with me," Valerie teased.

"First things first. So how about dinner at my place, let's say Saturday at eight? I will make you the best salmon you have ever eaten."

"I was kidding. You are on, I could use a change of pace. Now how will I find your place?"

"I will pick you up at the farm at eight. You are staying at your parents farm, aren't you?"

"Yes, I am."

I always hated everyone knowing everything about one another here. That was one of the reasons I moved away.

"Dress casual. If the weather permits, I will take you out on the lake for a boat ride."

"You have a boat?"

"It is not a big one, just a thirty-footer. I live on the lake. It was my parents' place. I bought it when my dad retired. They moved to Florida last year."

"Was your dad a doctor too?"

"He was a cardiologist."

"Sounds like we will have fun. I will see you Saturday night then. I am looking forward to the night away." *It will be nice to have an intelligent conversation.*

"Valerie, I am looking forward to the beautiful company." He shook her hand while watching every movement of her body.

Valerie walked back to the elevator.

"I will go back upstairs with you. The coffee is too strong today anyway. Have you made any long-term plans?"

"Doctor—"

"Valerie, call me Jon."

"Okay, Jon. I don't know what I am doing yet. Getting out of the forest, I see what I could not see before. I think my job had me snowballed. I believed whatever they told me to believe. I think God allowed this shaking in my life to change me."

"Valerie, God has a way of getting us on track. That's for certain."

"This has been a season of seeing things I never saw before. I had fun and worked hard, but, Jon, I abandoned my family in the process."

"Sounds like you're growing."

"I know I am. Painfully."

The elevator button sounded, and the door opened.

I wonder why he asked me how long I would be here. I hope he doesn't think I am date material.

Valerie headed out the elevator shaft to the left. Her father was in room 424. She braced herself for the shock that could come. When she walked in the door, he was fumbling with his fingers. Fluid was drooling down his cheek.

"Dad, how are you feeling?"

Her dad turned to the place he thought he heard the voice but was not looking at Valerie.

Valerie walked to the direction he faced. "Dad." She waved her hand in his face.

He smiled, saying nothing.

Valerie pulled her long auburn hair back, thinking, *What should I say? Words have always come so easy for me. But I have never been placed in a situation so personal before. I feel ashamed for not being there for dad when Bill died and mom found out she had cancer. I don't want to slip and tell dad his wife died.*

"Dad, I love you. I was so worried about you.... Your flowers are very pretty." Valerie bent over to look who had sent them. Tears began to flow; emotions that had been pent up couldn't be stopped. She couldn't even read the card. Turning toward her dad, she wiped her face on her shirt. The pain to see her dad crippled and unable to talk was almost more than Valerie could bear. She was good in crisis but fell apart when alone. She didn't want her dad to see her like this. She didn't want the questions of why he was there to come up.

"Dad, do you remember when you made me a dollhouse when I was seven? You placed it under the Christmas tree."

There was no response.

"Dad, are you hungry yet?"

Again, there was no response.

"I remember when you took us out camping in the woods one year. I got lost and you had to call the ranger to find me. Dad, I was so scared out in those woods. I felt so all alone. I also remember you reading me bedtime stories each night, and each Christmas, you bought the advent candle and we would do a Bible study each week." Valerie bent over the bed rail and kissed his forehead. " I loved it when you would read us the Bible with the fire crackling behind you. I miss those days. You are such a good dad." Valerie went to the window, looking down at the front entrance below. "I remember when we painted the barns and the house and I dumped paint all over everything. Bill never let me live that down. I also remember when you taught him to play soccer and baseball." *I haven't thought about these things in forever. I need to find positive things to say to Dad.*

"What about that time you took me to a daddy's dance at the park?" Valerie squeezed his hand. He gave her no response. "Do you remember when we did the pig roast and invited the neighbors over? What did happen that night, Dad? I thought I remember that someone took the pig roaster and you had to pay for it." She laughed at the memory.

She squeezed his hand again, and he squeezed back. He had a tear running down his face. No words came out of his mouth. She wiped the drool off his chin and took his hand again. This time, she rubbed it affectionately. She pulled a comb out of her purse and combed his hair. He had red hair much lighter than hers. He had a few gray hairs forming but still looked young and handsome. She wanted to wash his face. She had a face cleanser sample in her purse. She found a washcloth in the bathroom. She turned on the hot water and ran the washcloth under the water. She rang it out and took it over to her father. She poured the cleanser on the cloth and wiped his face. She turned the washcloth over and took the cleanser off, touching his face gently to see if it was clean. Again, he had a tear run down his cheek but spoke no words. Valerie sat there for hours, talking gently to her dad. When he looked like he was getting tired, she kissed him good night and went home.

CHAPTER 5

September 25:

I finally got the letter showing guardianship for Dad and favor with the IRS. They agreed to a lesser amount. Lord, I can see your hand of protection, favor, and mercy. I am ever so grateful for your love. I also thank you, Lord, for helping me find the life insurance policies. Both Mom and Dad are entitled to a payout. I can see your hand of protection, Lord. I hope someday the pain will diminish and I can use it for good for someone else. I guess I really can't be angry with Damian. He has never suffered a great loss before. You can't give away what you don't have. Meeting new people and

remembering old people and things from a long time ago has shaken me. I wish I could go back and rewrite a few chapters of my life.

Valerie set the pen down. *My memories are good of the times and people here. So why did I run?* She turned the computer on to check her e-mails.

Valerie set her computer back on the dresser. She had assurance that things were going to work out. She could finally rest. While sleeping she had a dream. In the dream, she was walking to the field to check the harvest. The sun at a noon position in the sky. Walking toward the field, the crops parted like the Red Sea did. She walked in and the crops had given off larger yield than normal. The size was at least double what should have been expected. She gathered a few kernels but couldn't handle more than that without a basket. Taking the few kernels inside, she boiled and tasted the soybeans, finding that the flavor was beyond her expectation. In the next scene in the dream, she had a flatbed full of the crop, and the field was still full. Awaking, she wrote the dream down in her journal. She didn't know the meaning for sure but knew it was good. She had no way of knowing how to interpret the dream. She doubted Damian, the pastor at the seeker church, would know. He seemed too self absorbed in his own life, she wanted to finish that nap. Trying to fall back asleep, she couldn't stop thinking about the dream. The scripture that nurse gave her a few days before came back to mind. She reread the scripture. This time, she read the entire chapters of fifty-four and fifty-five of Isaiah. She found great comfort in the scriptures, that many of the words came to life. God's character deeper than she had seen in the past. She felt that her dry ground was being watered, for all the seeking she had done seemed to be releasing a new level of awareness of God. She fell back asleep, awakening at seven thirty that night. She quickly arose and brushed her hair, put on some simple makeup, and changed her clothes. The weather had cooled down in the last couple of days. She chose a layered look. Jon had said to dress casual. She put on jeans and a blue

ROSALYN ZOGRAFOS

t-shirt with a light sweater. She wore her gold hoops and a simple necklace. She sprayed Beautiful from Estée Lauder on her neck and ate a few pecans to hold her over.

At promptly 8:00 p.m. she heard a car in the driveway, an old '68 Camaro. The paint job was ghost paint of blue, green, and purple. The angle of light determined the color you saw. She would have expected a doctor to drive a newer car. She had to remember that she was out in the country. The doctors in an rural area might not make the big bucks they do in the city. He's driving a hot rod, I would never have guessed that out of him. I would have guessed him to be more conservative than that.

Jon knocked on the back door. Valerie answered it, surprised as she opened the door. Jon was carrying a large, exotic bouquet of flowers, the kind you see in the Caribbean countries.

"This, is for you. Why don't you put them in a vase before we leave?"

"Doctor, you're so sweet. I love these kind of flowers. How did you know?"

"Every woman I know loves beautiful flowers. You are a unique woman, so I figured you would like unique flowers."

Valerie pulled a special vase from the china cupboard.

"Thank you, Jon. I really do like unique things. As a journalist, one of the perks is I get to see places most people don't. I get invited to five-star restaurants and win gift cards on a regular basis. My aunt thinks that is why some people were my friends."

"I will tell you that I will be your friend without all that."

"Right now that is all I can want is friends. I have no idea what tomorrow will bring."

"None of us knows. The Bible tells us that we shouldn't worry about tomorrow for it has enough worries of its own. Your dad is gaining color and strength, Valerie. Don't worry about him; he is a strong man."

"Thank you. It's been about six weeks. I hope he recovers soon."

"We are doing all we can for him."

"I know, Jon. Do you spend much time at home?"

"Not really. I spend a lot of time at the hospital and with friends. I am hoping that you will be friends with me."

"I could use some good friends. I have made mistakes letting the wrong people into my heart," Valerie said sadly.

"We all do that at times. Don't beat yourself up. You will have solid friends."

"Is your house very far?"

"I live not too far from here. Are you ready to go?"

"Let's go." Valerie grabbed her purse, locking the door on the way out.

The air felt so refreshing to Valerie as air flowed in the passenger window.

"It's beautiful out here. I never stopped to smell the roses when I lived here. I left and got caught up in the wrong things."

"I understand. I did the same thing my first four years of pre-med at Ohio State University. Luckily, my parents had a stronghold on my life and drew me back here before it was too late."

"So, Jon, did you like all the college stuff?"

"Well, it did prepare me for the long days and long hours. What about you?" Jon responded.

"I made many friends in those years," Valerie stated.

"I did too. In my field, they come in handy. We draw upon each other's experience on a regular basis. A few moved out of state, but most of my class stayed in the area. We get together a few times a year. One doctor has a getaway in North Carolina that we go to each fall. One owns a cabin on Lake Michigan that we go to in the summer. The rest of the time, we take a weekend away at a new location. I usually host around the holidays. That might be more difficult, as most the men are getting married and having children, but so far, we have not missed a year."

"That would be nice to meet a few times a year. My classmates ended up all over the United States. One went to China."

"Was that for journalism?"

"She was a nurse. She got a nice job working for some rich family. I forgot the entire story. Someone in the family was really sick or burned or something."

"Valerie, you sound stressed. Take a deep breath, and don't worry about anything. This thing with your parents has you upset. I understand why, but stress won't help you deal with it."

"You getting me out of the house was a good thing. Thank you."

"It is good for me too. We all need a change of pace once in a while. I rarely take a lady out, so this is a treat for me too."

"So why did you ask me out tonight?" Valerie asked. *What is his motive?*

"I asked you because I wanted to get to know you. I have enjoyed being around you. I think you are intelligent and pretty and are a nice lady. Have you noticed that there aren't too many people our age living close by?"

Turning his head, he watched her response. She, in turn, watched him without responding right away.

"I haven't been looking for people my own age, so I can't say I would give a correct answer, but I do remember that was a problem as a teenager."

"There are no correct answers right now."

Jon took her hand and squeezed it a little and let it go. They finished the ride to his house in silence. Valerie silently questioned his motives. *He was a good-looking man not much older than her, but why did he choose to make her dinner? It seemed personal.*

"We have arrived. My dad created that idea when he had the house built years ago." Jon parked under the covered driveway, got out, and opened Valerie's car door. He took her hand as she got out.

"The covering makes it nice for a cold night or when it rains."

"I like it. I have a garage at the back of the property, as you can see over there," he said, pointing to the garage.

"This is a neat setup. You have room for twenty or more cars. Did your parents entertain much?"

"My mom loved to entertain. She owned a catering company. She sold it when my dad retired. It gave her something to do with Dad gone a lot. She had plenty of opportunities to pick from."

"That is pretty cool. Do farmers hire caterers much out here?"

"They hired her for all kind of festivities: baptisms, graduations, weddings, and funerals. She also had my dad's wealthier friends hire her from all over."

They walked into the kitchen. The smell of freshly cooked food was in the air.

"Whatever you made smells really good. I am hungry," Valerie said, smelling the roasted garlic in the air.

"Good. We will eat. I think it might be too cool to go out on the lake tonight. Maybe another night. It would be nice to get out there one more time before putting the boat up for the year. Here. Have a seat," he said, pulling out a chair for Valerie that overlooked the lake. He lit a candle in the middle of the table. "I will be right back with the food."

Valerie watched as a boater moved past on the water. She was impressed. Jon quickly returned with a dish of appetizers: stuffed potato skins, fried cheese with dips, and artichoke dip with crackers.

"This is for you, my dear." He set the plate closer to her plate than his. He poured her a quarter cup of white wine. "I hope you like white wine."

"I don't drink it very often. I'm not big into drinking. My parents never had alcohol in the house, and I never picked up on it when I left."

"We won't drink much of it. I don't want you to think I am trying to get you drunk. The wine was only meant to compliment the food."

"You had better not," she teased.

"Valerie, tell me, do you plan on taking care of your dad once he comes home?"

"I haven't thought that far out yet. How long of a recovery should I expect him to have?"

"He will need supervision for three to six months. Since he's still is not talking, we don't know if it is just the trauma or if he did damage to his vocal cords in the accident. We will be running tests on Monday."

"Does that happen very often?"

"Each case is different, but, yes, sometimes people respond to trauma by not talking. It could be a fear. If the tests prove his vocal cords are fine, then we will have him see a therapist to get to the root of the fear. He is responding tonight better to his surroundings. So that is a good thing. Accidents are a strange thing, Valerie. They can cause emotional and physical problems for a long time."

"One of the nurses said he would need to see a new doctor." Valerie took one sip of the wine. Not liking the taste, she set the cup back down and picked up the water glass.

"I called in a specialist. I am not walking away from your dad. I want an expert to look over the medical file. Unless I tell you differently, there is nothing to be alarmed by."

"What did x-rays show?"

"He has a spot on his left lung. Because of the accident, we could not see it at first. We ran new tests Friday. His lung is healing. That is when we saw a spot. It could be scar tissue. That is why I do not want to alarm you yet. You have enough stress going on."

"So far, you have done a great job, and I have to trust your discernment." *If he didn't tell me, maybe there is more to it? I got to let fear go, this is about trusting God.*

"That's my girl. I like to hear that. I am just covering all bases."

"Thank you." Valerie tasted the artichoke dip, giving a, "Mmm."

"You are such a pretty girl. Don't you have any boyfriends or any hot guys on your trail?"

"I had a boyfriend. He flew the coup when I got the call about the accident."

"Then he wasn't worth it anyway."

"I wish I could have seen that before. I wish my heart would heal from the wounds he created." Valerie wrung her hands. Anxiety started to crop up. She turned and looked into Jon's eyes. Peace came instead.

"We learn from every experience we go through. God never wastes anything. As a doctor, I see all kinds of things, as I am sure you did as a journalist."

"Well, yes, I did. I always looked for the good side of everything until it happened to me. I have to admit that I am struggling with it. I have never let anyone see my struggle, but I do fall apart when I am alone."

"The accident or your boyfriend's behavior?"

"Both, but what I was referring to was Tim not ever calling me after that night. He turned thirty and I gave him a very nice birthday party. The rumor has it he and my best friend are now together. That betrayal hurts deeply."

"It will just make you wiser in the future."

"How?"

"I don't know exactly how. It just does. You see what you could never see before. I never had that problem before, but I have had coworkers stab me."

"What? As a doctor?"

"When I did my internship, I had a guy jealous of me and back-stab me. He tried to set me up to lose my internship."

"That's awful."

"It was at the time. I was lucky I had someone cover my back. They saw what he was doing and turned him in. He was kicked out for it. So, for me, it all worked out. Maybe for you this is the best thing, but you just can't see it yet."

Valerie let her guard down a little, getting the feeling that Jon wanted to enjoy this present time, not look into the future.

They finished the plate of appetizers. Jon took the plate into the kitchen and returned with the salad.

"Um, that looks good. I haven't eaten any salads since I returned home. I bought easy-to-prepare foods. Oh, this really hits the spot. That dressing is really good," Valerie said, taking a few bites. *It feels good to be pampered.*

"I am glad you like it. I made you a pint of the dressing to take home. I have a goody bag for you when you leave."

"Jon, you are going to spoil me."

"My bill at the hospital will make up for it." Jon laughed.

"Talking about hospital bills, I hired an attorney to look into the insurance delay."

"Don't worry too much about it. Companies are just waiting longer to pay. Your dad will be able to collect from the driver's policy until he has recovered enough to go back to work."

"I hope so. I have had to hire help for what I can't do. I will be out of income soon. I think one of my big stressors is a huge balloon payment Dad signed a year ago. I don't know where the money is going to come from. I don't know what the loan was for."

"When is it due?"

"In five weeks."

"Is there enough value in the house to use the house for a line of credit?"

"This loan is on the house already. I never paid enough attention to what my parents were doing before. I called them every few months for a few minutes. They tried to respect my choice for leaving the farm. It made my mom very unhappy that I left. Then their only son got drafted. Well, he didn't get drafted but was offered something he could not refuse and died in Iraq. This might be affecting my dad more than I thought."

"Valerie, all you can do is live in the now. The past is gone and can't be brought back. We will get to the issue with your dad. I promise. Eat your salad and enjoy the moment. Once the moment is gone, you can't retrieve it."

They finished eating salmon, roasted red potatoes with garlic butter, and fresh string beans and almond slivers.

"You're better than I thought you would be." Jon winked, as he shot the six ball into a side pocket.

"We played while I was in college. We had a group of six of us. We teamed up and played a group on the north side of Columbus once a month. I used to fool the guys the first time. They never expected me to be any good."

"Do you like table tennis too?"

"I am not as good at that, but I like it."

"Good. That is the next game we will play. I have to beat you at something. I can't have a pretty girl win at everything."

"You seem so kind and gentle. God seems to be important to you."

"I gave my heart to Jesus when I was nine. We had a group come into our neighborhood once a week on a bus. They would park at the end of this street and let the kids come on board and teach us the Bible. They gave us prizes for each Bible verse we learned."

"So they bribed you." She put the stick down and stood to face Jon.

"I guess so. It worked. My buddies and I would try to see who could learn the most verses. Later, we all ended up on Bible quiz teams together. I came in third in the state championship. In the process, it won my parents' hearts. They now serve God. They do work and witness trips in Peru twice a year. They have gone to Mexico a few times but like Peru better."

"Have you gone with them?" Valerie questioned, curious as to his heart for God.

"I have gone twice. I would love to go more often, but the two weeks away is hard. When I retire, I will do what they do. They actually train people down in Florida for the trips. They teach people how to do simple medical procedures."

"Like what?"

ROSALYN ZOGRAFOS

"Take blood pressure, temperature, and blood samples and give IVs."

"How long does a class like that take?"

"Just a couple of hours. I said it was simple stuff. Do you want me to teach you?"

"Like play doctor?" Valerie laughed.

"No. I am serious."

"Sure, but not tonight."

"Of course not, but you would be a fast learner."

"I bet I would be too. We have to be CPR certified to work at the Dispatch."

"That makes sense."

"Are you ready for table tennis?"

"You aren't going to beat me, are you?"

"Only if you are really bad."

The two played three games, Jon winning two out of three games.

CHAPTER 6

On Sunday, Valerie fed the animals before heading off to church. The drive was beautiful. The leaves were starting to change. The trees were filled with oranges, golds, and reds flowing through the trees.

She eyed Mason as she walked into the school building. He was standing at the end of the long hallway close to the entrance to the auditorium, wearing blue jeans and a red polo shirt.

"Hi, Valerie, how was dinner last night?"

"It was fun. I didn't tell you about dinner with Jon, did I ?"

"No. Jon told me he was cooking for you. He really is a nice guy."

"How you do you know him?" Valerie asked.

"What do you expect? Everyone knows everyone around here."

"That is so cool. Do you ever get together and do things?"

"A group of us has gone out on the boat or played pool in the basement a few times. Jon and I talk once a month. I called to get him to do another group night. That's when he said he had plans with you." Mason intently watched Valerie's eyes.

"I think he is pretty cool. He is doing a great job of taking care of my dad."

"Right now, you need all the friends you can find. A good support group is important to make it. Jon is a true gentleman."

"I was thinking the same thing on my drive here. I don't know how long I will be around here, but I do need to have a change of pace every once in a while. I had fun last night. It has been awhile since I played pool."

"We'll talk more after the service. I am helping out with the service today. Go find a seat and I'll catch up to you later."

"Hello, Valerie. Be right with you." Mason motioned with a finger in the air.

Valerie sat down and just waited, thoughts flooding through her brain. She had an hour before going to the hospital to see her dad.

"You keep questioning the wilderness. God says to look to him and he will direct your path in his time and his way."

"Do you read minds?" Valerie asked. She shifted in her seat. *This is getting uncomfortable. I barely know this man and he knows what I have been struggling with. Is that why he keeps looking at me so intently or is there something I am missing? No can't be, he's much older than me.*

"Did it feel like I was reading your mind?"

"You have no idea. I was lost in the service, pondering what God has for me and why I am here. I have been feeling guilty for leaving for school and never returning home. I have other emotions pulling at my heart about the night of the car accident."

"God knows when we are about to give up. He knows when we need to be encouraged. I would suspect that is why God allowed you to have entertainment this week. He knew you desperately needed it. You need to relax."

Valerie let out a stream of tears, gently taking out a Kleenex from her purse and wiping her face. Mason noticed, wiping a tear running down her left cheek with his right thumb. "It is okay. This is a traumatic experience."

"Thank you. You have been so kind to me. I took your advice and had your friend look into the insurance issue. He said they would have it settled in a few days. They told him the paperwork was misplaced."

"With computers these days, that shouldn't be the case," Mason said.

"I have arranged to go clean out my apartment in the morning. This whole thing has been very emotional. I feel like my whole life has been turned inside out. Yesterday, I called and cancelled the purchase of the flat I was buying. I lost my five-thousand-dollar deposit. I can't expect my dad to come to Columbus, and the flat wouldn't have worked with all the stairs."

"Would you like company for the trip? I could help you move. Working for myself gives me some freedom. I have a clear schedule."

"That would be nice. I filled up the farm truck with gas. I could pick you up at seven in the morning. It will be nice having a mature man around."

"I will meet you here at seven. You are closer to the expressway. How were you going to get the truck loaded?"

"I have male friends meeting me at the apartment in the morning. You can meet some of the men I hung out with."

"Do I get to meet Tim too?"

"No one has seen him or Carmen at church since the party. I have not heard from either of them. I am starting to let the hurt go. It was for the best. Meeting quality people has changed my view of what a friend should be."

"God knows what he is doing. The problem is us. We rarely understand until things finish what he was doing. Understand one thing: it all belongs to the Lord, even the problems are his."

"How did you get so secure in your relationship with God?"

"My dad died when I was thirteen. My mom had to fight to take care of us. I watched. God never failed us. We didn't have the luxuries, but our needs were met. My mom was faithful to tithe. She was a giver. I believe God honored that. In her time of need, God provided all the help we needed."

"How did you pay for college?"

"My dad set up a trust fund when we were born. I was short some, which scholarships paid for."

"That is awesome. I took out college loans to pay for mine. I am still paying on them. My parents didn't want me to go to college. They wanted a farmer's wife."

"Did they want more children?"

"I think so, but my mom had complications when she had me. She could no longer have more children."

"That's sad."

"My dad loved it when we were small. He took time to read to us and played a lot of games with us. It was when we got older that he backed off. We both had more friends than we should have. My dad respected that. He never pushed his way."

"I have been praying about his silence since he came to."

"What do you think it is?"

"I think he might be traumatized. I think he needs some professional help when he gets a little better. I would like to pray over him. I saw him yesterday and prayed for him before I left."

"That was so sweet. I didn't know."

"I was there from seven to eight. I knew you would be getting ready to go with Jon and I wouldn't be interfering. I sat and read the Bible to him. He had a few tears forming in his eyes."

"What did you read?"

"Psalm ninety-one."

"That was my mom's favorite scripture. That scripture gave her great comfort when Bill died."

"It had to be God."

"I want that closeness that you and God have. You have so much maturity on me."

"You will soon enough. It takes time. God sent me through battles—kind of like you are in now—to get me here. Remember, I am much older than you."

"Your faith is so strong. You know when something is God and when it is not," Valerie stated, matter of factly.

"In the past few years, I spent most of my time in the presence of God instead of socializing."

"Right now I would change my choices for what you did."

"Start now. There is never a too late as long as there is breath. God is challenging each of us for more. He will meet you where you are and take you on a journey."

"I am willing to do whatever he asks of me."

"He knows that already. He has some plans for you that no one else can or will fulfill."

"I feel so inadequate for his plan for me."

"Valerie, that's the good thing about God. He never sends you out without training you. This situation with your parents and your boyfriend are part of God's training for you."

"That is a good way to look at it. I should look for the positives that will come from all this. Maybe I can build a good relationship with my father. He deserves more than I ever gave him before."

"That sounds like a good goal. I must go, it was good talking to you." Mason shook her hand.

"Thanks for the encouragement."

CHAPTER 7

The truck was loaded, the apartment empty. Valerie bought the guys subs from the corner deli.

"Thanks for the help, guys. Tell everyone at the singles group hi."

Valerie couldn't hold back the tears. She gave Mark and Dan hugs. They both had been part of her church social group since she started going there nine years ago.

"Our pleasure. Soon, we will come to see you," Mark said.

"Promise?"

"Yes," Dan agreed. Shaking Mason's hand, he said, "It was nice meeting you, Mason. Hope you come back soon."

"Thanks for the offer," Mason smiled.

"Well, Mason, we should head out of here. Here are the directions for the cleaners. It isn't very far."

Valerie jumped out of the truck, making sure the cat was safely in the cage, taking several steps to the doorway of the dry cleaners. The last person she thought she would run into was Carmen. Carmen was on the cell phone, not paying attention to Valerie walking toward her. Clearly, she was talking to Tim.

"Carmen, why didn't you ever call me back?" Valerie asked sternly.

"Um," was all Carmen said, turning her head away in shame.

"I thought you were my friend. Is it true that you and Tim are together now?"

"Yeah. We are getting married." Carmen Turned her head toward Valerie, making a snarly face.

"So when did this all take place?" Valerie asked very loudly. *I am hurt.*

Carmen walked away and said nothing more to Valerie but went back to her conversation on the cell phone.

Valerie couldn't afford to lose it. She gave the receipt to the counter girl and took her dry cleaning, returning to the truck, tears running down her face.

"Are you okay?" Mason asked sympathetically.

"I will be if I am not now. That was Carmen. She admitted that she is with Tim and they are getting married. How could I be such a fool?"

"It won't last. I doubt they even get married. You are much stronger than all that. Don't hold it in and let it fester. Let it out. You will feel much better if you do."

Valerie let out the pent-up hurt as Mason held her head. It felt like comfort her father would give her—something she deeply desired right now.

Whiskers licked her hand.

"Thank you, Whiskers. You must miss Mommy."

The cat just looked at Valerie.

"Do you think God orchestrated that today?"

"You running into Carmen?"

"Yes."

"Probably so you could release it."

"Do you pray for me?"

"Every night."

"Why?"

"Because I feel that God placed you in my path for such a time as this. It is part of who I am. I stand in the gap for people on their journey. That is why I am at the church we met at."

"Let me ask you a few questions about Damian and his group." Valerie did not wait for a go-ahead but continued asking questions. "Who does Damian submit to?"

"They are part of a group called Willow Creek. They start seeker-type churches across the USA."

"Are they grounded?"

"You mean to ask are they mature?"

"Well, yes."

"They are for the immature, and I would say they are immature themselves."

"Mason, I like the fun, but I am uncomfortable deep inside of me. I have been thinking I should find a deeper church. I had a dream a couple nights ago that the group took me whitewater rafting and I drowned."

"That could be a good clue that God doesn't want you there. Where have you been thinking about going?"

"I heard that a good church was fifteen miles to my east. One of the nurses at the hospital told me about it. She came in one night and prayed for me. I felt a power rise up from the prayer. I was depressed. Afterward, I felt peaceful."

"Go check it out. I have committed to help this group for a few months. Damian and his wife, Elaine, have been pretty good to me. They have had me over for a few times. They are very nice people."

"I agree they are nice, but I am searching for something with substance."

"Why don't you sit down and talk to them? Ask them the questions stirring in your spirit."

"I will."

Mason's BlackBerry was singing a song. "Hello. This is Mason." Hitting the speaker button. "Valerie and I were just talking about you," Mason said.

"You are with Valerie? Good. I need her help. Kala is missing. We think someone broke in and took her early this morning," Damian said.

"What? Someone took your baby?"

"Yes. We don't know where to search or what to do. My wife is beside herself. Can I talk to Valerie?"

"Sure." Mason handed the BlackBerry to Valerie, just so it would pick her voice up clearly.

"This is Valerie."

"Valerie, I need your help. Someone has taken my thirteen-month-old baby. The sheriff in town doesn't have a clue where to look. I thought you might be able to help us."

"Pastor, we are about an hour south of town. We can come over there when we get in town."

"Thanks. Good-bye." Damian hung up.

"Damian asked us to come to his place to help find the baby. Maybe we should pray."

"Absolutely. Do you want to start?"

I really don't feel comfortable praying in front of Mason. I have never done this before. "No. I will let you."

"Father in heaven, you know the hairs on our heads and you know the thoughts before we think them. Only you know where this baby is and how to direct us to her. Father, guide our steps and lead us where only you can. Give us visions or dreams and the interpretation for them. We ask that you would calm Damian and Elaine and protect Kala from any harm. Send confusion to the enemies camp so that the plan cannot be completed. We ask that Kala be found rapidly and be returned without a hair being disturbed. We ask these things in the name of Jesus."

ROSALYN ZOGRAFOS

"Lord, I can't imagine the hurt and pain of a mother's heart right now. Heal the parents in a way that only you can. Give them grace and mercy to be able to endure. I ask that you would allow them to be strengthened in this midnight hour. You have said that blessed are those who grieve, for you will comfort them. We ask that you would comfort them and give them peace in this time. Amen."

Valerie felt drained from the events the last hour. She couldn't imagine how a mother would feel having her infant taken. She knew from training that most kidnappings were by people familiar with the house. She had a few questions she would like answers to.

"That was a beautiful prayer. It was filled with so much compassion," Mason said.

"I think I learned that from the accident. I have had a few nurses praying with me at the hospital. They have given me scriptures to read while I sit there. I didn't know it was changing me."

"That is awesome, Valerie." Mason touched her leg with his hand briefly.

The two drove in silence the rest of the trip.

Valerie and Mason arrived at a new ranch home built on an acre of land. An Escalade sat in the driveway along with a deputy car.

"Here. Let me help you out." Mason took Valerie's hand to support her while she jumped out of the truck.

"Thank you."

Damian opened the front door, his eyes bloodshot from crying.

"Thanks for coming, guys." He opened the door and held it open for them to enter. "Everyone is in the den. Can I get you anything to eat or drink?"

"I will take a water," Valerie said.

"Me too. That sub left me thirsty." Mason said.

"Pastor, who was the last person to watch the baby besides you and your wife?" Valerie asked.

"We have a babysitter come in a few times a week. The lady is about thirty-five. She lives a couple miles from here with her mom."

"Call her and ask her to come over. I want to talk to her," Valerie commanded.

"She wouldn't take our baby," Damian said.

"She might not have taken the baby, but she might know something crucial to get your baby back."

"Okay. I will call her." Damian pulled out a red BlackBerry and dialed her number. "Sharon, this is Damian. Can you call as soon as you get in, it is an emergency?"

"It was the voice mail," Damian stated, still looking at the phone.

"Pastor, did you ever notice anything strange about your babysitter, any boyfriends hanging around?"

"No, not really. It was Elaine who did most of the interaction with her. Let's go talk to Elaine."

Mason looked at Valerie. He knew she sensed something. Valerie nodded her head.

"Hi, Elaine, my name is Valerie Sharpe. I'm a journalist for the *Columbus Dispatch*. I am so sorry for your loss. Can you tell me have you gotten any ransom letters?"

"Hi, Valerie, nice to meet you. No. I fed Kala at about seven in the morning and put her back in the crib while I took a shower. When I came back, she was gone. My husband and I were headed out to Cancun this morning for four days."

"Did the babysitter know you were leaving?"

"Yes. We had talked about it on Saturday. I had her here for two hours so I could get my hair and nails done."

Valerie took notes as Elaine talked. *Pain for the loss griping at her heart.*

"Did she seem to be nervous about you leaving?"

"She zoned out on me at one point, as if she was someplace else. She's done that a few times recently. I figured it was just her money problems."

"What kind of money problems?" Valerie asked.

"She lost her job last summer. She has been working part time cleaning houses in the area. She lost her car this month. Do you think she took my baby?"

"We don't know that she took your baby. Did she ever talk about wanting to have her own baby?"

"She said she wanted to find a guy to have a family with. She really loves Kala. She was really good with her."

"You never mentioned anything about not hiring her to baby sit again, have you?"

"I am not sure. My husband's sister lost her job and wants to come here to live, so maybe we did."

"How long ago did that happen?"

"About two weeks ago." Damian plugged in.

Valerie ran her fingers through her hair. In the big city, the cops did a wonderful job at working the details out. Out in the country, they usually didn't see too many crimes. Maybe a farmer getting in a fight with his neighbor. Occasionally, an animal taken, especially pigs. What should I ask?

"Who was going to be watching Kala while you were gone?"

"My mom was going to watch her until we returned."

"Have you two taken many vacations and left the baby behind?"

"We go somewhere every other month."

"Isn't this a fairly new church plant?"

"We have been here for three months. Our parent church has been paying us for a year now, well, closer to sixteen months. We had agreed to start it in January but backed it up to June."

"Elaine, tell me, who else has been in your home with the baby?"

"My family, church members, and a few neighbors."

"Could you make a list for me with contact information?"

"Sure. I will have my husband help me."

"I have to get back to my dad, but I will be back later tonight for your list. I am going to run your babysitter's name through police records, if you don't mind."

"Go ahead."

Elaine took a step to give Valerie a hug. Valerie responded, moving toward her. They hugged. Valerie held Elaine for a few minutes, letting her cry. Valerie hunted for Mason. She found him in the kitchen, eating donuts.

"Mason, I need to get back to the hospital for a bit. I can take you home or leave you here. I plan on returning later."

"I want to go to the hospital with you. I think we need to pray for your dad."

"Mason, bless you. That would mean a lot to me. Pastor, we will be back. We will call before we return. In the meantime, I will run Sharon's name through the records if you can write her full name down for me."

Damian nodded, took a piece of paper, and wrote down Sharon Glover's name down with contact information included. "Thanks, guys."

"You are welcome," Mason said, walking out the door.

Valerie waved.

"You are really good at what you do," Mason said to Valerie, as he opened her door to the truck

"I have been passionate about my career. I am thankful I can help. The babysitter might be behind all this. I don't know how yet, but I will find out."

"Do you have connections to check her out?"

"All good journalists have good connections to get to the bottom of things. Many cases are worked alongside the police. Let me make a quick call while you drive."

"No problem. Are you going to eat anything before we get to the hospital?"

"I should. I am really hungry."

"I ate with Damian. Someone brought a few casseroles in."

"I saw you eating the donuts." He looked like he had eaten a few too many.

"I did eat one. I usually don't." Mason wiped his mouth with his lips, making a little noise.

"Detective Brown, this is Valerie Sharpe."

"Valerie, I heard you took a leave of absence. Is everything okay?"

"Yes and no. I will tell you later about my leave. Right now, I want to see if I can get you to run a name for me. I have a pastor in the town my parents live in with a kidnapped baby. The babysitter might be involved. Her name is Sharon Glover." Valerie looked out the window of the truck. *My problems look small compared to Damian's right now.*

"I will run it and call you back. You still at the same number?" Detective Glover asked.

"Yes."

"Have they called the FBI in yet?"

"With all the trauma, I never asked."

"Give me an hour."

"If I don't answer, leave it on the voice mail."

"Okay, Valerie. Good to hear from you. You sound great."

"Thanks for the compliment."

"I will call you back, my fair lady."

"Thanks." Valerie shut the phone and turned her attention to Mason.

"Valerie, do you think Kala could be in a barn somewhere?"

"Is that what you sense?"

"Yes."

"After we go to the hospital, we can map out the farms close by. It is a good thing it is not very cold out tonight. I don't think she was taken for ransom money. I think it was personal. Someone wanted a baby and found a way to take her. I forgot to ask Elaine if she had a key to the house or if there was evidence of a break-in."

"Damian said there was no evidence. The sheriff looked all over the property for clues and found none."

"Which means it is likely someone they trust."

"From what Damian said, the sheriff had no clues at all. You seem to be on track much better than he was."

"You have to keep in mind that they don't get cases like this in the country. I work writing stories of this kind of thing all the time. Cops are my pastime. We talk the case in and out."

"You are quite a lady, I must admit. Tim must have been a fool to let you go."

"That is his problem now." A level of strength rose in Valerie. She was grounded and knew what she had to do. She started the truck and put it in reverse.

CHAPTER 8

"Dad, it is Valerie," Valerie whispered in his ear. She waited to see if he would respond.

He opened his eyes without speaking.

Mason took his hand. "Jacob, would you mind if I pray over you?" Jacob nodded in agreement.

"Valerie, take his hand. We are going to pray for complete recovery. If he is willing to receive, God wants to bring healing to him tonight."

"Dad, that would be great."

"The Bible says where two or three are gathered in his name, he is there. Praise you, Father. It is in your glory and your presence where healing can take place. So we ask for your glory to come down into this hospital room. Open his mouth to speak. Break off every chain trying to stop and block him. Heal him from the inside

out this night. In the name of Jesus, we pray." Mason opened his eyes. He took a breath and looked at Jacob squarely in the eyes. "Now, Jacob, speak."

Silence filled the room.

"Will you get up and walk for us?" Mason asked him.

Jacob nodded his head. He took Mason's hand to steady his body weight.

"Jacob, I am proud of you," Mason said.

Valerie was shocked. Her dad hadn't walked since the accident. *Now to get him to talk.*

"Dad, that was awesome. I understand that you and Mason have been meeting secretly?"

Jacob nodded his head.

"Dad, how are you feeling?"

"Groggy," Jacob responded.

Valerie looked at Mason and Mason at her. They smacked their hands together in a high-five.

"Would you like us to leave so you can sleep, Dad?"

He nodded his head. Taking his daughter's hand, he gave it a squeeze.

"I love you too, Dad." Valerie kissed him on the forehead and left the room with Mason following her.

Leaving the hospital, the phone rang.

"Valerie, it looks like your Sharon Glover has mental issues. She was hospitalized a year ago and released to her mother's care. Her mother's guardian over her. It is very possible she could have taken a baby. If I were you, I would go without calling them."

"Will do. Thank you so much. I will call you back in a few days and keep you informed on what is happening."

"Thanks. I got to run. A hot issue just came up. Call me soon."

"Detective Brown said that she has been hospitalized for mental issues before. Can we stop over there before going back to Damian and Elaine's?"

"You bet."

Mason knew where Sharon lived. He stopped there before heading on. When they pulled into the driveway, the house was dark. There were not even any outdoor lights on. It was evident that no one was home. Valerie motioned to drive back by the barn. No life was stirring back there either. So they headed on to the pastor's house. Maybe they would have some news.

"Should we get the sheriff's department to get us a list of the barns in the area?" Mason asked?

"That is a good idea. Do you know anyone here?"

"I went to school with one of the deputies. I will call him when we land."

"This is like teamwork. Cool!" Valerie smiled.

They arrived at the pastor's house. Damian answered the door. He looked more settled than he did a couple hours earlier.

"Come in, guys. Elaine went to lay down. I doubt anything will happen to find Kala tonight. Did you find anything out?"

"Well, Pastor, I found out that Sharon has been in a mental hospital. She was released about a year ago. Her mother is her guardian. Did she ever tell you any of that before?"

"No!" Damian said with anger.

"Damian, is the deputy still here?" Mason asked

"He left right after you did."

"I am going to go in the other room and call my friend who works for them. I will be right back."

Neither Damian nor Valerie paid any attention to Mason leaving the room.

"Valerie, what do you suggest?"

"I suggest that we search all the barns in the area in the morning. If we can get a list of barns in a five-mile radius, we can split up and go search for Kala."

"Could that be dangerous?" Pastor asked.

"It could, but I doubt it is. She has shown no signs of being violent on record yet. Many crimes committed are by the mentally ill."

"We do record checks for all the people working with our children at church. I can't believe I never thought about doing it with Sharon."

"Pastor, tragedy is a great teacher. I have learned to grow up since my parents had their accident. It reveals who is for you and who is against you. You also learn skills you didn't know you had."

"I'm sorry for your loss, Valerie. I should have been more compassionate with you. I never knew what it felt like until today. I would never wish this on anyone," Damian said.

"Me either," Valerie said, watching Mason return to the room.

"The sheriff's department is getting a list together for us. They think there are twelve barns. Two have been abandoned, and they will hit them at sunrise. It is more likely to be there than where someone lives. They have put an APB out on Sharon. They want to at least question her. They called the neighbors across the street. They said no one has been home all day at the Glover home."

"I wonder where they went," Valerie said.

"Did Sharon say anything to you about leaving town for any reason?" Mason asked.

"Not that I remember," Damian responded.

"We are going to go home and get some sleep. I will call you after seven in the morning. If something happens before then, call me. Good night," Mason said.

"Good night," Valerie said. She too could use the sleep.

"Can I take you out for something to eat?" Mason asked Valerie, as they left the house.

"Sure."

"You need to eat."

"I have leftovers in the fridge. You can have some with me."

"Okay. That might be faster. Do you think someone else could be behind the baby being taken?"

"Do you have anyone in mind?"

"Not really."

"It could be lots of people. It could be family, which I doubt. It could be someone from church, or it could have been someone watching the house." Valerie had enough thinking about a missing baby for the night. "I made corned beef and cabbage last night. Does that sound good?"

"That sounds really good. I haven't had that in months."

Valerie pulled the truck into the barn. She didn't want her household goods being exposed to the weather. She locked the door to the barn.

Valerie went to bed and lay there thinking about the turn of events. While she was sleeping, she had a dream about the baby. When she awakened, she could not remember what she dreamed. She knew that in her dream was a key to find the baby before it was too late. She did know that the woman in question was not a part of the dream and neither was a barn. That puzzled her. She wanted to get up the hospital early and talk to Jon about her dad. He did his rounds between seven and nine in the morning. She dressed without showering or putting any makeup on. She grabbed a protein bar on the way out along with a bottle of orange juice. She would get coffee at the hospital. She hoped Mason would not mind if she did not go out to the barns this morning. She would call him after meeting with Jon. She found Jon on the third floor.

He welcomed the interruption.

"Hey, girl. I am glad to see you are back. How was the trip?"

"It was one long day. On the drive back, Mason got a call that the pastor's baby was missing. I thought Sharon Glover might have something to do with it."

"Sharon couldn't. She's been in the hospital with her mother since yesterday early morning. Her mother had a heart attack. Sharon drove her over here at about six thirty yesterday morning. She's still here. I saw her already this morning."

"I had a feeling I was wrong about her taking the baby. If the babysitter didn't do it, who did?"

"I don't know. Wish I could help you on that one. I hear Jacob was up walking last night for the first time. I will see you in your dad's room." He touched her arm affectionately and walked back into the room he was in before she came up on the floor.

Valerie took the elevator up to her dad's room and found him waking up. He'd been sleeping at least twelve hours a day. She would guess it was because of depression from the current events. She'd rather not see him on any more medication than absolutely necessary.

"Dad, can I get you anything?"

He shook his head, taking her hand. This time, he rubbed it gently, looking into her eyes. He winked at her and then patted her hand. Valerie's cell phone rang. She forgot to turn it off.

"Hi, Mason. I'm at the hospital."

"Hi, Valerie. I called to tell you I have meetings with clients and won't be going out looking for Kala. The sheriff said they wanted to go alone anyway. They felt that was safer for all involved."

"Mason, Sharon is here in the hospital and has been since early yesterday morning. I had a dream this morning about the baby. When I woke up, I forgot it. The barn wasn't part of it. There is something else to this baby ordeal, maybe a family member."

"It could be. Damian and his wife are not from around here. Her parents live south of Columbus I think. I am not sure about his parents. I'll call you later. I have to run and meet up with one of my clients now. Have a great day."

"You too."

Valerie returned to the bedside of her dad. "Dad, so much has happened, right now, I want to know how you feel."

"So-so," Jacob said.

"Hey, you talked. The doctor will get down to what is ailing you. I love you, Dad." Valerie just about slipped and mentioned her mom dying in the accident but didn't feel that that would be wise.

"Mmm," Jacob said.

Valerie sat holding Jacob's hand for what seemed like forever. The doctor came in, and she let go.

"Am I interrupting something?" he teased.

"Oh yeah," Valerie teased back.

"Jacob, I am going to take your vitals and see if we can't get you back on track. How are you feeling this morning?"

"With my fingers, of course," Jacob said.

The doctor tried not to laugh. He didn't want to create a scene over Jacob not talking before.

"I see we have a sense of humor this morning. You must be feeling a little better."

"Mmm." Jacob looked between Jon and Valerie.

"Come on, Dad. He is here to help you." Valerie looked at Jon to see how he was going to react. He seemed to always be level headed.

"Jacob, we are going to take you downstairs today for a few tests. You might be able to go home in a couple of days if all is well. It would make me feel better if you were talking on a consistent basis. We might have to put you in a nursing home for some rehab to get you to walk. I understand from the nurses last night that you did walk a little in the room. I have a physical therapist scheduled to look at you this afternoon. Forester will determine what you can and can't do. Your blood pressure looks normal, and your heart rate has returned to a good place. You no longer have a fever, which is good."

"Did he have a fever before?" Concern crossed Valerie's face.

"Yes, he did. He had an infection in his lung where it was punctured. The fever was pretty high for a few days. We pumped him with antibiotics, and it looks like it worked just fine," Jon said.

"Looks good, Dad. Doctor, will he need to be in a wheelchair for a while?" Valerie asked.

"I would think so, but we will know that this afternoon. I do what I am good at and leave the rest for those who are experts in other fields. Jacob I will see you later." Jon walked out with Valerie following him.

"The insurance company contacted me today. All is set. You will be receiving a check with benefits in a few days," Jon said.

"Does that include the check for my mother's life?"

"From what they said, I think so. I think you are home free on that now. Someone in the hospital put the wrong code in the box. That is what held up the issue."

"Thanks, Doctor," Valerie said with gratitude. *Getting the insurance turned around would help in getting those overdue bills paid.*

"Anything for you, my dear." Jon winked and walked down the hall.

Valerie returned to the room. "Dad, that's a good report. Things are looking up here. We will see what happens with your appointment with the physical therapist this afternoon. If the check comes from the insurance company, I might be able to pay all the bills. I thought I would hate coming home, but, Dad, it is changing me. I see life from a new perspective. I was all caught up in things that faded away. There is a simplicity here that I am enjoying."

"Good. All I want is for you is to be happy, Valerie. Your mom and I tried to provide a good life for you."

"Dad, I am so sorry for upsetting you before. I was self-centered. God's teaching me how to be Christ-centered. I am thankful to have Godly parents. You did all the right things, it was me."

"Mmm," Jacob responded.

CHAPTER 9

Three FBI men had been called in to find Kala, they were flying into Columbus airport. A driver had picked them up at the terminal, driving them to the country home on Route 34. They first addressed questions to the parents. They wanted to get the story straight. They'd start the search first on the premises and then move out from there.

"Peters, go get prints from the baby's room," Quad said firmly. Peters was a seasoned man on the team.

"Yes, sir," Peters said, walking back to the open door to Kala's room.

He took agent Talbot, the newest agent, in with him to meet with the parents. They had formed a list of questions while flying over from Oregon.

"I am Agent Quad, operating Chief from the FBI. With me is Agent Peters, who will be dusting the house and property of all prints. Agent Talbot will be questioning you for any details in the last twenty-four hours. We want to hear everything you have done and everyone you have talked to. I will set up communication equipment in the dining room. Agent Talbot, the floor is yours."

"I can't remember all that," Damian said to Elaine.

"Honey, you have to try. Take your time. This is important," Elaine said.

Agent Talbot took a deep breath, wiped the sweat off his forehead.

"Let us start with yesterday morning. Can you tell me how the day started? Oh. I am sorry. Sunday morning details."

"Kala awakened at about six, I think. I was the one to get up and feed her. I put her in the playpen beside me and worked on the sermon for that morning. At about seven fifteen, Elaine came in and took her out of the playpen and played with her. She took her back to our bedroom and gave Kala a bath at about seven forty-five. She brought Kala back to me, and she took a shower. After she dressed and was ready, I took a shower and dressed. I remember Elaine making us waffles. We all sat down and ate. Kala had a few bites with some orange juice. I helped Elaine clean the dishes up. I printed out something for the service while Elaine read the Sunday paper. We then headed off to church at about eight forty-five."

"Damian, do you normally leave that early?" Agent Talbot asked.

"Yes. We have to oversee some of the setup. Elaine takes care of the nursery on Sundays. We get there early so others coming to help have an adult to watch the little ones. I pray over the crew and make sure that what they have brought in so far is placed in the right spots."

"What time is the service?"

"It starts at eleven and ends at noon."

"That is simple," Agent Talbot said.

"For the farmers, it gives them time to take care of the animals. I was never an early morning person, so it works for me too."

"So, go on with your story."

"After the service, I had one of the guys take over the cleanup, replacing everything in the trailer. Elaine and I met her parents in

Columbus's north side for lunch. We put Kala in the backseat with her car seat and a DVD of VeggieTales. She fell asleep not too far along in the ride. Elaine and I talked about Cancun and what we needed to do to finish packing. We had a few errands we would need to do before our trip. We were at Ernie's from one thirty-five until three fifteen. We then headed home. I was going to leave Elaine home with the baby and run the quick errands. I dropped the girls off at the house. I waited for them to enter the house and left. I went on to Walgreen's to pick up suntan lotion. I headed west to drop off paperwork requested by a friend."

"What kind of paperwork?" Agent Talbot asked.

"He asked me to research a company he is going to invest in. The company is in bankruptcy. He wanted the last year's investment portfolio."

"Where would you get that?"

"I dabbled in that before starting the church. Let's just say I have connections."

"Where else did you go before returning home?"

"I went to the grocery store for some ice cream. I wanted to surprise Elaine."

"What time did you arrive home?"

"I got home at about six. I found both the girls sleeping in the master bedroom on the bed. So I went into the den and watched football. Elaine got up at about seven thirty. She made supper, warming up leftover pasta and beef. We ate and I helped her clean the dishes up. We watched TV and went to bed."

"Now, tell me about the morning Kala disappeared," Agent Talbot said.

"Elaine woke up to the baby crying. I fell back asleep. I woke up to Elaine screaming that the baby was gone."

"Elaine, tell me about the morning the baby disappeared. Give me as much detail as you can remember."

"Kala was crying in her crib. I got up, made her a bottle, and rocked her in the den. I played with her a little and changed her diaper. I lay her back down at about seven, and I went to take a shower. I planned on waking Damian up. I didn't hear any noise coming from her monitor, so I went into her room to check on her. She was gone. I started screaming for Damian to come quickly. He ran in the room in his underwear and started pulling blankets off her crib. He looked in the closet and went from room to room, looking for her. I sat in the rocking chair in shock for several minutes."

"Tell me what happened after he had searched the entire house."

"We called the sheriff. He was here in less than ten minutes. He had his deputies search each room and the property."

"What time was that?"

"About seven forty-five," Damian said.

Agent Peters came into the room. "I have the rest of the house dusted. I will be going out to dust the windows and the entrance doors."

"We will be asking more questions later. For now, we will be talking to the deputies and the sheriff and comparing information. Tell me, have you been contacted by anyone about the baby?" Agent Quad asked.

"No one. Nobody has called us in the last twenty-four hours or so. Family has called to see if she has been returned. That is all I remember."

"Elaine, have you had any calls?"

"My college roommate called last night. She lives in Tennessee. She couldn't possibly have anything to do with it," Elaine said.

"Tell me, who knew you were taking a trip?" Agent Talbot asked.

"Our families knew, and two people at the church office knew we would be gone. The babysitter knew. She's here on Wednesday and Saturday afternoon while we take a date afternoon. We told her not to come and why. I play racquetball on Thursday mornings with an old friend. He knew. I told the lady at the drug store who checked me out. I don't remember her name," Damian said while scratching his head.

"How did you buy your tickets?" Talbot asked.

"Online. I buy them all that way." Damian shook his head.

"How often do you take a vacation?" Quad asked.

"We go every other month. We don't want to get burned out."

"Doesn't that add up to a lot of money?" agent Talbot asked.

"I got paid quite well to start this church," Damian said.

"How well is that?"

"They pay me seventy K plus full benefits. I get six Sundays and two weeks off during the year. As long as I am back by Sunday, I can take all the time off I want."

"Sounds lucrative," Agent Quad mentioned quietly.

"Is there any pattern to the time off, like exactly every eight weeks?" Agent Talbot asked.

"Not really. It does work out more or less every eight weeks most of the time though," Damian said.

Elaine was in shock. She heard what was being said but couldn't respond.

"I would like you to tell me about your relationship with Elaine," Agent Talbot said.

"We get along just fine."

"How long have you been married? Where did you meet?" Agent Quad asked.

"We met six years ago at Wheaton College. We dated for two years and got married. I was a senior, and she quit school after her junior year. We were married for about two years when she got pregnant. I was pastoring a church in Grand Rapids, Michigan, until this opportunity came up. Kala was a month old when our group offered us this church plant deal. We jumped at it. The pay was good, and it would get us back to a less stressful environment."

"Elaine, tell me, how does Damian treat you on a day-to-day basis? Is he respectful of you?" Agent Talbot asked.

"Most of the time. He does have a temper. He gets mad when he doesn't get his way," Elaine said.

"Recently any problems?" Talbot asked.

"You think Damian took our baby. Why would he do that?" Elaine yelled.

"We have to ask these questions. We are not at all suggesting he did any such thing. I know this is painful for you, but we are almost done for now," Talbot said.

"Well, he got mad when I ordered a new comforter set from Elder-Beerman last week. It seemed to be the end of the world to him. I thought our finances were solid and all going well, but by the way he acted, you would think he lost his job," Elaine said harshly.

"Thank you for your time. We will be back later. For now, relax as much as you can," Agent Quad said.

Agents Quad and Talbot walked out the front door. They found Peters finishing the last window.

"Let's get out of here," Quad said.

The three men got in the car that had been waiting for their return.

"That was excellent work, Talbot. You are learning fast. You might be on to something there. That man seems to be a little controlling of his wife."

"I was thinking the same thing. Let's pull the phone records and credit card usage for the last two months. Peters, I want you to check into his past history. Talbot, run a bureau report and see if anything shows up."

"Peters, did you print the SUV?"

"No. Maybe I should have. Why don't you tell them to not go anywhere until we return?"

"That is a good idea, Peters. I want to see what they told the sheriff's department and see if the stories match. When did he start the church?"

"I heard the sheriff say three months ago," Talbot said.

"Talbot, I want you to check into the church's financial records. His behavior with his wife over a bedspread is a little much. He might have a huge debt he is trying to cover. Also, check and see if there is life insurance on Kala," Quad commanded.

"Yes sir, boss," Talbot agreed.

"Peters, I want you at that house until I tell you to come back. We are going to set up surveillance equipment to see if he did it."

"Yes, sir. Is the driver aware that I am going back?"

"No. I will radio him now," Quad said.

CHAPTER 10

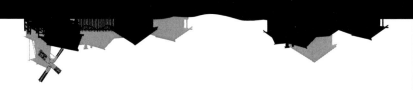

"Jacob, I will make the arrangements for you to be taken to Angel's Nursing Home. I will find out how fast they can take you. It is imperative that you be given proper care for your legs to function again. They also need to keep a watch on your lungs. There has been some damage that will heal under the right conditions," Forster, the physical therapists said.

"How long will he be there?" Valerie asked.

"I would expect up to six weeks. We will be doing physical therapy twice a day with him. After he returns home, he will be continuing for another month or until he is back to new," Forster responded.

"Do I need to do anything with the insurance company?"

"No, that will be handled by the hospital. I understand your concern. Dr. Jon mentioned the problems you already had. Insurance companies like to be a pain in the neck. It gets them out of paying

claims sometimes. Some won't do the effort it takes to get the bill paid. I am going to get the whirlpool ready for you. I have an assistant who will be helping you in and out. After the whirlpool, we have a short therapy for you Jacob. We are going to do small movements with your limbs. I promise it won't hurt today. I have prescribed some items that will be delivered to your room later today. I want you taking salt soaks. We are going to put you on a natural joint complex, and I want you taking fish oil. It will help your body heal. Any questions?"

"Not at the moment," Jacob said.

"Here is my card. Feel free to call me with any questions. I am sure over time you will have a few. Valerie, I am also going to give you a card for our support group. It is through Mercy Hospital. It is free, and I would suggest you take us up on it. Dealing with trauma like this can be very difficult. You can call and get the schedule for meeting times that work with your schedule. You will meet people in the same situations you are in. It always help to have people around you who understand."

"Thanks. I have found out what it is like to not have the support. It has been hard."

A young man came and wheeled Jacob to the changing room, leaving Valerie alone with Forster.

"Valerie, he will be in therapy for at least ninety minutes. You can go get something to eat or sit in the lounge. We will take him back to his room when we are done. I promise to take good care of him."

"I am sure you will. Everyone here has been wonderful. I never knew nice people existed like this." *From looking at your arms and wide shoulders I am sure you can handle my dad.*

"It is what we get paid for. Enjoy your day."

Valerie decided to go see Elaine.

On the ride to the Wade house the phone rang.

"Hello. This is Valerie."

"Valerie, I have story for you to cover. It is right around the corner from you. It is making headline news. Some pastor had his baby taken yesterday."

"Yes, I know. I was there last night, Shelly."

"Perfect. Will you cover the story?"

"Sure."

"The boss approved a full salary to be reinstated as long as you stay on the story. We want the real scoop."

"No problem. Can you ship me some office supplies?"

"I will get a mixture of everything you could need out today. I will overnight it."

"Good enough." Valerie gave her address.

"Oh. Valerie, keep track of your gas receipts and food. The boss will reimburse you."

"That helps. Thanks. Is everything else in the office okay?"

"The new kid blew a big story. We never should have let a green journalist do such a story. It was my fault. I let the kid talk me into doing it in your absence. We miss you, Valerie. How is your dad doing?"

"Much better. He will be transferred to a nursing home soon. He is not able to do much walking, and he has vocal cord damage from the steering wheel hitting his throat. He is going to make it, and so am I."

"Are you doing okay?"

"Sure."

"That's my girl. Keep me posted. I will call you later."

Valerie started the engine; pulling out of the hospital parking lot. When she was a mile away, her phone rang again. This time, it was Tim.

"Hello?" Valerie said softly.

"Valerie, I am so sorry for what I did to you. I don't know what got into me. I guess I allowed Carmen to suck me in. She made a real fool of me. I am so ashamed for what I did to you."

"Tim, we all have been played for a fool."

"Valerie, I miss you so much."

"Tim, you never called after I told you about the accident. It has been six weeks now. Why are you calling me now?"

"I want you back."

"Tim, you ignored me for six weeks. You never came to the funeral, never sent flowers or anything. You didn't take my calls. You even slept with Carmen. What has gotten into you? Isn't your virginity important to you?"

"I know now what I lost. I want to talk to you."

"Tim, I bet Carmen dumped you, right?"

"Well, yes, she did."

"Tim, this whole situation has allowed me to see. I am sorry. I don't want you anymore."

"Have you found someone else?"

"Tim, you do understand that my dad has been in a coma for six weeks. Where would I find time to date anyone?"

"You always were so organized. You could fit it in and still keep things going. Look how you did your job at the *Dispatch*. You dated me and did a lot of church functions too."

"Thank you for the compliment, but I am not dating anyone. Unless you call my father's doctor and an older man at church helping me a date."

"Valerie, I said I was sorry. Why can't you forget it, and let's start over?"

"Bye, Tim."

Valerie made a right turn and drove to her parents' house.

I wish he would have called some other time, now I am upset. My heart is racing and anger is starting to rise again. How could I love him so much but be so angry with him?

She called Ceil to find out what she might have heard.

"Ceil. Hi. It's Valerie."

"Hi, Valerie."

"Ceil, did you ever go to the printer where Carmen works?"

"She quit two days ago. I heard she got into a big fight with the owner. I didn't pay too much attention to her story. But then I heard her say she was moving away. Her father has cancer. I forgot where she said she was going."

"Ceil, Tim called me and asked me to take him back. I ran into Carmen at the dry cleaner just the other day. She said they were getting married. This was the last thing I expected right now."

"As the stomach turns. You didn't tell Tim you would take him back, did you?"

"Of course not. He ignored me for six weeks. What kind of fool do I look like?"

"I never thought of you as a fool. Hey, I have to go. I am out the door for a job. Call me later."

Aunt Rose was right. Carmen was jealous and really didn't want Tim. If she wanted a relationship with him, she would not have dumped him so fast. What motive did Tim have for dating Carmen? She wasn't educated and didn't have a good, solid job. She was like a stick. She was flat front and back. She had a tendency to be negative. How did she seduce him?

Quickly, Valerie ran into the house. She grabbed her laptop and recording device. She grabbed her professional camera for photos. She grabbed her work bag and a calming tea. She opened the fridge and found an orange and a yogurt.

That would be lunch for the day. She promised herself a good supper that night. *I don't care how I got it, even if I have to go grocery shopping and pick a few things up. I'm going to eat a real meal tonight.*

By two thirty, she had arrived at the pastor's house. Several cars were parked in the long driveway. One had out-of-state plates. She expected it was family. She knocked on the front door. A man she had not met answered.

"Hi. I am Valerie. I am here to see Damian and Elaine."

"Oh, Valerie, come in," Damian yelled from the other room. He came in to introduce Peters to her. "Valerie, this is Agent Peters from the FBI. He will be here for a while. Thank you for all your help yesterday. I appreciate you looking into Sharon's background. I am sorry to hear her mom had a heart attack."

Valerie nodded her head.

Damian was a little too up for a man who lost his baby. It seemed strange. Valerie had worked plenty of cases like this—well, two. None of the other parents had been like this. They had been more subdued and in shock.

The TV was on in the den. Elaine was parked on the couch, watching a movie. She looked like she was going to die. Her face revealed despair. She barely looked up when Valerie walked in to talk to her.

"Elaine, I am so sorry for what you are going through. This has to be very painful."

"My baby, my baby, my baby. She is my only baby." Tears flooded Elaine's face.

Valerie pulled a travel pack of Kleenex out and handed it to Elaine. She sat down on the floor in front of her.

"I want to help if I can."

"Help me find my baby," Elaine begged.

"Can I ask you a few questions?"

"If it finds my baby, ask away."

"Was your baby born healthy?"

"Perfect health."

"Was anyone in your home besides family in the last couple of months, not including the babysitter?"

"We had an informational meeting here three weeks ago. I also hosted a MOPS meeting last week."

"Can you find the list of people who where here those dates?"

"That should be simple enough. We have the list on the computer for both. I will print it out for you."

"Elaine, tell me, has Damian been supportive in this ordeal?"

"He has hugged me a few times and told me we will get her back."

"Has Damian always been faithful to you?"

"Of course. He teases me about finding another woman, but you know he couldn't do that."

"Did Damian have any side business going?"

"Not that I know of."

"Ms. Sharpe, why are you asking her all those questions? The FBI will be handling the case from now on. You don't need to worry about it," Peters said defensively.

"Have any of you talked to the media?" Valerie asked.

"No," Peters said.

"Do you know if the sheriff department has given any statements yet?" Valerie asked.

"That I can't say for sure. You would have to ask Sheriff Hodges about that. They were here on the case yesterday. They took the first statements," Peters said.

"Agent Peters, did they find non-family fingerprints?" Valerie asked.

"'They are still at the lab. What are the questions about?"

"I have been asked to write the story for the *Dispatch*."

"Oh," Peters said, stopping for a moment to think. "You should talk to my superior, Agent Quad. He will be back here in a couple hours. They are digging up information. Have you written anything yet about this story?"

"No. I was just assigned the case a half hour ago."

"Here. Would you like some coffee?"

"I brought some calming tea."

"That sounds like something I should be drinking. My boss gives me the grunt work to do now that a flower child has arrived."

"I understand." *I probably shouldn't have said anything.*

"If they gave you a case like this, it doesn't sound that way."

"It was convenient for them. I am on family leave of absence.

"I am sorry to hear that. I guess you understand being in the cooker, don't you?"

"Yes, Agent Peters, I do. I can't imagine being a parent and having my child taken from me."

"It sucks," Damian said, as he entered the room.

"I am sure it does. Again, I am sorry for what you are going through," Valerie said with compassion.

"Thank you. It seems like everyone around here is blaming me for it," Damian said.

"You are just the closest to it. That is all," Valerie said, *hoping he couldn't see questions about his involvement. I don't see a motive, and can't imagine a father doing it, but you never know. Before too long, I'll need to go talk to the sheriff, glad at least to know his name.*

"Elaine, is there anything I can get for you?" Valerie asked.

"No. You have been so sweet to me. The ladies at MOPS brought food in if you are hungry help yourself. We have more than enough to go around. Did you meet my brother yet?"

"No. I saw an out-of-state plate in the driveway."

"He might be sleeping. He drove all night long. He came in from Florida. He was on a business trip."

"That was very nice of him. Listen. I am going to head out. It looks like the FBI has this under control. Damian has my cell number. If you need me for anything, just call me." Valerie gave her a hug and turned to leave.

Damian stood up. "Hey, how is your dad doing?"

"He came out of the coma. He will be transferred to a nursing home soon. It will be a long recovery process."

"Do you plan on staying around?"

"It is too soon to tell. The people here are great, but my job is in Columbus. I will let you know once I figure it out."

"Valerie, thank you so much for being here for us," Damian said.

"I will keep praying for you. I found it helps," Valerie said.

Agent Peters walked her out. "I am impressed. Most journalists are cold and heartless. You have them eating out of your hand. I am going to talk to Quad. I think we should hire you to help us on the investigation."

"Agent Peters, I didn't come here for a story. It just worked out that way. I didn't ask the boss. The boss asked me."

"Let me talk to Quad. If you feed us what you find, maybe we can reciprocate back."

"That works for me. Have you talked to the sheriff to compare the two questionings?"

"Quad is doing that right now. He will be here when he gets done."

CHAPTER 11

It had been a long time since Valerie had been by the county offices It was a small building with two offices and two jail cells. The Sherriff Department was on the left side of the building.

It couldn't leave much room for the FBI to be working from. I never worked on a case that involved the FBI. Peters seemed to welcome me after finding out who I was.

She entered the double doors. Inside was a security door. She pressed the buzzer and waited a few minutes. A short chubby guy let her in.

"I bet you are Valerie Sharpe. I have been expecting you."

"How did you know I was coming?"

"Your boss called us a few hours ago. We needed to investigate you to make sure you were clean."

"Wow."

"Come in. We were going over the evidence we have so far. My name is Agent Quad. I am in charge of this investigation. This is Agent Talbot. He is new with us, but don't underestimate him. He is sharp as a tack."

"Nice to meet you."

Valerie shook their hands and sat down where Quad pointed to an open seat. They were in a board room that could seat about eight people. The room was behind the front office and adjacent to the jail cells.

"Peters called and said you had been to the house. Did he tell you the baby seat is gone from the Escalade?"

"No, he didn't."

"We found third party finger prints in the baby's room. The prints do not match Sharon or any of their family members. The front door was used to enter, but nothing was broken. We found a key made at Lowe's on Sunday by Damian. He paid for it on a credit card. We have checked phone records and requested a full voice playback for the last two weeks. Several calls have come in from an unidentified person.

"Damian was over his head in debt. He made a business deal with a man who went out of business two weeks ago. The home has a one hundred and twenty-five percent LTV loan, then the value of the home drastically dropped. We checked into the new church. It is not pulling in much money yet. We are checking into the parent church to see if he has been threatened with his job yet. Friends of Damian's are making high-risk loans. We are digging deeper into that one. It looks like he owes one of these friends a large sum from two years ago. It also is on record that he was asked to leave his last position in Grand Rapids, Michigan. He pays six hundred dollars a month for the Escalade and sixteen hundred for his house. They have forty thousand in credit card debt. He is member of Lifetime Fitness about twenty miles from here. He had a reckless driving ticket six years ago, but somehow, he escaped going to jail. He has had two speeding tickets in the last eighteen months on his record. He never graduated from Wheaton College. He went there for three years; got involved in his friend's financial business; and, two years later, got the job at the church in Grand Rapids.

"Elaine has two charge cards years old. Both are in good standing and rarely used. She has no bad driving record. Her name is not on the house, his credit cards, or the checking account. She has not worked since they got married. Damian is her first and only man. They have been in and out of counseling. She has three close friends. Damian has fifty contacts in his e-mail account. We are digging deeper into those records. We should have that back in the morning. Do you have any questions?"

"I am impressed with how fast you got all that information."

"It was teamwork. A story like this can make or break my job. If I move fast, I look like a hero. The press will eat a story like this up. I can't afford to foul it up," Quad said.

"Off the record, do you think he did it?"

"Valerie, do you think he did it?"

"I thought the babysitter did until I found out she had been at the hospital since six thirty in the morning Monday. I am not sure what to think right now. I want to write a fair story."

"Right now, all you can write are facts. The facts will unfold as time goes on," Quad said.

"Boss, weren't we going to head back to the house?"

"Yes. We are done here for now. We need to talk to the couple again. Talbot, I will be with you in a few minutes. I have something I need to handle first. Why don't you guys go get something to drink at the 7-Eleven? I shouldn't be too long."

"Looks like you are stuck with me now," Talbot said teasingly as his eyes roamed up and down Valerie's body. He had been sizing Valerie up.

"I could do worse. So you are the one who questioned them earlier?"

"It was the first time he has had me do it."

"He must have confidence in you."

"He keeps telling me that."

"So how did you choose a career in the FBI?"

"I could ask you the same question."

"You first," Valerie insisted.

"I loved solving crimes when I was very young."

"I loved writing when I was young."

"So there we have it. So tell me, Valerie, are you with anyone?"

"I look like I am alone now, don't I?"

"Cute."

"I knew what you meant. I am teasing you. No, I am not with anyone. Could I really be fair to a man?"

"If you found the right one, you could."

"What is the right one?"

"That is up to you to answer. Each person looks for different qualities."

"Talbot, I have no desire yet. I want to enjoy the moment. I am still young. I have many years before I need to worry about my biological clock ticking. Are you interviewing me for a job?" *This guy is a little much, fun to flirt with but get real dude.*

"No. We are just passing time. He told us to get lost. Remember?"

"Yes, he did."

"Maybe we could go to dinner sometime while I am here."

"I am hungry now," Valerie said.

"Let me go ask and see if he will let me go. I would love that."

In a few minutes, Talbot returned. "He said as long as you drop me off at the pastor's house, I could go for ninety minutes. By the way, call me Bruce."

"Okay, Bruce. I was planning on eating a good dinner tonight. I would like the change of pace," Valerie said.

"I hope you know a good place to eat."

"I am going to take you out by the highway. The atmosphere isn't all that good, but the food is decent, there is not much to choose from out here in the boonies. There is an old truck stop and this place. The truck stop is good for breakfast foods."

"Let's go. I understand you work for *Columbus Dispatch* and Damian and Elaine called you in the day the baby was taken."

"Yes. Isn't that amazing? I didn't expect a break like this."

"So tell me about the accident."

"I was told my parents were returning from a church function. They were out east of town. They came to an intersection in which they had the right of way. A seventeen-year-old had been drinking. He never stopped. He was also left of the center lane. The EMS said my mom was dead when they arrived. My dad was thrown from the car and banged up pretty bad. He was in a coma until a couple days ago. I should be getting a call soon for them to transfer him to a nursing home nearby."

"I am so sorry for your loss. Looks like you are coping quite well."

"I don't feel it, but maybe I am doing better than I thought. Tell me, Bruce, is there any more to this baby story?" *I don't feel comfortable with so much personal talk.*

"The facts can sometimes look one way and then turn out to be something completely different. But to answer your question, Damian is our prime suspect. We know he could not have done it alone. But there is a motive."

"How could a father get rid of his baby?"

"Desperate people do desperate things. I could never do it. Look at it this way. He might have sold her for money. Maybe knowing she would not die, he could soothe his conscience. He might not have personally done anything to have her taken, but it might have been a trickle effect from a business deal."

"Do you think he owed money and sold the baby?"

"I am thinking that might be what happened."

"What about his flippant behavior?"

"That just might be his personality. You never know. Each person reacts to the same thing in their own way. I don't want to be too quick to judge him. I do, however, see that he has some financial issues that are pretty big, which leaves a motive. We will see what kind of evidence shows up over the next few days."

"What about the baby? She could be dead by then."

"I doubt it. I think she was taken to be sold. She is at the top of the age bracket, but babies bring big dollars."

"I never thought about that."

"No ransom note has appeared. She's not meant to be returned."

"That is what you get paid the big dollars for."

"Who you talking big dollars to? I don't make any more than I bet you do."

"You never know. I guess both of our jobs have an element of risk to them."

Valerie parked the car. Bruce told her to wait because he wanted to open her car door for her.

CHAPTER 12

Valerie was almost ready to send the story. She wanted to reread it to make sure everything was precise. She sent the e-mail with the story attached. It flowed from her heart. She asked Shelly if she could do a piece about a mother's loss. She would wait for her reply. She called the hospital and found out that her father would be there for another two days until a bed was available. She called the support group number and found a support group meeting Tuesdays at seven o'clock. The ages of the members were close to hers. She opened a text message from Jon asking her to go out to dinner and a play with his friends that weekend. He told her he would call her that night for an answer. The cell phone rang. It was Bruce.

"Good morning, beautiful lady. I wanted to call and say thank you for last night. The company was great, and the food was good. Are you coming to the pastor's anytime today?"

"Why? Do you want to see me?"

"I am on guard duty here for the day. No new clues have come in yet. We did order a forensic team to come in and search the house. They should be here in a few minutes."

"I will be there this afternoon sometime. I have a trip to the hospital, and a heads-up for my next article."

"Is the article about me?"

"Well, of course, Bruce. It is about how the FBI is full of heroes."

"All kidding aside, I hope to see you today."

"Hey, have any TV cameras shown up yet?"

"Late last night, a crew was here. We didn't tell them much. They asked a couple questions about Elaine and Damian. They did a shot of the home and property."

"Thanks for telling me. I ordered pictures to go along with the article. The family had a photo taken last month. That should be current enough."

"Good job. We didn't even know that. How did you get that info?"

"I called the photo shops in town this morning. I was just lucky. The photos haven't been released yet to Damian and Elaine."

"Do you know if they are done?"

"Today, the lady said they had requested them to be mailed. So it was perfect timing."

"How is she getting you the photo?"

"E-mail."

"That works out well. Listen. I got to go. There is movement in the house."

Valerie shut the phone.

I really did enjoy my time with Bruce last night. It was too short. It had given me enough time to write the article and dig for new leads. I didn't feel Elaine could sell her baby, but Damian maybe. She felt that to him, being a pastor was about a title and a business deal. He didn't have a heart for the lost or helping people find their savior. He was arrogant and prideful.

Valerie started looking for more information on those seeking titles. She downloaded a few chapters of some books dealing with surrounding issues to that. One she liked a lot was Frank Viola and George Barnes's Pagan Christianity. While she was reading, her boss called her.

"Valerie, I love the story. The boss said you can write the article you want. It's a good humanitarian story. Do you think Elaine will agree to do it?"

"I will find out. I will go there today and talk to her. I think she will if she thinks it might bring her baby back alive."

"Good job, Valerie! We have one more story just north of you that we want you to do. A military plane blew up late last night. I have not been able to get all the details yet. I will e-mail them to you soon."

"Do you know where it happened?"

"I will have to get the location for you. Thanks for doing such a good job. You are making me look real good."

A second story would be pushing it. I'll need to take my laptop with me.

She headed first to the hospital. Jon would be done with his rounds so she wouldn't be seeing him. She checked to see if her dad needed anything. He was in physical therapy. She sat in his room, finishing some of her research. She got the e-mail to the plane site. It was about an hour north, close to Mansfield. She would head up there after talking to Elaine.

She got a text message. It was Mason checking in. He asked if she was going to be around later that night and said he wanted to meet with her. She texted him back and said that she would but she just couldn't be sure what time. She told him she was working on two stories. He sent her a message back to call him when she was free. She thought she had better eat before leaving the hospital. So she headed down the elevator to the basement. Upon reaching the basement floor, she saw Jon across the room. She waved. He came excitedly running.

"Hey, girl. I didn't expect to see you down here today. I thought I had missed my chance to harass you until tonight."

"I didn't think that was fair, so here I am. Harass away."

"I was teasing you."

"I know."

"So how about Saturday night?"

"If I can get my stories to line up in time, I would love to go."

"Are you telling lies now?"

"That didn't sound good. I have a military plane that blew up that I have to write about. They don't know what caused it to blow up yet. I am headed up there this afternoon."

"I wish I could go with you."

"Me too. That would be fun. Besides cameramen, I have always worked alone."

"We can change that for you."

"How do you plan on doing that?"

"It could be arranged, you know."

"I suppose so." Valerie took that as joking.

"I have to get back to work. Call me later. Please."

"Okay. But I won't be able to talk long. I am working late."

Valerie ordered a BLT and a salad. She grabbed a V8 and paid for her meal. She hoped her dad would be back in his room when she got up there. If not, she hoped he would return soon. She ate and returned to the room. Within a couple of minutes, they were rolling her dad back in. The orderly helped him get back up in the bed and then left.

"That was a longer session today, Dad."

He nodded his head. He patted the hospital bed, motioning for her to sit by him. They did that when she was young. Valerie liked to sit by her dad wherever they went. They sat in silence for a long time. Valerie looked at her watch and saw that it was time to go.

"Dad, do you need anything?"

He shook his head no.

"Dad, I'm writing two stories. I won't be back tonight. Sorry."

Valerie had forgotten her professional camera and needed to head back home. She would grab the mail and put it in the house. She found two checks from the insurance company. One was for the disability income for four weeks, and the other was life insurance on her mom, double indemnity from the accident. It was more than she had expected. With her paycheck, she would be able to pay off his large loan. She grabbed the camera and took a bottle of water with her.

She found Elaine taking a nap when she arrived at the house. Bruce had said that she had laid down more than an hour before. Valerie concluded that she was depressed. So she went looking for Damian. She found him searching the Internet. He quickly exited out, so she had no idea what he was looking for. His time on the Internet was being watched by the FBI, so they would know whatever he was wanting to hide.

"Damian."

"Yes?"

"Could I ask you a few questions?"

"Sure. Have a seat. Here. Let me clear that off for you," he said, removing the stacks of papers lining the chair so she could sit down.

"Damian, how does all this feel to you, losing your only baby?"

"Of course it hurts."

"I know it has to hurt. Has this affected your relationship with Elaine?"

"No, I wouldn't say it had."

"What if they don't find her alive?"

"She has to be alive. I know it."

"But how can you be so sure?"

"I feel it."

"Damian, where does God come into all this?"

"What do you mean?"

"How is God helping you through this difficult time?" *He doesn't realize that has nothing to do with my articles, I want to know what kind of relationship he has with God.*

"God has nothing to do with it."

"Do you think Elaine will be getting up soon?"

"Elaine hasn't been sleeping at night. She might not be sleeping now. You can open the door and check on her. She is a sound sleeper, so if she is sleeping, she won't hear you."

"I think I will do that. Thank you for answering my questions."

"No biggie."

Valerie found Elaine looking out the window. "Elaine, do you mind if I come in?"

"Please do. I could use someone to talk to."

"I am sorry for your loss. I have been praying that God return the baby."

"Thank you. It seems like you are the only one praying around here."

"Aren't you and Damian praying together?"

"Are you kidding?" Elaine asked.

"We get these ideas of what a pastor should look like. It is funny that they rarely ever look like our model," Valerie said.

"I have never felt such deep pain. I feel like a part of me has been ripped off my body. She is my flesh and blood. Who could take my baby like that?"

"We hope to find out and bring her back safely."

"I can't complain. Everyone has been good to us. The FBI is doing all they can."

"Are they getting in your way?"

"Not really, but it does seem strange to be going through this and have your house filled with people you never met before."

"Elaine, when the time comes and you want to get out and do something, call me. I would like to be your friend."

"Thank you, Valerie. That means so much."

"I found new friends in my crisis. Mason has been wonderful. The doctor has been too."

"In time, I might be ready for your help. This minute, I feel so much pain that I don't know if I can take it much longer."

"God won't take you too far. He has a way of taking us to the end and quickly bringing us back. You will make it, Elaine."

"Thank you. I needed to hear that."

"Damian encourages you, doesn't he?"

"Not really. He is so caught up in himself, to be honest."

"I am sorry to hear that."

"We have been doing counseling for a long time. It only changes me."

"I have heard that God changes us first. Women are more relational than men. Have you ever read the book *Men Are from Mars, Women Are from Venus?*"

"No, but I have heard that it is good."

"I think it brings a good perspective for the differences between the two sexes."

"It might help me."

"Elaine, would you mind if I do an article from a mother's heart to her missing child?"

"No. That is fine with me."

"Is there anything you want the readers to know?" Valerie asked.

"That things happen no matter what status you live in. I never thought something like this could ever happen to me. We are middle class. There is no money for a ransom."

"That is a good point."

"You can tell whatever you think is right."

"Elaine, has the FBI talked to you about their findings?"

"Not really. They are here but aren't talking to us."

"Are you aware that you two are in financial distress?"

"I wouldn't know anything about that. Damian pays all the bills. He leaves me out of those issues. I know he was offered a good salary to come here. We had just lost our job in Grand Rapids when the offer came in."

"Who made the offer for you to come here?"

"I am not sure," Elaine said.

"Why would your mother church chose such a small town?"

"I don't know. I have questioned that too."

"Are you happy here?"

"Pretty much."

"Do you ever regret marrying Damian?"

"Sometimes, but what am I going to do, leave?"

"Elaine, I have met some very nice men since I have been here. I am not suggesting you leave Damian but that you make some friends. Having a support group is important in times like this."

"One of my girlfriends will be here tonight. She is flying in from Colorado."

"I am glad. You need that."

"Thank you."

"I am going to head out. I have another story I have to go work on. If you need me, call me." Valerie hugged Elaine.

"Thank you for everything," Elaine said softly in the hug.

Valerie hunted for Bruce, wanting to say bye. She didn't know how long the FBI would keep a crew there. She doubted if it would be too many days.

"Hey. I was hoping to see you," Bruce said.

"I just wanted to say bye. I am headed north for another story." Valerie shifted her weight.

"One cup of coffee first. It won't take long."

"Okay."

CHAPTER 13

The story with the military plane wasn't as big of a deal as Valerie thought it might be. The plane developed a hole in the gas tank. The last mechanic to work on it noted that the gas tank needed to be replaced before flying again. Somehow, it was flown without being certified. The plane was flying from Georgia to Sefridge in Michigan. She was able to quickly get the information and get out. She took footage of the crash site. She got the names of men on the plane and those involved before the flight took off. Before her drive back to town, she texted Jon. She said she would go out with him Saturday night. He immediately texted her back, asking for her dress and shoe sizes.

I don't want to talk about this with a text. I'll call him.

After the call to Jon she returned Mason's call from earlier that day.

"Hi, Mason, this is Val."

"I was hoping you would call soon. How about dinner?"

"Sounds good."

"Meet me at the diner by the e-way," Mason said.

"I'll be there in about forty-five minutes."

Driving back to the country, she pondered over the things that Elaine had said. It left more questions than answers. She was going to ask Bruce what Damian was looking at on the Internet. She had not gotten a phone number, so she hoped he would still be there in the morning. Earlier, he had called off a local number. She wasn't sure whose it was. She guessed it was a line the FBI hooked up.

On the drive back, she prayed for all the parties involved. She prayed that God would open up the location of where the baby was. She prayed that the person responsible would turn themselves in before the baby was gone for good. She prayed for her dad's healing and that God would use it to take her farther to grow where she was. She asked God to give her wisdom to know what to do.

Should I return to Columbus and full-time on the job? Am I ready for a relationship?

After praying, she drove in silence, hoping to hear back from God. The still, small voice spoke to her to stay with her father, that God was in control and would work it out. Valerie felt peace flow. She knew that she was on the right path. Her dad was going to need her help to keep the farm going. Columbus was no longer a desire anyway. She was starting to like the laidback life. She would enjoy the new people God had laid across her path. She felt like she and Elaine would be friends someday. She arrived at the old truck stop.

"Hi, Mason."

"Valerie, thanks for coming. I ordered food." The playful look was not there. He was straight faced.

"It feels good to sit, not having to go anywhere for a bit."

"A hard day?"

"I wouldn't say hard. Just many pieces needing to come together."

"How is your dad?"

"They are moving him on Friday to a nursing home."

"Have you been back to see Damian and Elaine?"

"Yes. I was there yesterday and today. Why?"

"I don't know how to do this."

"Spit it out, for crying out loud," Valerie said louder than she should have.

"Valerie, I talked to the sheriff. He told me that the stories don't add up. He said that what Damian said the day the baby was taken was not what he told the FBI. He also shared with me the debt problems. I checked with the leaders who placed him here. They have talked to him about letting him go. The church is not growing the way they expected. They sent a couple in as spies, and they were not impressed. I am not saying Damian did this, but it doesn't look very good."

"Things are rarely what they look like. We can't accuse him without any evidence. Right now, it is all circumstantial. There is nothing solid to point at him. Did you know he had a side business?"

"Not until now. I thought that his only thing was the church. I should have guessed that his heart really isn't there."

"You have been to their house before this happened. Has he always been indifferent toward Elaine?"

"He has always been self-centered, if that is what you mean. I don't think he is trying to hurt her. He is bossy with her. She tolerates it, but I can tell she is not very happy about it."

"Mason, I wonder if she saw that before she married him?"

"She is in love with him. You know the saying that love is blind. She might have thought she could pull him out of it."

"She doesn't seem to be in love with him now."

"Look at what happened. You can't let emotion drive a relationship. One day, you would stay; one day, you would leave," Mason said.

"You might be right. I haven't been in many relationships."

"That is an improvement. I am glad to hear that. I was worried about you for a while."

"I am like a cat. I have nine lives. No. I mean to say that you toss me in the air and I will land on my feet. The ride in between landing and tossing me might not be pretty."

"I would say you are level headed. You would have to be to be a journalist."

"You know what they say about accountants? Every bean has to be accounted for."

"In today's world, that has to be a good trait."

"Of course it is," Valerie teased.

"I am sorry for the way we met, but I am glad you are here."

"That is a nice thing to say."

"You are good company. This area has many men but no women your age besides Elaine."

"I hope you are wrong. I start my support group next week. I was hoping to have some women my age in it."

"How far does it go?"

"They cover the entire county. The meeting is twenty miles from here."

"That is not too bad."

"What do you think they will do about church on Sunday?"

"Damian called in a guest speaker. They have a pastor from one of the other churches coming."

"I didn't think he would be up to it."

"I suggested he do that. He doesn't need the questions from all the people right now either."

"Mason, do they ever do communion?"

"Not since I have been there."

"Doesn't that seem odd?"

"Maybe. I have been placed there to pray for them. I am not condoning what they stand for."

"I am glad to hear that."

"God can use us wherever he plants us. I don't have too many choices out here in the country, you know."

"I guess that is a drawback. In the city, you have a church on every other corner. You pick the denomination and you have it within a ten-mile radius," Valerie said.

"Have you ever thought about how God feels about having so many denominations?"

"I was reading an excerpt from a book today making me look at just that. How did we get so far out of balance, Mason?"

"I guess we listen to society. It dictates things it shouldn't."

"I was caught up in it. I didn't even know. God pulling me out and bringing me here might have saved my life. I value life in a new way."

"That is awesome. God knows how to get us on track. I have seen it in my own life. I know that this will change Damian and Elaine."

"Hopefully not in a bad way."

"Not what I meant. They have enough foundation to eventually pull them back to center. They both came from a Christian college."

"I hope that means something to them," Valerie said, not confident it would.

"Our job is to pray for them."

"You're right. I hope they can make the marriage work after the crisis."

"You and Elaine are about the same age. Maybe you can be of help to her."

"I am trying."

"Give her a little time. She is a nice lady."

"I would like to get to know her."

The two ate without talking for a bit.

"When we get done, I am going to go check on Damian Mason said.

"Let me know if there is anything I need to know."

"How did the story turn out?"

"The bosses are pleased."

"That is always good. I am thankful I don't have any bosses."

"You have plenty of clients."

"They can be a pain too."

"What do you do when you go on vacation?"

"Work hard before and after. I don't take many vacations for that reason. I can't take January to the end of April off."

"Why January?"

"Year end. I am closing out their books. I have a few staggered clients who do their year end other than fiscal years."

"That is smart."

"I try to work smart. Having to crunch is not fun. For the most part, things have worked out well for me."

"That is good," Valerie said.

"It looks like your job is working out well for you too."

"I never expected to be able to write in the country."

"It probably gives you a clear head."

"You might be right. I will find out as the trauma goes away."

"Your dad is going to be fine. It will take a little time."

I sure hope so."

"Look how you were able to be compassionate with Elaine because of the accident. Thanks for coming out. No. Leave that. I want to pay."

"If you insist. I can turn it in for a business expense," Valerie said.

CHAPTER 14

Letters poured into the newsroom. The public wanted to know more about the kidnapping. The story was hot. The headlines showed the recent photo of the family. The paper printed both stories. The backup story was in the headlines with the mother's heart placed on page four. The military plane story also was on the front page, with a shot of the burned-out wreckage. Pictures of the deceased followed on page two. Stories of the lives of the men had been included by another journalist. Valerie assumed they came from the air force records. They had used what she had written as the headline and used the rest to compliment her story. She was the only writer given credit. That made no sense. It was a dog eat dog world. Why would her boss do that?

At eight o'clock, her cell phone was buzzing. It was Shelly.

"Valerie, you did an outstanding job. We have had a hundred and twenty e-mails about the story from yesterday. The paper got calls this morning already about today's paper. They love the angle. Keep it up. The boss said he was going to give you a bonus."

"Cool. Any new stories for me to follow?"

"Stay on the baby."

"Who finished my article on the plane wreckage?"

"I had them forward the information yesterday afternoon. I had that written and ready to go. The press just had to plug it in."

"Thanks, Shelly." Valerie sat down on the couch in the living room, turning the news off.

"You deserve it."

"You could have taken credit for it."

"Not this time. I owe you, kid. You got the boss on my good side. You keep up the good work, and I will keep your back covered."

"It's a deal." Valerie looked at the phone before dialing Damian and Elaine's house phone. Peters answered, "A camera crew is here from ABC. They are interviewing Damian and Elaine. I'll have Elaine call you after they are done," Peters said.

Out of all the men, Valerie had not gotten to know Peters very well. She figured she would give it a couple hours and take some food with her and go see the pastor and his wife. Peters might have a different take than Talbot and Mason. It was hard for her to imagine a father selling his baby, no matter what the circumstances. She knew Elaine would not hear of it.

She hacked into Damian's computer and verified that he indeed had bought the tickets for a trip. He had bought cancellation insurance. Records indicate that he always bought the insurance. She verified a life insurance policy on the baby and on Elaine. The FBI had forwarded the names of family members to her. One by one, she did a background check on each one. There was nothing unusual about Elaine's family—no divorces and no early deaths.

Damian's family was a little more colorful. His parents had divorced, and his dad spent time in prison for embezzlement charges. His older brother had a DUI a couple years before. His sister was caught selling drugs a few years before. She was under eighteen, so they only sent her to a juvenile home. She closed the laptop. *I'll run to the hospital and check on dad and then go see Elaine. Camera crews should be gone by then.*

She found her dad to be talking more words than the day before.

"Hi, Dad! How are you feeling today?"

"A little better. The doctor gave me an anxiety pill. It seemed to be helping. The doctor thought my talking issue was fear related."

"It must have been. That makes perfect sense. Who did that?"

"They sent me to a psychologist yesterday afternoon. He came up with that diagnosis. He feels like I need to have therapy twice a week for a while."

"I am glad to hear you talking. Can you tell me why you took a large loan out?"

"With the foreclosures, I had an opportunity to buy a new section of land cheap."

"So did you buy the land?"

"Yes, I did. It is the forty acres west of us. Honey, tell me you figured out a way to pay for it."

"Well, Dad, you are in luck. The insurance money came in. I added my paycheck, and, yes, the loan is paid for. Now I have an appointment with the IRS to renegotiate your bill with them. Mason said he would go with me. I might have to sell some of my portfolio to get that paid for you."

"Honey, I have most of the money sitting aside. It is in the house."

"Dad, you have to be kidding me. I have struggled all this time working hard to do this for you. What a relief."

"Honey, I am so proud of you. I always knew you would come through in a time of need. Honey, did you find the Mutual Standard Insurance policy?"

"No, Dad."

"The policy is on both your mom and me. It pays out fifty thousand dollars in case of a death and double indemnity. Once we get that paid, I will pay you back what you used to pay my bills. We will pay the IRS and all the credit cards."

"Dad, I paid the credit cards. The only outstanding debt is the IRS. That is not one to play with. I got them to agree to work out a settlement. With the guardianship, I have flexibility you would not have with them. The fact that you have not been able to work the last six weeks helps. I am just glad that the amount you owe them is not that much. I have to show them that I have used my own funds the lady said. I have the cancelled checks."

"Honey, I only owe them last quarter's taxes. There shouldn't be any penalties and interest yet. The tax bill was due the week the accident happened."

"Dad, I don't know about those things. I get my taxes taken out of my check. I file at the end of the year and get a refund every year. It is that simple."

"Honey, I have investments I have to pay on quarterly. The farm is calculated at the end of the year."

"So where are the investments at?"

"I am part owner of the dairy company."

"That makes no sense. You were delivering organic dairy products to the restaurant in town. You own a dairy too?"

"I am part owner. It is not organic. I keep the two separate. The organic products have a specific market, but it is much smaller than this dairy."

"Who does the dairy sell to?"

"The dairy is selling to manufacturers of food products. We don't have to have labels or public awareness. It works out. With me selling on a small scale, no one would think that I am part of this dairy. Some of the local farmers would treat me differently if they knew. I am a silent partner. I get profit-sharing checks every quarter. It has been a money-maker ever since I got into it."

"I should have known you better than that. I was questioning your money skills."

"Honey, I never wanted your mom to work for a mean boss. So I had to be creative to make enough to live on. I have put some away in foreign banks, but it isn't much. I bought into the dairy when one of the guys was going through a divorce. He needed money to pay debt off and attorney fees. Now he wants to buy me out."

"Would that be a good idea or not?"

"Not yet. The money will flow if I am working or not. With the accident, I will collect disability for a few months, but I can't work the farm. Luckily, things slow down in the fall. We can get Bob to fix the equipment for us. A new guy came to town who we can use to harvest the animal feed. It will still be cheaper than me working and not collecting the money."

"Sounds good, Dad. Do I need to stick around?"

"The question is not do you need to—but do you want to?"

"Why do you ask that?"

"I have seen the way two men look at you, my dear."

"Maybe. I have a date with Jon for this Saturday. Last night, Mason and I had dinner and talked about the baby case. There is nothing there, he is Bill's age. "

"What baby case?"

"Oh, that is right. I never told you. There is a new seeker church in town. The pastor had his baby kidnapped this week."

"Is that where you met Mason?"

"Yes, Dad, it is. Aunt Rose was worried about me, so she took me there one Sunday morning."

"How is Aunt Rose?"

"She was up to see you a few days ago. I guess she hasn't been back since you came out of the coma. She is fine."

"I am glad you and Aunt Rose connected. She is a fine lady. She has always been good to me and your mom."

"Dad, does it upset you that Mom is gone?"

"Sure, but what can I do about it? You could have told me. I would rather have heard it from you than a nurse."

"I know."

"Your mom and I had a lifetime of good memories. Did you know that we knew each other since we were three?"

"That is a long time."

"She was my sweetheart then and always will be."

"I hope someday I find a guy as sweet as you."

"You will sooner than you think. The city is not a place to find nice men, but in the country, the men are sincere. They don't play games here. They can't. Everyone would know. There is safety in a small community that is unknown in the city."

"Tell that to the pastor and his wife."

"Honey, I doubt someone from around here took that baby. Investigate their roots outside of here."

"That sounds like good advice."

"Find out where the couple came from. Find out where their family all lives. And I bet in the mix you find the person with the baby."

"I will work harder at that. I researched the family members this morning. Nothing jumped out at me. Maybe I should check into the church they came from in Grand Rapids, Michigan."

"Do it, honey."

"Dad, I am so glad we had this talk. I have to go to the pastor's house and gather more information. I have another article to write."

"They are letting you do it from here?"

"Due to the story being right here, they are."

"That is another one of God's blessings."

"I am finding that out too." Valerie kissed his forehead before moving out of the room.

Jon walked in. "I was hoping to steal a glimpse of your beautiful daughter."

"You don't have to worry about stealing anything. She said you have a date set up for Saturday night. You treat her right," Jacob said with a firm tone.

"Yes, sir. So I see the Xanax we prescribed worked. How are you feeling today?"

"Better. My muscles are feeling better."

"Good. Valerie, how are you doing this cloudy day?"

"Better now that I see you."

"Cool. We might have it made for Saturday night, Jacob."

"You two have fun."

"Jacob, they are going to assign you a traveling doctor once you get to the nursing home. I will still be going over your charts once a week for the next month. If you need anything, call me. The nursing home I have set you up with is the best in the tri-county area. I doubt you will have any complaints."

"Will I still be doing the aqua therapy?"

"Yes, you will. They have a similar system there. I have also plugged you in for the infrared treatments. It will help the body heal quickly, and you will have more energy. It helps break up the scar tissue, which reduces pain. Let me get your vitals. Blood pressure is good, and so is your heart rate."

"See you Saturday night, Jon," Valerie said.

"I will pick you up at five."

"Sounds great."

"Did the outfit show up yet?" he asked, turning back in the doorway.

"No. I forgot about it. It might be there. I will check later. Thank you."

"My pleasure. If it doesn't fit, call me. I will have them send another one out."

"Is this coming UPS?"

"No. It is a friend's store on the north side of Columbus. I had her make you an original designer dress in colors I think you would like. Let me know if that bothers you."

"How cool is that? Do you do that for all your dates?" *What a special thought he made, I bet it was because he didn't think I had very many clothes here.*

"I don't date much, Valerie. I have never seriously dated anyone."

"I see."

"It is a good place for you to be. I mean, getting out. I am only trying to help you reduce stress."

"That is what they all say." Valerie left on that note.

CHAPTER 15

Valerie made a stop at the store to pick up some sleep aids for Elaine. The body can only go so many nights without sleep. She bought her some calcium/magnesium to calm her down. She bought a combination that had melatonin too. She picked up a roasted chicken, potato salad, and coleslaw. On the way out, she grabbed a case of water. They would have food for another meal anyway.

She drove to their house, finding Damian raking leaves. "Elaine is in the house. Go ahead and go in."

The FBI was gone. A young lady was sitting at the kitchen table. "Hi. I am Valerie." She held her hand out to shake.

"Hi, Valerie. I am Jessica, Elaine's friend from college. Elaine's in the tub. She'll be out soon. She's been in there a long time."

"Is she feeling any better?"

"She is taking this pretty hard. She won't eat, and she can't sleep."

"I brought her something for her sleep issues. Oh. Here, I brought some food. I will go back out and get the case of water."

"That was great thinking. We ran out of bottled water last night. Food pickings are getting slimmer," Jessica said, as she walked toward the car to take the water in.

"When did the FBI leave?" Valerie asked.

"They picked Peters up at seven. I am not sure if they are coming back or not. They were pretty good to us. They had food catered in yesterday."

"So when did you arrive?"

"I got here at about four yesterday. I can only stay for two days. I was hoping she had someone around here to keep a watch on her. I see that she has that."

Elaine came strolling out of the bedroom. Her hair was wrapped in a hair towel. She was wearing a bright-red robe.

"Good morning, Valerie."

"Are you feeling any better?"

"I still am struggling, but not as much."

"Good. I bought you some sleep aids. I hope they work. I found that a good night's sleep cures fifty percent of anything. I can deal with tough issues as long as I have had enough sleep."

"That was sweet of you. Thank you."

Jessica walked over to the food Valerie brought. "She brought fresh food too."

"I don't know how to show you my grateful heart."

"Elaine, I have been there. No one knows the pain and the loss until they too have experienced something of this magnitude."

"That is true. You have been so kind to us."

"Is the FBI done?"

"Who knows? They didn't say anything."

"I am going to go out and talk to Damian. Is that okay?" Valerie asked.

"Sure."

"Damian, can I talk to you while you rake?"

"Suit yourself."

"Damian, do you have any idea who would take Kala?"

"I wish I did. I would kill the SOB."

Valerie was shocked at his descriptive talk, but if her child was gone, maybe she would be angry too.

"Do you know that you are their prime suspect?"

"Isn't that who they always look at?"

"There is evidence that you are in financial trouble that could be motive to sell your baby."

"I am going to tell you, Valerie, I didn't sell my baby. I don't know who did."

"Did you purchase a key on Sunday?"

"I did, to give to a neighbor in case something happened while we were gone."

"But it is not the first trip you have taken. Why the key now?"

"I changed the locks after I had a worker in the house painting a few weeks ago."

"When asked who else had been in the house, why didn't you mention the painter?"

"I forgot all about it. The FBI never asked me about the key to trigger the memory like you did," Damian said with a tear forming in his eye. You could see remorse. He looked very sad for the first time.

"Damian, I understand that you have connections to high-risk business adventures?"

"I went to school with a guy who owns a financial company. I have done some work for him on and off."

"Did you tell the FBI that?"

"They didn't ask me."

"What did they ask you?"

"They asked about the day before Kala disappeared, what we did, who had been in the house, those kinds of questions. They asked about my relationship with Elaine."

"What did you tell them?"

"Not much I guess. I thought we were happy. Maybe I have been a jerk all along. Elaine hates me. I can't give her the support she deserves." Damian held his head down.

"Why? Because you don't know how?"

"I was never raised to be sensitive like that."

"You know she needs you."

"I am learning. I have no business leading people when I can't lead my own family. I couldn't protect Kala. How can I protect a group coming to hear me speak?"

"Damian, that is something you have to work out over time."

"I am thinking about leaving the church and working on me for a while."

"Might not be a bad idea. Crisis has a way of teaching us lessons. I am not the same woman I was when I got the call about the accident."

"Valerie, I am sorry. I failed you too. I was cold to your problem. I could have at least let you vent."

"Probably so, but that day is gone. God has been wooing me to a gentle spot in his heart. Damian, I was so stuck on the city living. Now I have a new set of values."

"I need a new set of values. I need my family to mean more than appearances."

"Have you asked God to forgive you?"

"No, but I should."

"Let's do it now."

"You lead. I will follow."

"Repeat after me: Father, forgive me for not putting you center stage," Valerie prayed.

ROSALYN ZOGRAFOS

Damian repeated, "Father, forgive me for not putting you center stage."

"I repent for allowing my own agenda to take control over my life and it costing me my Kala."

"I repent for allowing my own agenda to take control over my life and it costing me my baby girl. Oh, Jesus, I can't bear this anymore. Take this guilt and shame and replace it with your presence. Teach me to be compassionate with my wife and others. Teach me to trust in you. Give me a humble heart to be pure and holy so that I can be a vessel of your glory and your honor. In Jesus's name, I pray." Damian turned and looked Valerie in the eye, "Valerie, I can't thank you enough. I had blocked all that in. I wasn't able to let it go until you prodded me."

"Damian, sometimes we all need help. It might not look like much, but the hand we offer to a person in need might be all it takes to bring change. Mason did that for me. Then God brought the doctor to show me attention. The little things made a huge difference for me."

"God has used you to teach volumes to me, Valerie. If you ever move back to the city, will you promise me we won't ever lose contact?"

"I would like that, Damian. I am going to go back in and say bye to the girls. I have a story to write."

"The first three have been excellent. I hope this one is too. Good luck, Valerie."

"Thanks, Damian."

As Valerie was walking back into the house, she got a call from Shelly.

"Valerie, we have three leads on the baby. The pictures printed in the paper have caused many to call. We are inundated with calls, letters, and e-mails. You have been the highlight of the paper. I will call you to keep you informed on what happens with the leads."

"Where do they thinks she is?"

"She was seen in an airport in Utah. The flight had come from Columbus two days ago."

"Wow! That is great."

"It was your good thinking that might have found her."

"I am glad she is still alive. I interviewed Damian, he couldn't have done it. As much as the evidence looks that way."

"Your instincts are improving. I will talk to you later."

Valerie turned back to tell Damian. She saw his eyes glued to her face.

"She was sighted in Utah at an airport. The flight was out of Columbus. Whoever took her wasn't too smart. They had to know the closest airport would be watched."

"Thank God. Do they know how she was taken yet?"

"It doesn't sound like it. Whoever had her at the airport might not be the same person who came in the house."

"That is true, Valerie. It was all because you printed the family photo. I had my reservations about it, but I see you were right."

"It is what I get paid for. I will tell Elaine."

"Good."

Elaine was dressed sitting at the kitchen table.

"Elaine, I got a call from the paper. They have had three leads on Kala. They sighted her in a Utah airport. It is a matter of time now before they find her, but she is alive. I have to go write my article. If you need anything, call me."

"Thank you, Valerie."

Jessica stood. "It was nice meeting you, Valerie."

"You too, Jessica."

Jessica hugged her, and so did Elaine.

Valerie called Mason from her car, wanting him to know Damian didn't do it.

"I got a call from my editor. They have three leads on Kala. She was sighted by three people in a Utah airport. The FBI is working on the leads. They left the pastor's house at seven. They had to have known about the leads. Why didn't they tell Damian and Elaine?"

"Maybe because they think Damian is in on it."

"That could be true. I had a heart-to-heart with Damian. I don't think he did it. I could see the remorse on his face. He doesn't know how to show emotion. I think you will find a new Damian emerging. Hey, how is your day going?"

"Pretty good."

"Unless you have anything more for me, I am going home to write."

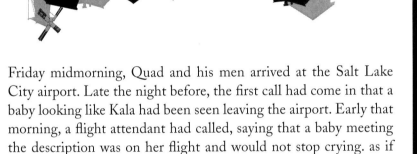

CHAPTER 16

Friday midmorning, Quad and his men arrived at the Salt Lake City airport. Late the night before, the first call had come in that a baby looking like Kala had been seen leaving the airport. Early that morning, a flight attendant had called, saying that a baby meeting the description was on her flight and would not stop crying. as if she was with a stranger. She was wearing mismatched clothes. The man with the baby didn't have a diaper bag and didn't seem to know how to handle a baby. When she got in, she saw the paper, raising red flags.

A passenger sitting next to the man with the baby also called this morning. It was a businessman returning from China. He slept most of the time and didn't pay too much attention to the man but was drawn to the beauty of the child. He said the man was about forty. He assumed it was a grandfather but didn't know.

"Okay, boys. I want Peters to question the employees. This time, I want Talbot to dust for prints on the seven twenty-seven. It's at gate thirty-three B. The man in question was sitting in seat sixteen D. Scour for all the evidence you can find. I don't care if it is a hair. I am going to get the GPS chip installed in the baby activated to find her location. That should take us within a few blocks of her. It's too bad Damian never told us she had a chip from the beginning."

"Okay, boss," Talbot said.

"Ten four," Peters said.

Peters went to the gate where the flight had come in. He found three employees working the area. They should have taped off the gate and rerouted the rest of the flights to another terminal. The next flight was close to leaving. He tried to get the attention of one of the workers at the gate but was unsuccessful. There were fifteen people standing in line so he would just have to wait. While he waited, he used the men's room and stopped and bought a cup of coffee.

After questioning employees and showing them a current picture of Kala, he would move down the hall to the exit doors. The man was said to not have had any luggage. The businessman said he was not at the luggage claim area.

After a few minutes, he found the counter empty of patrons. All three employees stood at attention when he approached the counter.

Peters flashed his badge. "I'm Agent Peters."

"We were expecting you, Agent Peters," one of the workers said.

"Have you seen this little girl recently?" Peters asked.

"I was working the counter Monday when the girl came through the gate with an older man," Clyde said.

"Did you see the man closely?"

"No. I am sorry I didn't," Clyde said.

"I wasn't working Monday. It is my day off," Stan said.

"Well, how about you, Brenda?"

"I am not sure where I was, but I didn't see her," Brenda said.

"Clyde, did you notice anything strange about them?"

"No," Clyde said.

"Which way did they go?"

"There is only one way out of this terminal. They went that way." Clyde pointed to the open hallway.

"Was there any carry-on baggage?"

"Not that I saw. He was empty handed except for the little girl," Clyde said.

"What did the man look like?" Peters asked.

"He was wearing old, torn jeans and a flannel shirt with a t-shirt underneath. He had sandy-blonde hair, wire-rim glasses, and a round face. I would say he was five eleven and two hundred and ten pounds. He looked scruffy to me," Clyde said.

"Was the baby still crying when they exited the plane?"

"No."

"Thank you. Here is my card in case you remember anything more. Have a good day, ladies and gentlemen."

Peters had been informed that he could find the flight attendant in the lounge area. The pilot would answer any questions he had via the satellite. He was out of the country for three days. It was unlikely that the pilot had paid any attention to who was on the flight, but it was worth the chance that he might have seen something. After going the wrong way coming off the escalator, Peters found the lounge for the flight employees. He knocked on the door. A lady named Lita answered. She had her name badge on her dress in plain sight.

"Lita, I am Agent Peters. I would like to ask you a few questions," he said, showing her the badge.

"Sure. Come in. The lounge is quiet right now. Here. Have a seat." She showed him a small table for two.

Pulling out the chair for Lita, he sat himself down. She offered him something to drink. He declined.

"Is this the baby you saw on Monday afternoon on flight thirty-four sixty-seven?" Peters showed her a photo of Kala?

"It sure is."

"How can you be sure?"

"It was her big, round blue eyes with the long lashes. Most babies don't have long lashes."

"What did the man look like?"

"I would say forty-three to maybe forty-five. He was a smoker. I could smell the cigarettes on his flannel shirt."

"What color was the flannel shirt?"

"It was a red plaid with yellow and blue and green in it. He had a old, white t-shirt underneath. It was holey on the edges and yellowed. The man smelled like he had not showered in days. Ash blonde hair. His eyes were hazel I think."

"Did he have any glasses or anything that would mark him in any way?"

"He had glasses. I think they were gold rimmed. He had a scar on the left side of his face. He also had long hairs in his eyebrows that were obnoxious and a mole on his left cheek."

"Did he look like he was trying to disguise himself in any way?"

"I would doubt it. He seemed oblivious to the world," Lita said.

"Any carry-on luggage?"

"Not that I saw. He did buy an apple juice, and the little girl drank a little bit of it."

"Did he seem to be mean to her in any way?"

"Not really. She wasn't happy to be with him though. She cried for most of the flight. She did fall asleep at one point for a while."

"Here is my card. If you think of anything new, call me. My cell is always on."

"It was nice to meet you, Agent Peters."

"It was my pleasure. Do you mind if I stay in the lounge to contact the pilot?"

"No. Of course not."

"Thank you for your time, Lita."

Lita left the lounge. Peters sent the picture and questions over the wireless connection. He waited for a reply. He was hoping to talk to the pilot. He sat waiting and waiting with no response.

Quad was successful getting the frequency to the chip placed behind the left ear of the baby. It was a matter of time to get the location. It was showing that she was still in the area. The chip installed was a genius idea for locating people. It really wasn't meant for this kind of thing but was useful.

"Boss, I found a note under the seat with a phone number and a few letters on it," Talbot said to Quad.

"Good. We will send it to the lab for examination. What is this, a gum wrapper too?"

"It was jammed in the side of the seat. Here are the hairs I found around the seat," Talbot said.

"How many prints did you find?" Quad asked.

"Several. Some are overlapping and not clear enough."

"All we need is one good one. Good job, son. Let's get Peters and get out of this airport. I will call and release the plane for the next flight. Meet you at the gate in ten minutes." Quad turned and walked away.

"Get in, guys," Quad said, gesturing to the red SUV. "Let's get this show on the road. So tell me, Peters, what you found," Quad said impatiently.

"I could not get a clear identity from any of the flight attend-ants or crew. I was not able to get the pilot to contact me back. The descriptions the desk clerks gave are vague. The guy is stocky, about two hundred pounds, and has blond hair and hazel eyes. He is wearing a dirty white t-shirt with a flannel shirt over it and torn jeans, wild eye brows and a mole on his cheek," Peters said.

"That is something. The baby is still in the Salt Lake area. The chip did activate, and it is within ten miles of here. She was found on radar a few minutes ago. We will have to go back to the office to get a clearer location off the office system," Quad said.

"Since when did they start putting chips in babies?" Talbot asked.

Quad told him, "It is a fairly new thing. It is part of the agenda pushed to stop terrorism, or that is what they tell the people."

"I didn't know that. I still think the dad has something to do with the kidnapping," Talbot said.

"I think so too, maybe that is why he never told us about the chip." Peters said.

"I think you boys have it all wrong. What if his debt problem made him a target for the baby to be taken and he had nothing to do with it?" Quad asked.

"I doubt it, boss," Peters said. "Something is wrong with this picture."

"Then I hope you are wrong. I don't want to believe he did that to his own child," Quad said as he yawned.

"Boss, you have put too many hours in to think clearly. You need to take a break," Talbot said seriously.

"Let's get this back to the lab and go get some food. I am hungry and tired. We have put some long hours in this week."

"We always put long hours in. Why is this case any different, Quad?" Talbot asked.

"I am a father, and I could never pull a stunt like that. I just don't want Damian to be the…" Quad lost his train of thought as a car pulled out in front of them. He had to swerve to miss it.

"Where do people learn to drive? We could have been hit," Quad snapped.

"Good thing we are back at headquarters." Talbot snickered.

CHAPTER 17

"From A Father's Eyes" story was sent to Shelly; Valerie quoted Damian on the interview. She talked about the remorse she had seen in his eyes. She told how he had repented for letting his family and his church down. She wasn't sure if Shelly would print it. It was pretty conservative. The readers had eaten up the story about a mother's heart. Shelly had forwarded the best of the e-mails to Valerie. She opened an e-mail from the owner of the *Dispatch*.

"Valerie, I am impressed with your great writing. I particularly like the personal touch given to Kala. If I can be of assistance to you, please contact me. Hugh."

"Valerie Sharpe, thank you so much for writing the candid story about baby Kala. I too lost my baby through the hands of a stranger. I was at the local grocery store. I walked away from my six-month-old in the dairy dept for only a few seconds to grab milk and eggs. I was

stunned to think someone was quick enough to get my baby out of the cart and out of my eyesight in a short amount of time. The media was hard on me for allowing a stranger close enough to kidnap my baby. I never saw my son again after that afternoon. I went into a deep depression and could not function in my daily duties. My husband left me for another woman. Reading your articles has allowed me to face my own loss and let it go after eleven years of mourning. Thank you. Katie T."

Valerie had to wipe the tears from her face.

She found an e-mail from Jon.

"Has the dress arrived yet?"

She had forgotten to look. Valerie got up to see if it was on the porch. She found a blue dress box with a beautiful gold bow sitting next to the door. Opening the box, she found a beautiful salmon-and-gold gown. A pair of matching shoes accompanied the dress. She couldn't wait to try it on. She had never worn an outfit that beautiful before. The dress was an A-line strapless with a gold sash. She tried it on. It fit perfectly. It showed off her slim waistline. The dress made her look like a goddess with her red hair. She put the shoes on and walked into the bathroom, where a full-length mirror was over the door. She absolutely loved the dress and couldn't wait to wear it the next night.

"Jon, this is Valerie. The dress is drop-dead gorgeous. The shoes fit too."

"Good! I will talk to you later. I have a patient I need to take care of now." Jon ended the call.

Valerie stretched out on the bed to think for a bit. Instead, she fell into a deep sleep. The dream about the baby returned. This time, she got up and wrote it down before falling back asleep.

"I saw a man take money and sign a contract. The man who gave the money was in the shadows. I could not see who he was."

She went to Meijer's, the closest store around. The farmers were lucky to have a store like it close. While she was shopping, she received a call from Shelly.

"Valerie, the piece on Damian was good. I'm going to give you the contact number for Quad. See if you can get more about Utah."

"Sounds good. What is the number?"

"432-555-1212."

"Thanks, Shelly," Valerie said.

The house phone rang.

"Valerie, have you seen the news?" Mason asked.

"No."

"Turn on ABC. They dug into Damian's past, and they are making the story out to be really bad."

"Did they find the baby yet?"

"No. The chip was a dead-end at this point. The news said there must have been a glitch in it, or someone tampered with it."

"I have ABC on. I will have to go to the Internet and catch it there. The story just ended."

"Have you eaten yet?"

"I went grocery shopping earlier and did a little cooking. I ate a couple hours ago. Well, it looks like four hours ago. I must have fallen asleep watching *Fireproof*."

"Do you want to meet for dinner?"

"If that meets your approval. I have some anointed music I want to give you. I bought an extra for you."

"That would be nice. I'm spending more of my time alone with God than I ever did before. New music would be very nice."

"I saw this couple last year for New Year's Eve with a buddy of mine. The depth of worship was powerful."

"Cool. Where do you want to meet?"

"Do you mind if I bring dinner over? I promise to behave."

"I am sure you would. That works for me."

"I am sorry it took me so long to get here. Here. Take this bag and I will get the rest of the food from the car," Mason said, as he handed a large, plastic bag to Valerie. "I brought stuffed peppers, salad, and fruit compote for dessert. I will be right back."

"I never knew you cooked," Valerie said with surprise.

"I don't tell too many people that secret. Maybe when we are done, we can watch that movie you mentioned earlier. You look wiped out. I promised to not stick around late. You look like you could use a good night's sleep," Mason said with compassion.

"I am feeling the emotional drain from not only my own loss but everyone that this news story is affecting. I have not been sleeping very well. I keep having dreams about Kala. I cleaned out the bedroom of my mother's things today. That was pure torture. It made me an emotional wreck."

"I want to help you forget about the work for one night. Just a few hours."

"Okay."

"If you set the table, I will get the food ready."

"It is a deal."

At seven the next morning, she was wide awake, ready for a new day. She first turned the computer on to see what response she had from Shelly. There were too many e-mails to count. She found the one from Shelly and opened it.

"Valerie, you are doing great with the story, but what happened to the FBI details?"

"Oops," Valerie said to herself.

CHAPTER 18

Valerie took a bath. It was long overdue. It was Sunday, and she was not going to be pushed by anyone. Whatever her computer held for her could wait. Soaking in the tub, her thoughts kept going back to Jon and his convictions for a pure place to really worship God. Valerie had been happy by little offered in churches. That was all she knew. But somehow, she was being drawn to more. She wanted more of God and less of her. Until Jon talked frankly with her, she had no idea of how badly botched up things had gotten. What was happening in churches was far from biblical. Jon pulled the Bible out and showed her scriptures that revealed that taking a title was far from God's intent. He showed her where, in the New Testament, Paul said they should give what they could. Jon made the example of his income with 10 percent versus what God tells him to do. He said the obedience factor far outweighed tithing for him.

As she stepped out of the tub, her phone rang. She would dry off before returning the call. Right now, she needed to take care of herself. She dressed and put a glaze in her hair and then dried it. She quickly put face powder and mascara on. She was ready to rock and roll. She found the phone in her purse looked at the last call. It was the nursing home. She called them back but could not locate the person who had left the message. She hoped all was well with her dad. She had skipped a day. She had not seen him since Friday. She talked to him on Saturday and told him that she would be by the next day. He agreed.

She turned on the computer to check her e-mails. It was another day of hordes of mail. She looked for the ones from her bosses and opened them first. There was nothing special. Just a thank you. They were compiling the articles from the week to put in Sunday's paper. A copy of what ran was enclosed. Valerie didn't care to read it. *Something was changing. I always put work first, so why the backing off now?*

Dialing the nursing home, she found the original caller.

"Your dad wants his PJs and robe and a few clothes. Will you be bringing them over today?" a woman asked.

"I will be there later this afternoon," Valerie said.

Relief flowed through Valerie. She shut the computer case, turned on the worship music, and lay on her bed. She felt God more powerfully than she ever had in a church service. God was healing Valerie right where she needed it.

"Father, I humble myself before you and ask that your will be done. Heal my broken heart. Remove the pride from my wounds. Remove anything that hinders me from moving closer to you."

Scouring the Bible for a word from God, she read from Isaiah to Psalms, finding all kinds of nuggets. When she read Isaiah 54:2, God allowed her to see that he was enlarging her tent, strengthening her and digging her deep. She had an understanding of why God allowed her mother to die. It was to save her, in a sense. She was to be saved to save others. She had been of some help to Damian and Elaine. How many more in the future? What would God use to take her deeper? She remembered a scripture Mason had made reference to: "Either you fall upon the rock or the rock falls upon you." She would rather be humble and allow God to have his way than to be chased.

At a little after noon, Mason called.

"Are you okay, Valerie?"

"I think I am better than I have ever been. I have been soaking in all of God that I can get. What are you up to?"

"I was hoping to take you out after church."

"I really don't want to go anywhere today. Why don't you come here and I will cook for you?"

"Okay. I will be there in less than a half hour. Can I bring anything?"

"Just yourself. I have the house stocked with food."

"Okay."

Valerie wasn't much of cook, but she had learned a lot from her mom years ago. She would fry some cabbage, make some steamed potatoes, and fry the chicken breast she had bought on Friday. It would be fairly easy. Chopping the cabbage, she sliced her finger. She cleaned it up, placing a Band-Aid on it to keep it clean. The back door bell rang. She was glad to have company on a spiritual level far beyond her previous friends.

"Come in, Mason. The flowers are beautiful."

"For the most beautiful girl in town."

"Well, thank you on both notes. I love flowers. These are so beautiful. Where did you find a bouquet like this?"

"Farmer's market yesterday. I liked them and hoped you would too."

"I love it. Where is the farmer's market?"

"I will take you next Saturday. Deal?"

"Deal."

Mason followed her into the kitchen. "Can I help you finish all this?"

"I cut my finger. Otherwise, I would have been done by now."

"I will finish cutting the cabbage. You cook the chicken. Looks like the potatoes are done."

"Turn them off. What kind of seasoning do you like: this one or that one?" She held up a Mexican flavor or a French herb mix.

"Let's do the French herbs. Damian and Elaine weren't in church this morning."

"I didn't think they would be. Was the guest speaker any good?"

"He spoke on forgiveness from Matthew eighteen."

"I bet that was good." Valerie made more of a question than a statement.

"Something has been stirring in my spirit for a long time. It is gaining magnitude recently. I have been really thinking about taking what the Bible says and finding like minds to worship together. We would not use money for a building or salaries but for the community needs. So many are losing their homes and jobs. Valerie, this might sound strange, but God has been speaking to me to give the money to those in need. The church does a great job of making sure the poor have a turkey dinner on Thanksgiving, but what about the other days of the week? I want to start a pantry where the community as a whole can give or receive."

"I think you need to talk to Jon more about all this. God is leading him to something similar. Last night, we talked in great detail of what God is leading him to do. He feels that God wants him to be a part of organizing an organic church, not religion but purely God doing it. I was really impressed with what he had to say."

"Really? I had a dream many months ago that there were four of us who took the step. In time, many joined us."

"Mason, I think that is really awesome how God is moving. I didn't go to church because I was pondering the same things. I wanted to really think about the ideas that Jon placed in my mind last night. He brought up how obeying God takes us much further than doing duty. It convicted my heart. As a matter of fact, I repented today for allowing pride and wounds to take me off course," Valerie said.

"You think God might be leading you to be a part of this?"

"I think it is very possible. I am no longer putting my job first but placing God in a place he should have been years ago. Mason, I played games. I didn't want to see it, but I did. I went to church for the socialization. Now is not about the people at all for me. I want to really worship my creator, for he loved me first. He placed me on a path that I would not have chosen, but I am very glad to be here. I have had the best time with you and Jon. I want to make friends with Elaine. On Tuesday, I get to meet more hurting people. I hope I can make some female friends there too."

"Valerie, you are a special woman. You are holding up under crisis very well. I am proud of you."

"This new woman is God's creation. For the first time in my life I am receiving God's love. That is what is changing me."

"You bet. Hey, it looks like the chicken and cabbage are both done."

"Well then let's eat."

Valerie placed the food on the table. She placed two flowered placemats, plates, and silverware down.

Mason took her hand, "Lord we thank you for this food, bless the hands that prepared it. In Jesus name amen."

"Mason, I have to go see Dad this afternoon. Do you want to go with me?"

"I would love to. I think it is time to pray over him again."

"I like that."

"This food is good. I didn't think you could cook."

"I was raised on a farm, right?"

"Well, yes. That is true."

"All mothers should teach their daughters to cook. I am no exception to the rule. Coming home has brought me back to my roots, cooking being a part of that."

"You let the secret out and all the men in the county will be at your doorstep."

"Well then don't tell them. If you don't tell, I won't."

"Promise?"

"Who are you afraid I am going to tell? I don't have many friends here. Just you and Jon. Oh, that is it. You are jealous."

"Well, maybe. I think you are great. I hope you never leave. I hope none of us hardheaded men ever make you want to leave."

"I hope so too. Don't get any ideas about me, you are ten years my senior."

"I think you are sweet. I think your mother would be very proud of her daughter if she could see you now."

"Maybe she can."

"I guess we will find out in heaven, won't we?"

"Can we change the subject for a minute or two?"

"Sure."

"My dad has a birthday coming up. I really don't know what to do for him. It would be easy to go buy him a watch, but he wouldn't give two nickels for that."

"Valerie, you have a creative side. Make him something he can keep for the rest of his life or something to use."

"Like what?"

"Let us both think about that for a while"

"I can't take him out to eat yet. Clothes are no big deal. So what would be nice?"

"I take it you are asking me as a man?"

"Yes. Of course."

"He will be coming home next month or so. Do something to the house to make it ready for him."

"That is a great idea. They are thinking he might still be in a wheelchair, but the doors aren't wide enough. The house will need some work. Now that his money has come in, I can use mine for the repairs."

"Don't put yourself in any trouble."

"What? Spend money I don't have?"

"Yes."

"I am good with money. I made decent money as a journalist, and I saved it too."

"Do you plan on working for the *Dispatch*?"

"It is working for me at the moment, but I might have to free-lance in the future."

"This baby story was a big help, wasn't it?"

"It was God's providence in action."

"I guess he does place us at the right time in the right place. Look. He put you here right now."

"That he did."

"Do you want me to help you clean up so we can go see your dad?"

"I will do it when we come back. I should be getting there now.

On the way to Angel's Nursing Home, Mason freely talked to Valerie about his convictions of the path God was leading him on. Valerie knew that the three of them needed to talk together soon. She had not been drawn like they had, but her spirit agreed. There was spiritual change in the air.

"I have some books that might help you on this new journey. Would you like to borrow some?" Mason asked.

"Pick one for me to start with."

"I will bring one over in the next few days. It looks like some excitement is going on at the nursing home," Mason said, pointing at the ambulance out front.

Valerie waited at the nurses' station to check in.

"Your dad is down the hall to the left in room one forty-five. He is finishing up with Forster in physical therapy. He will be back in his room in less than five minutes. You can wait in the lobby or in his room," the old nurse said and walked away.

She went in his room and left the articles on the bed. The room was clean and fresh.

"What are you thinking, Valerie?" Mason asked.

"How boring it will be here for my dad. Look at the walls and floors. It is almost all white. It is a good thing he can see the trees outside to have some color around here."

"Men don't think that way. We couldn't care less what color it is as long as it is clean."

"Is this the way you decorate your home?"

"I will have to invite you over to have you see for yourself. I don't have much color either."

"Men."

"Valerie, you know you can't live without us."

"Could I at least try?"

"If you insist."

At that comment, Jacob rolled in the door. Mason was embarrassed as he turned around and saw him.

"What is my daughter insisting on?"

"Nothing, Dad. So, they don't have staff pushing you around like the hospital?"

"I guess not. He picked me up here and brought me back. I am getting more movement in my leg."

"I am glad for you."

"Mason, it's nice to see you. Is my daughter treating you well?"

"Yes, sir. We were just teasing each other. I am sure it might not have sounded good if you came in only on the end of it."

"It is okay. I am used to Valerie being a flirt. She was like that as a young girl. She got that trait from her mother."

"I love that about her, sir."

"You can call me Jacob."

"Great, Jacob," Mason said. "I wanted to come along and pray for you again."

"I am ready."

Mason took Valerie's hand, and Valerie took her father's hand. Mason led in a short prayer asking God for complete restoration of his body and his spirit.

"Jacob, have you ever been filled with the spirit?"

"No, I haven't."

"Would you like me to lead you in a prayer?"

"Sure."

"Father, we ask in the name of Jesus to fill Jacob this hour with your Holy Spirit and give him evidence of that through the power of tongues."

It was as if a power circuit had been turned on. Power was flowing through Jacob. He was speaking in a foreign language he knew not of. His body was trembling. That lasted for a few minutes. When it ended, Jacob looked at Mason.

"That was powerful."

"Yes, sir. That is your new prayer language. It will fill your spirit up when it is low."

"I could use that. This has been hard."

"Valerie said they had you in some therapy?"

"I am in group sessions here, and I have a physical therapist come in here once a week."

"Are you noticing any changes?" Mason asked.

"It is a process. I am doing better. I am less depressed. The therapist is helping me work through the grief."

"That must be tough."

"For us guys, it is. We don't move with change the way women do. My wife showed her feelings much better than I. She cried and let it out when Bill died."

"Maybe you should too. It is not wrong for a man to cry," Mason said.

"I know. It is just hard for most men to do it. We have been conditioned to be a certain way."

"Valerie and I were talking about that with church issues today. What makes us do the things we do? Is it habit and training?"

"I tried to not do that with my children, but I am sure I did."

"What, teach them traditions?"

"Yes."

"I think we all do it to some extent. I do it with my clients. I get them in the habit of giving me their paperwork on the third of the month and doing their income tax the same time each year. I shop the same days of the week and wash my clothes on Thursday nights."

"Have you done that for very long?" Valerie asked.

"Since I went off to college. I started my own habits."

"Getting in the habit of doing something is not always bad, Valerie protested.

"No. My point is that sometimes we do things without really thinking about why."

"I would agree," Jacob said.

"Jacob, have they told you when they are going to let you come home?" Mason asked.

"No, not yet. Guys, I hate to cut this short, but I need to take a nap."

"Let me give you a hug, Dad. I love you. I will call you in the morning. Have they connected a phone in here yet?"

"The number is on the phone. I should have had the nurse give you the number this morning. I am sorry, Valerie."

"It's okay, Dad."

Mason shook his hand and said bye.

"Your dad is sweet."

"I love him, but thank you. Thank you for coming to pray for him. It feels like you are my older brother, looking out for me."

CHAPTER 19

Valerie's cell phone rang. She didn't recognize the number of the cell calling her, but it was a local number.

"Hello. This is Valerie."

"Valerie, this is Elaine. Something is really wrong. In the middle of the night, Damian had three friends show up with a semi and move us out. He then drove me to my parents and dropped me off. He told me to forget about Kala. He said it was over. He's been acting very strange for months now….. I am so upset." Elaine sobbed in between sentences.

"That was middle of last night?"

"Yeah. The guys got there at about two thirty. He packed up what he wanted, I guess. Some of our stuff is still there. The guys came in with packing boxes and boxes of packing paper. The men

quickly wrapped up the items that were breakable. We were out of there by five thirty." Elaine blew her nose.

"You must have left a lot behind to move everything in that amount of time. Do you know where he is headed?" Valerie asked, concerned.

"I don't have a clue. Do you think Damian had anything to do with the baby being taken?"

"I didn't think so after I talked to him a few days ago, but this doesn't sound good, Elaine. What can I do for you?" Valerie paced her floor, walking from the kitchen to the living room and back.

"I am in Columbus, so I am a ways away. I guess pray for me. Check into the whole thing and get to the truth. You will have a great story on your hands. Whatever you find out, just promise me to tell me before you print the story."

"Elaine, you have my word on it. Now, is this the cell number I can reach you at?"

"Yes. This is my cell number. Unless Damian shuts the phones off, that is how you can reach me. Let me give you Mom and Dad's number. It is 740-555-3487."

"I am so glad you called me. I am so sorry, Elaine. I wish you would not have to go through this."

"Thank you, Valerie. You have been a true friend in a time of need. I will call you if I hear anything on this end."

"Good night, Elaine."

"Good night, Valerie."

What could be going on with Damian? Did he plan to leave her and disappear with Kala? It was p*ossible, but where was Kala now?*

Valerie rushed home to check out her e-mails. She had plenty of e-mails from readers but nothing from Shelly. She called Shelly.

"Shelly, this is Valerie."

"You sound upset. Is everything okay?"

"I just got a call from Elaine. She said that Damian had his friends come in last night in the middle of the night with a semi and pack most of the house up. He then drove her to Columbus and dropped her off. He told her to forget the baby. Do I dig in and write another article?"

"Absolutely. This makes him look guilty as sin. This might be a great break for the *Dispatch*. Has she talked to another paper?"

"No. She wants me to do it."

"I will put Camdon on research for you. I will have him track the credit card purchases and check deeper into his background. I will call you with what we find. Good job, Valerie. Have a good night."

"Thanks, Shelly."

The deadline was 1:30 a.m. Valerie hoped to go home and sleep, but with the new development, she had work to do. She needed to verify that Elaine was telling the truth, if the house was really empty. The home was two miles from her current location, a lucky break. With it being dark out, she might not be able to see much.

She pulled in the driveway. The Escalade was gone. Pulling her large Maglite from the trunk, she looked in the only open window not covered with blinds, the kitchen window. Sure enough, the kitchen table was gone. Shining the light into the family room, the furniture that once sat there was missing too. She shined the light back into the kitchen to look at the counters. Even the appliances were gone. It was evident that the occupants were gone.

Her next move would be to get the sheriff out there. She called the office, requesting an officer meet her there.

Temperatures had dropped to forty-three degrees. She waited in the car to stay warm. She plugged the computer into her cigarette lighter, turning it on. She had received an e-mail from Bruce Talbot a couple days ago, letting her know that they knew nothing more and were returning to Oregon. She responded to his e-mail, telling him what she had found. She requested any information that would help her find Kala. She told him about the call from Elaine's cell phone and gave him the number so they could verify the information. She told him that she was waiting for the sheriff to meet her at their abandoned house. Bruce responded quickly.

"We suspected he might have something to do with the case. This new development might be what we need to connect the dots.

I will send the file over to you. For the story's sake, only print what I have highlighted. We don't want all the information to leak out. Don't make any accusations yet. On a personal level, I hope I can see you again in the future. Bruce."

She typed back to him, "I hope so too. As far as the story is concerned, I don't want to create havoc, but I know I have to write something."

A young deputy pulled in the driveway. "Hi. I am Tom. Are you Valerie?"

"Yes. I got a call thirty minutes ago from Elaine, the woman who lived here. She told me her husband had a group of male friends show up at two thirty in the morning with a semi and load the house up. He then dropped her off at her parents' house in Columbus, Ohio. She gave me the number where you can reach her. She is pretty distraught."

"Let's take a look." He pulled out a long metal piece, putting it in the door and turning it a few times. The door unlocked. He flicked the lights on. "Let me look first to make sure it is safe."

"Okay." Valerie wouldn't argue.

"Come in. It is clear. They left a lot of debris. They must have left in a hurry. Even the towels in the bathroom are still hanging. And look, Valerie. The closets still have most of the clothes."

"Let's look and see what they took of Kala's. If he had any-thing to do with the baby being taken, he would want her stuff, wouldn't he?"

"He might not take it to create more suspicion."

The two entered Kala's room. The room had been stripped clean. A couple diapers were strewn across the floor along with a few other small items, but the furniture was missing and so were all the clothes. They entered the master bedroom. Valerie opened the large walk-in closet. All of Elaine's clothes were hanging, but most of Damian's had been taken down. The master bath had all the toi-letries in the cabinet and linen closet. Two towels were hanging on the towel rack. The room looked like nothing was touched.

"Let's check the den out. That is where Damian spent most of his time," Valerie said.

They found the computer and media desk missing, but the huge desk was still there. She opened the drawers, finding the articles once there gone. The large, black leather sofa still occupied the room.

"Tom, does it look to you like he might be moving someplace where he doesn't have the room for everything?"

"That was exactly what I was just thinking. This man has problems. Let's go see what they left in the kitchen."

"Sounds good to me."

Valerie opened a few cupboards, the simple basic needs of a kitchen were gone. Food was left, and so were fancy dishes and china and such. Most of the pots and pans were gone.

"Tom, is it possible for me to get more information about Damian and Elaine and this case?"

"I will have the sheriff call you. That would be up to him. As far as I know, we haven't dug into the case past the first night. Once the FBI got involved, we backed off."

"I would like to access files to see late payments, money owed to anyone around town, who the man was that he met with the day before Kala was taken, that kind of thing."

"Let me page the boss. Sheriff, I am out here at the house where Kala came up missing. The house has indeed been cleared out. Can I let Valerie access our files for an article for the *Dispatch*?"

"Get her e-mail account. I will send over what I want her to have."

"Give me your e-mail address. The sheriff will e-mail you the information tonight."

Valerie gave him her e-mail address.

"Sheriff, it is Valerie@Dispatch.com. Okay. I will tell her."

"He will have the files to you within the hour. He said whatever you do, don't make this office look bad."

"Why would I do that?"

"It is just what he said."

"Thank you, Tom. I appreciate your help. Have a great night."

Valerie walked to her car. She had work to do. She was tired, but sleep would have to wait. The answering machine light was blinking when she got home. Valerie pushed the button to hear the message.

"It is Aunt Rose. I was calling to make sure you are doing well. I just came back from my trip. Call me when you can. I love you."

Valerie cleaned up the dinner dishes, vacuumed the house, and put things back in order. The hour was almost up. She turned the computer on and saw that she had a e-mail from Carmen. *What did Carmen want?*

"Valerie, I was hoping you would help me. I lost my job, my dad died, and now I have nowhere to go. Can I come stay with you? Carmen."

I'll deal with that later. No apology. Just wanting help.

There was the e-mail Valerie had been waiting for. Valerie said a quick prayer before opening the e-mail. The first document showed that he was over sixty days late on his house payment.

There was a copy of a questioning of a Norman Blackwell. Valerie had to read the entire document to figure out that he was the man whom Damian had gone to see on Sunday. She would research Norman and see what came up. Damian's credit report had indeed been pulled, he had in excess of six hundred thousand dollars of debt. That was a lot of money for a pastor. It held a list of credit card holders; two banks; and the lease on the Escalade, was thirty days late. The report showed a checking account at City National Bank. He owed an attorney five thousand dollars and had a dental bill left unpaid, but no amount was attached.

Valerie did a search for the legal office and found that it was in Grand Rapids, Michigan. She found their website with a contact name, so she sent an e-mail requesting information. She would contact the bank in the morning about the mortgage and see what they had to say. The Escalade was probably the best bet for them to locate Damian. It had an OnStar system that could find him quickly. She would e-mail Bruce and mention that. Elaine had said that she was not a part of the financial decisions. There was no use asking her about that again. She did, however, want to know if Damian drove Elaine to her parents' in the Escalade or the semi. She dialed the number she had been called from earlier.

"Elaine, this is Valerie. Can you tell me if Damian took the Escalade with him or what?"

"He had a friend take it somewhere to dump it. He said he could be tracked by it too easily," Elaine said.

"That was my thought too, doggone it. Thanks."

"No problem."

That did clarify that Damian was out on the run. He had to be up to something to run like this. Valerie got an e-mail back from Bruce at 11:20 p.m. They had found the Escalade abandoned in the woods thirty miles from town. She had her article. She would include the picture of the house. She was allotted a finder's fee on cases like these. She would offer a reward for anyone turning in evidence to the return of Kala or information leading to an arrest. That was likely to get a big response.

CHAPTER 20

"Men, what have we found so far?"

"We located the Escalade in a State Park. The keys were tossed under the floor mat. I have the men bringing it in and getting it fingerprinted. We will scope it and get all we can on it."

"That sure makes him look guilty. For such a promising future, he sure is messing up," Quad said

Agent Talbot put together a profile from Elaine's information.

He passed the profile to his boss. "This is what she could remember. Two of the men were Jack and Solomon. She said he had known them for many years. They were from out of state somewhere. She is hunting to see if she can get us more on those two men. The next two men she said she'd never seen or heard of before. They worked, but neither of them talked. These two men are the men who took the SUV off the property. She thinks they might be

local men, but she's never seen them before. She said they were young, maybe eighteen to twenty-one. She said they looked to be brothers. Both had blondish hair."

"Did any money pass hands?" Quad asked.

"Not to her knowledge. She said she was rather shocked when she heard male voices and came into the kitchen area and they were boxing things up. She was rather shaken. She said Damian told her to go back to bed and that he would wake her up when she needed to be up."

"Cold guy," Quad said.

"She said she didn't go back to the bedroom, but Damian took her by the arm and forced her to go, so she finally went. She called her parents on the cell phone."

"I guess they weren't surprised when she showed up then," Quad said.

"I asked to talk to the parents. I have to call back at noon today," Talbot said.

"Good work. The grandparents can tell you more maybe. Ask what they thought of Damian. Also, see if they know these men. Ask if Damian ever asked to borrow any money from them. I also want to know if they have heard from anyone about Kala."

"Wouldn't she have said anything?" Talbot asked.

"She is in shock right now. She won't be thinking clearly. First, she lost her baby. Now, the man she trusted betrayed her. Her information is not one hundred percent reliable. Once she calms down, she will remember more," Quad said.

"The bank contacted him last Friday about his overdue house loan. They asked him when he would be able to make the last two payments. The lady said he hung up on her. He never responded to her. That seems strange to me. He closed his checking and savings accounts in town the day before he left. We pulled his phone records to find out who he has been calling. I don't think he has been using his own phone or calling from the house. We would have heard the calls on our phone tap. He had less than five hundred dollars in both accounts. I'm tracing his credit card use. No luck there. I also notified state police in the states around Ohio to be looking out for the semi. Talbot, did Elaine have a description of the semi?"

"She said it was too dark, but it looked new and dark. She thought it might have been a blue or black Peterbilt."

"I want you to call her back and ask about what the cab inside looked like. That will tell us a lot."

"Yes, sir," Talbot said.

"Talbot, this afternoon, I made a reservation for you to fly back to Ohio. Lisa at the front desk will have a package ready for you in an hour, including cash. Bring me back receipts. After Agent Peters searches the records at Wheaton College and the local high school through the last five years of graduating classes, I want you to see if you can find the men. I reserved a car for your use. Any questions?"

"Do you want me to make copies of the composites?" Agent Talbot asked.

"Send them via e-mail. It will be quicker than the copier. We are having problems with it. A repairman will be in shortly. Men, go and get 'im. Don't let me or Kala down."

"Yes, sir," the two agents said in unison.

"I was hoping he didn't send me back," Peters said.

"I am glad he's sending me back. My instincts may have been right all the time."

"It isn't over until it is over. I have seen cases take sharp left turns many times, but I have to agree Damian seems like a schmuck."

"If he sent the baby out to only catch up to her, what motive did he have?"

"Taking her from Elaine?"

"That seems a little drastic, doesn't it?" Peters asked.

"People do the strangest things, you know."

"Have fun. Tell that cute redhead hi for me."

"I hope to see that cute redhead." Talbot said.

"I'll bet you do. I will send the info over as soon as I get it."

"Thanks, Peters."

Talbot finished what he was working on, cleaning off his work area and making a few short phone calls to let those in need know he would be gone. He had a neighbor take care of his cat, Alley. He cancelled his groceries delivery and called Jack, with whom he played tennis. He was disappointed that he couldn't win in the rematch that night. Talbot left the office and took the elevator to the first floor, where Lisa worked. She handled details for all the offices in the building. She was young, maybe twenty-two. Talbot had his eye on her, but another man beat him to the punch. He stepped out of the elevator and found her on the phone.

"No, sir. I will handle it, sir. Well yes, sir. No, sir." She put a finger in the air to tell Talbot one minute. "I would be glad to do that for you, sir. Yes. I already handled that, sir. Good day to you too."

"Quad asked that you be given a thousand dollars cash. He felt that you might need to bribe someone to tell the truth. If so, give the name and reason on the yellow slips provided in the envelope. I have a reservation at Northwest going out at two twenty in the afternoon. A car will be ready in ten minutes to take you home and then on to the airport. We have you staying at a Quality Inn a few miles from the crime scene. He had me order a Focus for you."

"I get luxury this time."

"That is what he does when he doesn't go. He cuts the budget on the men."

"Thanks for the warning. Bye, Lisa."

"Bye, Talbot. Be good."

Talbot noticed the driver pulling up to the building. He waved bye to Lisa as he picked his computer up.

"Do you have any bags to put in the trunk yet?" the driver asked.

"No, sir. But I will after we go to my apartment. I live two miles from here."

"The car's already been programmed for it."

"Well, good."

The drive to the apartment was fast. Traffic was minimal because of the time of day. It was approaching one in the afternoon. Talbot grabbed a pre-packed bag and returned to the limo. Approaching the entrance to the airport, it was 1:32. He boarded the plane. He searched the contents of the manila envelope. He found instructions to research the crime scene; photos of the tire tracks, Kala's room, and the den; to meet with the local bank that held the mortgage;

attend services at Damian's church, and to note any unusual behavior. Peters was contacting the men who had hired him to investigate his status. Did he quit? Was he fired? When was he hired? What did they pay him? Had they had any problems with him? After arriving at Columbus airport, Quad arranged for a meeting with Elaine and her parents, asking them to prepare pictures of Damian and Elaine. They were meeting at an Applebee's north of the city. It would be suppertime. Talbot put the papers back in the envelope. He was sure the task was not bigger than his capacity. He felt the pain the family had to be feeling. They must have trusted Damian in the past, so why the radical change in behavior? Elaine's family wasn't wealthy. They were middle-class citizens. Money could not be a motive for Damian to get a payoff there. Bruce Talbot sent an e-mail to Valerie.

"Let's get together and discuss the case. Pick the nicest place to eat around. Send me an e-mail or call me. Bruce."

He didn't expect an immediate response in the middle of the day.

"I have no idea where to meet. Ask your computer and let me know," Valerie responded.

Peters e-mailed Bruce the matches to three of the men. The two local men were brothers, Anthony and Sal Ingola. They were eighteen and twenty years old. Both dropped out from Mark's Catholic School. Anthony had bright green eyes distinctive in the pictures. Sal had a mole on his right lower jaw. He hoped that the other two composites were completed before he met with Elaine and her family. He wanted her to verify that they were the men. If they were, that would be their next search. He would hunt the area for the men. It was much easier to track someone down in a rural area than in the big city. Out in the middle of nowhere, everyone knew each other and their business. He searched police records to see if there were any prior arrests. Both men came up clean. He searched work records and marriage licenses. There were none. He searched family records to see who they were related to. He might find some history there. He quickly found that their father was Joseph Ingolia, who had died three years before. From school records, that was the same time they dropped out. What had the boys been doing for three years with no work records?

CHAPTER 21

It was Wednesday, mid afternoon. Valerie awakened after only sleeping four hours to a possible abscessed tooth. Her entire right side was swollen and in major pain. She looked up the family dentist's name and made an emergency appointment. She really had no choice. She could not wait to go to Columbus to see her regular dentist. Pain was not an option to endure any longer than necessary. She had tried putting an ice pack on her jaw. That relieved a little pain but not much. She had taken four Advil, hoping the pain would go away. She called Shelly and left a message for her. Until she felt better, she was out of commission. She hadn't even turned her computer on to check e-mails. That was a true sign that she didn't feel good. She turned the volume down on the cell phone so she would not be disturbed by the noise. She didn't care who called. She didn't want to talk.

After going to see the local dentist, Valerie arrived back home. He had given her a day's worth of pain killers and a shot of an anti-biotic—tetracycline she thought he said. He had written two pre-scriptions she could fill in the morning. She wanted to go back to bed. The Tylenol 4 would make her drowsy. She should be able to sleep. She took the painkiller with a glass of water and climbed into bed. Within a short time, she was in a deep sleep. She awoke to a hard knock at the back door. She looked at the clock. It was six thirty in the evening. She put on a robe and answered the door.

"What's up, Mason?"

"Are you okay? You don't look so good."

"I had a dental procedure today. I don't do so well with major pain."

"I am sorry to hear you are not feeling well. Maybe I should go." He was more fishing for an answer than making a statement. "I will call you maybe in the morning or later in the day."

Valerie went to shut the door and saw his disappointment "I am sorry. I just don't feel well. I am going to go back to bed. I was up all night working on a story and then the tooth pain woke me up."

"I hope you feel better." Mason left the porch, sad.

Valerie shut the door and returned to bed. She slept all evening and all night.

She woke up at five the next morning feeling like she had lost a day of work. Valerie showered and dressed. She had much to catch up on. She would send Shelly an e-mail letting her know she was back with it. There must have been five hundred e-mails in her inbox. She couldn't read them yet. She whipped off a short e-mail to Shelly that she had had a root canal. She expected to be close to a hundred percent in a day or two. She read the list of e-mails and opened them based upon priority. Agent Talbot sent her an e-mail. She opened it and saw that he was requesting her company the night before. She responded back.

"Bruce, I am sorry to have waited so long to respond to you. I had a dental issue knocking me out of commission yesterday. I would love to meet with you. Let me know where and when. Enjoy the day. Valerie."

An e-mail from Shelly let Valerie know that the baby story was getting major coverage on Headlines News Channel. The national TV channels had been broadcasting the picture of Damian and Kala, asking for information leading to finding them. Valerie opened several e-mails from readers, none of which gave any clues to where they might find Damian or Kala. The e-mails were all from the area. Valerie doubted that Damian stayed in the Ohio region. For all she knew, he had fled the country with the baby. He had connections with people with money. He might have been flown in a private jet. National news was in Kala's best interest now.

It was too early to write the next article. Valerie needed new information. Valerie wanted to visit the nursing home, but they didn't allow visitors until nine. She didn't know when Mason would get out of bed and she didn't want to call him before he did, so she finished reading the rest of the e-mails. Two from the area had seen the semi. One said that the driver bought gas at the Pilot at the expressway entrance. It described the man who got out of the truck as wearing a black knit cap. The other e-mail said that they saw the semi going north on the expressway. That made no sense. Columbus was south. If they had dropped Elaine off, they had to be going south. Another e-mail had come from Carmen asking again if she could come there to live.

She responded with, "I have forgiven you. However, it is not wise for me to let you back in to a close place in my life. I wish you well and will pray for you. Valerie."

Jon had sent her an e-mail: "How about dinner again this Saturday night? Casual. I will take you out to a movie and dinner. Let me know. I ache to be with you again. Jon."

She responded with, "It would be my great pleasure. Val."

At the end of the long list was one she had missed. It came from the boss above Shelly.

"Great job on the baby abduction story. Phil."

Valerie closed the computer. It was seven thirty in the morning. She was sure it would be acceptable to call Mason back. She dialed his number. He answered on the second ring.

"Are you feeling better, Valerie?"

"Yes. Thank you. I ended up sleeping for about fourteen hours."

"I was hoping we could go out this weekend."

"I have plans on Saturday, but Friday or Sunday would work."

"Valerie, you are such a beautiful girl. I would like an opportunity to win your heart."

"Mason, you know that I might leave the area and go back to Columbus soon. You are also much older than me. You are like a big brother to me."

"I was hoping I could change your mind."

"I would like to go out no strings attached. Until I figure out what I am doing, I can't make a commitment like that. Can we go out as friends only?"

"Valerie, I am an all-or-nothing kind of guy. I think I am falling in love with you," Mason said.

"Mason, I am uncomfortable with that right now. I think you are a great guy, but romantic love isn't how I see you."

"Is that how you see Jon?"

"It is different. Jon didn't ask me out romantically. He never pushed me to make a decision, but, yes, I think I could see him in that light. I know he makes me feel whole and alive and free."

"Valerie, how do I make you feel?"

"I feel like you are family, like a older brother. I just haven't looked at you from a dating thing. You are the same age as Bill, my brother."

"If you change your mind, call me." Mason abruptly hung up.

That was part of the problem. Valerie felt that Mason wanted to control her in some remote kind of way. She felt pressure, which she was not in need of.

She had not called Aunt Rose back from a few days before. She knew she was an early worm. She dialed her number, half expecting her to let the answering machine get it.

"Hello. This is Rose."

"Aunt Rose, I am sorry to not have called you."

"You're young and have a life. I was up to see Jacob yesterday. He said you never called."

"I know. I had a root canal yesterday. It kinda kicked my butt. I was in bed most of the day."

"Are you feeling any better?"

"Yes, I am. I have to go get two prescriptions filled when they opened this morning, but I should be good."

"So, Valerie, did that Mason ever sway you to stick around?"

"Are you in on that too?"

"What do you mean?"

"Did he put you up to all this?"

"What are you talking about?"

"Aunt Rose, I just talked to him. He came over yesterday when I was in bed, sleeping. I told him I would call him back. I called him a few minutes ago. He wants to seriously date me. He is very upset that I have had two dates with the local doctor."

"I didn't know that. How is that going?"

"Aunt Rose, we have just been having fun. I do have to tell you that he does make me feel wonderful. I feel alive, appreciated, and free. I don't feel like he would control me in any way. He is supportive and loving. He is a great cook too."

"What is wrong with Mason?"

"Nothing is wrong with Mason. He just assumes I want to be what he wants. He shows up without making an appointment. He is much older than me. He makes me feel like I am a sister or a buddy. There is no spark there. I appreciate all he has done for me, but now I feel like he tried to push his way into my heart. That is not how I want it to start. I don't want Mason to assume a relationship. He told me from the start he was there to help me and be a friend. I want to feel special. I want to feel like a man took the time to figure out what would make me feel cherished and loved. When I went out with Jon, the local doctor, he did that by having a special dress made for me. He wasn't insecure, it allowed me to see I have cut myself short in the men I have gone out with in the past. I am not wanting to push any relationship right now. It is just opposite of Jon. Jon took me out with his friends. He never once referred to me as his girl or anything that would lead me to believe he was pressuring me. He hasn't held my hand or kissed me, and he hasn't asked me if I might be leaving him in the dust."

"I see."

"Aunt Rose, what was dating like when you were young?"

"Much different than now. Back then, only the loose girls dated more than one man. I doubt we even thought we had choices like you do now. Valerie, you have your whole life ahead of you, a great career. You don't need a man to take care of you. When I was your age, we needed our father and then a husband to take care of us. The women around here didn't go after careers."

"Is that what upset Mom so bad about me leaving?"

"I think your mom wanted you to stay with the local values. She knew that you going off to school would change your world, which it did."

"I can't imagine how I would have turned out had I stayed here. You're right. I have choices."

"Mason is okay."

"I see his heart for others, but Jon has that too, plus a whole lot more than that."

"Can you come for dinner tonight?"

"Sorry, Aunt Rose. I am working on a story. I have an appointment with an FBI agent tonight."

"Another date?"

"Kinda. He is awful cute and very intelligent. The bottom line is that he has information I need. Just because I enjoy getting the information doesn't mean anything will come of it. "

"Watch yourself. He sounds like a big city guy. They know how to twist a girl's heart inside out."

"Come on, Aunt Rose."

"Suit yourself, but don't say I didn't warn you. Have a nice day. I have a swimming class in twenty minutes that I am off to."

"Bye and thank you."

A few hours passed. Valerie ran her errands. While she was at the nursing home, Jon called.

"Beautiful lady, how are you?"

"Better now. I had a root canal done yesterday."

"You could have called. I would have come over to take care of you."

"Mason did show up. I chased him away."

"Good girl. I have an offer from some friends of mine. They have a place on the lake up north. They have given us an invitation. Are you interested?"

"From what time to what time?"

"We'd leave early Saturday morning and return on Sunday afternoon. They have a guest bedroom just for you."

"Jon, it sounds perfect. I would love to get out of here. The fall colors would make for a pretty ride."

"I am glad you said yes. I will pick you up at eight in the morning. Is that too early?"

"No. It is great. I look forward to seeing you, Jon."

"Likewise."

Valerie breathed in happiness. She loved the way Jon made her feel. She couldn't wait for the weekend to come. She dreamed of what they would talk about. Would it be the spiritual things he had brought up last time? She hoped so.

Soon after relaxing at home, Bruce called. He said that he would pick her up in an hour.

CHAPTER 22

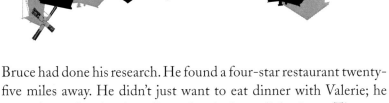

Bruce had done his research. He found a four-star restaurant twenty-five miles away. He didn't just want to eat dinner with Valerie; he wanted to enjoy the time. Sure, they had to talk business. That was part of the connection between them. They had something that went beyond the professional manner they had met through. There was a joking, playful side they shared. Even if they never had a relationship, Bruce wanted Valerie as a friend. She was a good lady.

He freshly showered and put on clean clothes. He had already made copies of the information he was allowed to give her. Quad had agreed to give her the composites and the interview details from Elaine and her family. He had copies of the banking information and pre-foreclosure status. He was even given permission to tell about the two local men whom he had tracked down to being the same men. Unfortunately, they disappeared. He found the country

address easily by following his GPS. That was one of the benefits he loved: the gadgets they were given. This was federal business, so by every right, he had the right to use it. He was a few minutes early. He guessed by her behavior that that was a good thing, not a negative thing. She was precise in all that she did. He parked the car close to the front door and then realized that the door was not used. There was a sign saying to go to the back door.

He knocked on the back door. Valerie came running cheerfully. She opened the door all smiles.

"I hope that means you are glad to see me."

"Yes. I have been looking forward to this all day. I am glad you are driving. I took a pain killer two hours ago. They make me loopy."

"You might be fun being loopy. For now, we will stay safe and I will drive. I found a great place to eat. It will be a little bit of a drive, but we can talk on the way. Anything I can get for you before I hop on the freeway?" he asked while he opened her car door.

"No. I am good."

"I copied the sheets that Quad approved for you to print in the paper. You are the first media with this information. That should give you some brownie points."

"I do my job to the best of my ability. I don't do it for brownie points."

"I figured that out already."

"Did you talk Quad into giving me the info?"

"I didn't have to. You made a mark on him. He was impressed with the way you do business. I asked. He said yes. End of story."

"Wow."

"We have the most pieces yet in the last twenty-four hours. Two of the four men live in the area. Actually, they live three miles from your farm. Sal and Anthony Ingolia, they are two brothers. Both dropped out of school when their dad died. They got hooked up with a man stealing catalytic converters. The two boys have been cutting the converters off and selling them to this man. They disappeared after the move on Monday. They both lived with their mother. She hasn't seen them since."

"Was the man in trouble?"

"The sheriff arrested him yesterday. We didn't know the connection until this afternoon. Another lead gave us the connection. I have been somewhat successful at checking it out. A junkyard in the next county was taking the converters. One of the employees identified one of the boys."

"That might or might not be accurate."

"I know. I also met with Elaine yesterday with her parents. She identified one of the brothers. She said she didn't get a good look to see the other's eyes. She thinks they are the same men but can't be for sure. She gave me a letter from the bank holding their mortgage. The letter was dated two weeks ago. It stated that they were sixty days late. The letter notified them that if the payment was not made by ninety days, they would start foreclosure proceedings," Bruce said.

"Did that bother Elaine?"

"She is more upset over losing her daughter and Damian being a con."

"I feel bad for her. She really is a nice lady."

"I agree. We have not gotten to the bottom of why Damian would pull such a stupid stunt."

"Have you checked into him flying out of the country?"

"Not that I am aware of. I would never have even thought about it. What made you think about it?"

"If he took Kala, he can't stay in the United States for very long without them finding him. Maybe he has property in an offshore place. It might be why he quit paying the bills."

"I will have Quad check into that. He would know how to do that." Bruce parked the car.

"Past your training, Talbot?" Valerie said as she shut the car window, the outside to the restaurant was beautiful.

Bruce walked around and opened Valerie's car door. Walking Valerie into the restaurant.

"Yep. I am not ashamed to tell you that. I am not that good on the research side on the computer. That is where Peters shines. He is excellent at it. Let me go make that call. I will be back." Bruce slipped to a corner of the alcove waiting area.

"Okay." Valerie said as he walked off.

Valerie took in the view of the high-class restaurant that Bruce had taken her to. It was set up like Medieval times. It looked like a huge castle. Each booth had burgundy velvet drapes that could be closed for more privacy. Mahogany wood tables filled the center of the room. Candles burned on each wall post. The lighting was just right. It was a romantic atmosphere. She wondered if Bruce knew that when he brought her there.

"I am back. Thank you for waiting. Good thing I was fast. I didn't have to hunt you down."

"Where am I going to go, run from the hunk that brought me to a castle? Are you going to save me too?"

"What a romantic thought. I doubt you need saving. You are too strong for all that, but it would be fun trying."

"Yes, it would. There are plenty of places to hide and watch you seek me out."

"I am glad you approve. This is pretty cool. I didn't know the atmosphere was like this. I just asked for the best food around. I was given this place, so here we are. The food does look good, and it smells even better."

"Bruce, it indeed does smells good."

"Back to our case. I asked Elaine's parents if they had ever heard Damian talk to business partners. They said briefly, but they doubted they heard anything worth talking about. I pressed them further. He had taken a call at the restaurant the day before she was taken. He set a meeting for Sunday later in the afternoon."

"That is the guy he met. We already knew about that," Valerie said.

"I know, it was a dead end. I questioned her about the other two men. I asked Elaine if it is possible that they went to college together. She said no. We have not figured out who they are yet."

"Quad is sure he wants to run their pictures?"

"He said yes."

"I see that the composites are rough. They might help us. They might not. I will run them."

"Elaine gave me better photos of Kala. They were taken by her phone camera the day before she came up missing. I have the link to the photos here."

"I saw that."

"We had calls sighting a man with a baby girl in Florida yesterday."

"At an airport?"

"No. It was a drug store," Talbot said.

"Did they find the semi used to take his things out of the home?"

"Not yet. We are working on the plate. We have a partial plate number, but it doesn't match the vehicle used. The plate was called in stolen from a truck stop in Indiana. Yes, we are searching Indiana for leads."

"Damian could have paid the local men to do things to knock you off course."

"He has gone to extensive trouble. We found his cell phone. It was in the trash at a truck stop that they fueled up at."

"Don't tell me it was here," Valerie said.

"He ditched it and filled the tank to full. I questioned the man on duty. He doesn't remember who paid the truck's gas bill. He said he has a hundred truckers an hour. He did remember it was cash. It was an eight-hundred-dollar fill-up."

"You would think he would remember that."

"Not really. With diesel fuel high, all the fill-ups are up there."

"Maybe when he quit paying his bills, he was setting money aside to take off. Damian might have this planned for months. If he were to disappear, it would take a huge amount of money?"

The waitress came to the table. "Hi, my name is Candy, and I will be your server today."

"I put the order in an hour ago. I am Agent Talbot."

"Oh, yes. I will bring it right out. Do you still want the appetizer tray?" the waitress asked.

"Yes, please. And two glasses of white wine, please," Talbot said confidently.

"A man of mystery tonight," Valerie said.

"You are on a tight schedule needing to work on the story when we get done."

"Sounds good to me. So are you going to tell me what you ordered?"

"Not until it comes. Then you can taste it. I will tell you it's a variety. If you don't like any of it, it is okay. There is plenty to choose from. Back to our case. Damian transferred money via wire to an account out of the country. We are working on verifying the location of the account."

"Was it sizable?"

"Yes. We don't know where he got his hands on that much money."

"Where is his dad now? Is he still in prison?"

"That is a good question. I will have Peters check into that. I never thought about his dad being connected to this."

"It is possible. He might be laundering money for his dad or that businessman he met with on Sunday last week."

"You should come work for the FBI."

"Why? So we could be together?"

"It would be nice, wouldn't it?"

"We do have fun together." Valerie leaned into Bruce, with her left hand on her face.

"You are a gorgeous lady. Look at your beautiful red hair, your green eyes, and your thin waist."

"You can look, but do not touch. You might find that I took karate lessons long ago."

"Did you really?"

"Don't touch me and you won't find out."

The waitress brought out the white wine and a large tray of several appetizers. The tray had to be fourteen inches wide.

"Thanks, Candy. What is the best one on the tray?" Valerie asked.

"I like them all. You two enjoy. I will bring out the next course in a little bit. If you need something, I will be over there." Candy pointed to the bar area.

"Ooo la la. That is good," Valerie said, taking a bite of escargot.

"If I come back to town, will you go out with me again?"

"What are you going to do to come back to town?"

"Beg and plead, Quad."

"Sure, I will go out with you again, unless another guy beats you to the punch."

"Do I have any competition?"

"I have many chasers. I have had a local doctor be very nice to me."

"That's not surprising Valerie, you are great. You have a great sense of humor."

"Thank you."

"The restaurant deserves its good rating. I would love to eat here again," Bruce said.

The two sat in silence for a few minutes and devoured the tray of food set before them.

"I would have thought you were hungry."

"I was hungry. Not now," Valerie said.

The waitress came back and brought a large Caesar salad with two plates.

"Can I get you more wine?"

"No. We are good. But how about more water?" Bruce asked.

"Good choice."

"Not at all. How can I find out who you are if you are drunk? I order the glass of wine to complement the meal, not to manipulate you. You are safe. I am not looking to take advantage of you. I like your company. I could sit here in public with you for the rest of my life."

"That sounds safe to me. I am going to be full before the main course comes."

"So you will have leftovers to take home. We don't have to eat it all here. We can save some salad for later."

"Sounds like a good plan. So am I allowed to write the piece on the money transfer now?"

"Quad said you could, but you could also drag the story out each day if you want.

I know I can't keep you out late tonight, but maybe in a day or two I can."

"I won't be around this weekend."

"A date?"

"Yep."

"With the doctor, of course."

Valerie nodded her head.

CHAPTER 23

Anticipation bubbling over, Valerie wanted to hear more of Jon's vision of the future. Nationally, things had gotten pretty bad. Change was at every corner. It was only the power of God that could correct every wrong. If God could bring change in Valerie's life, he could do it in the nation. After all, it was God and God alone that brings us life and restoration. From the surface, Jon had a professional demeanor, but underneath, he brewed with the things of God. His passion for Christ drew Valerie past anything she had known from any other person. She valued his relationship. She fed the animals and took the organic eggs to the restaurant. She finished packing her overnight bag. She picked up a gift to take to the hostess of the house. It was a beautiful glass votive centered in fall-colored flowers. The florist had carefully put it in a cardboard box for Valerie. She hoped it was well-received. At exactly 8:00 a.m.,

the back door bell rang. Valerie ran to meet Jon. She didn't think her smile could outdo his, but it did.

He gave her a big hug and said, "I missed you. I am glad you took me up on the offer."

"I am glad you asked. I'm ready for a new beginning." Her words shocked her. *I didn't know I felt that way. Am I saying I wanted a relationship with him?*

"Let me take your bags. I rented a full-size van. It will be more comfortable for the trip. I am bringing home some items from up north anyway," Jon said.

"I will carry this. It is a gift for the hostess."

"You can set that down on the floor. It can't go anywhere. Anything else we need to take?" Jon pointed to a spot perfect to hold the flowers.

"Just me," Valerie teased.

"I couldn't dare run off without the best woman. You bring new joy to my life."

"I was thinking the same thing this morning about you, Jon. I don't remember when I have been so excited to go somewhere. I guess the life I thought was so great really wasn't."

"That happens. When you find real life, you find out that the past was not all that it was cracked up to be. I have been doing a lot of thinking on those lines myself. I stopped and got you a Starbucks coffee. I hope you like it."

"I didn't know there was one around here."

"It is about five miles east of here. Okay, so I went out of my way to bring you coffee. I hope it's not a bad thing. The drive will be a long one. Hey, it is good to see you. How is the story going?" he asked, as they both hopped in the van.

"I got it wrapped up enough to go away for the weekend. They are putting a huge article in Sunday's paper. We think Damian went to the Dominican Republican, first to Florida and had a friend take him over in a boat. They are confirming all that now, he'd been transferring money there for a few years."

"Even before the baby was born?"

"It looks like it. It started out a few thousand a year but grew to big sums of money. Damian is involved in something making him big money. Him not paying his bills is baloney."

"But Elaine didn't know about any of it, did she?"

"Not that anyone can tell. She looks clean, which is good for her sake. When they find him, she will have full custody of the child. The feds say they will try to track down where the money was coming from and anything that doesn't need to be returned will be Elaine's. I talked to her late last night. She said that she plans on staying at her parents' house. She is going to go get a job. Her mom will care for Kala. She filed for divorce this week. The legal advice she got told her it was the safest way."

"I wonder if Damian was connected to the mortgage-lending-industry scam. Didn't I read that his partner went out of business last fall or late summer?"

"Yes. That was brought out the first few days. No one ever said what they were into specially. Just financial investments."

"I saw your dad last night. He's coming along well. We expect he'll be home in two more weeks. I have the hospital ordering the home equipment he is going to need, a wheelchair, and a hospital bed. Being out in the boonies, it takes a little longer than in the big city."

"It should take what, one extra day?"

"It actually doesn't take extra time. I just don't want equipment to be used for another reason and him be out in the cold. It happens. Rarely, but it does happen. Have the disability checks come in yet?"

"I got two checks. One was the life insurance on my mom, and the other was for the car. They sent me a letter that the checks for dad's disability would be sent out in seven days. They will be retro to the day of the accident. The letter said it comes from a separate department and takes about eight weeks to get started. What happens to people who live paycheck to paycheck?"

"It can be tough."

"Jon, I have been thinking about what you said about starting an organic church. How, when, and where are you going to do that?"

"I have to trust the leading of God. Everything we know to be true is changing. God is shaking things and bringing correction to his church body. If it is out of timing, it won't work. And if it is my agenda, it will fail. It has to be God. God is bringing those to be a part of this. You might be part of that."

"I think I am. I wake up in the middle of the night with dreams about groups of people worshipping God in a way I have never seen."

"It is exciting, isn't it?"

"It is. I have to tell you the truth. I couldn't wait to be here with you now to talk about this. I feel like I am a magnet being drawn to a piece of metal. Your spiritual depth and purity makes me want more of God."

"That is how God does things. It is never how we would expect or in the timing we would choose. When things line up, you can always see that his ways were perfect. I could never be God. You know, I look at how God uses me as a doctor. It amazes even me. I see miracles that defy science each day of the week for those who believe in him. Even your dad was one of them. The puncture in his lung and the infection he got from that should have killed him, but it didn't."

"You never told me how serious it was."

"God told me not to," Jon said, as he looked to see how she would react to his statement. He knew that medically, it was irresponsible.

"I am glad you obeyed. I don't know that I could have handled it then. God did miracles in me too. I gained strength. It seems almost overnight."

"I know. I watched God do it. Did you know I prayed for you every day?"

"Until you had me over for dinner, I didn't know you were born again."

"You would have seen it or sensed it over time. That is really how we know when someone is a child of the king. It is not our words that define us but our actions. Our spirits know. Your spirit can also detect when someone is not doing the right thing. Even when what they say is accurate."

"Jon, you are so wise."

"And you are so beautiful inside and out. Did you know the word *beauty* is really about our spirit?"

"I had heard that it is not the outward but the inward."

"That is the truth. How is that coffee?"

"It is very tasty. You know it will make us have to stop more often."

"That gives me more of an excuse to look at you as we walk in."

"It is hard to watch me and the road? Is that what you are saying?"

"You got it."

"What time will we be up there?"

"Two PM. Tamika is making a prime rib, garlic mashed potatoes, and more. I went to medical school with John, her husband. You will really like them. They are kind and gentle people. He has a practice on the west side of the metro Detroit area. They bought this cabin this past summer really cheap. When the housing market took a crash, they took advantage of it. I haven't been there yet, but Tamika said it is large and beautiful. The couple that owned it went bankrupt. I guess his business as a builder couldn't stand the drought. She said that he built the house himself, adding the best to it. The side that faces the lake is all windows. That has to be pretty in the morning and at sunset. I don't know how they get away from losing heat in the winter."

"We can ask them how cold it gets. I guess they might not really know yet unless it has gotten much colder then Ohio has."

"It is about ten degrees colder," Jon said.

They sat in silence for a few minutes. Then Valerie spoke.

"Jon, why am I so comfortable with you and not with Mason?"

"I can't explain that."

"He asked me out this weekend. I was glad I had plans with you. I feel smothered or controlled or something by him. He says so many right things, but somehow I don't really trust him."

"Maybe he is desperate for a relationship. I am not. I know that if you are the one for me, we will both know it. Until then, I am going to enjoy the company of a godly woman."

"Well put. That is why I am comfortable. You don't try to force things to happen. You let it flow where it needs to. I really like that you are secure."

"I like that you are secure too. I see so many wonderful traits in you. I doubt you even know all the wonderful things you are."

"I am a good journalist. I am kind and considerate of others."

"You are very passionate about life. You are strong and wise. You're loving and witty. I bet you're even good at managing money and life's affairs," he said, as more of a question than a statement.

Valerie picked up on it.

"My parents taught me how to save money when I was less than five years old. It stuck with me."

"I figured as much. You have excellent traits. You are a beautiful flower ready to blossom."

"Oh, thank you. Hey, next rest stop, I need to use the facilities. The coffee did its trick."

"Me too," Jon said.

They both were quiet until it came time to stop. The fall colors drew them into the beauty of the day. The sun was bright, and all was well with the world.

CHAPTER 24

Jon had been driving for an hour Sunday morning when Valerie got a call from the nursing home.

"We will go straight to the hospital. It will be a while. I am still in Michigan. Okay. Call me if something changes. Thank you. Bye."

"My dad fell out of bed this morning. A nurse found him at about seven, but he had been on the floor a long time. They are transporting him to the hospital," Valerie said.

"Valerie, let's pray for him."

"Can you start and I will finish?"

"Your Word says that where two or three are gathered in your name, you are there. We invite you into this van. We come humbly before your throne first to tell you how much we love and adore you. Father, you have always kept us safe even if we didn't think we were safe. We ask that you would protect Jacob, bring him comfort and

healing in the name of Jesus, your Son. I lift Valerie to you. She is in your hands, clay ready to be molded. Allow her to see your providence and your love for her. Take her further then she has ever gone before. Lead her into a peaceful place. Heal the wounds. Comfort her as she mourns and bring her new life abundantly." Jon swallowed and then talked directly to Valerie. "I sense that God is moving you into a deeper place with him. He is asking you if you trust him. You don' t need to answer, but let it roll around in your spirit."

"Jon, I feel awful. I think God might have allowed this to humble me. I have gotten too involved again with my own thing and what I want. I think I need to repent."

"So go ahead and do it. The quicker the better."

Valerie shocked herself. She felt comfortable baring her soul to the doctor.

"God, I am so sorry for pushing you aside for my own thing. I got all wrapped up in the story about Kala that I didn't let you have center place in my heart. Let me be restored to the rightful place in you. Cleanse me and I will be clean. Thank you for that. God, now I ask that you would let me worship you in a fresh way that would honor you. Heal my hurts and wounds that I would be free. Then if I may ask that you would completely heal my dad. Lord, you are the great physician. You can do anything. I ask that your will be done on earth as it is in heaven. In the name of Jesus, amen." Valerie turned to Jon. "I feel so free. Hey, look. A white dove."

"It must be a sign."

"What does the dove represent?"

"The Holy Spirit."

"Jon, last night, I slept so good. I had this long dream that went on forever. I am not much to dream or at least remember them. What I do remember was that I was with a group of people I didn't know well, but I felt comfortable. We had gone to an amusement park, spent the day there. It was getting dark. We went to leave. We got into this convertible. The top was partly down and partly up. A machine came and snatched the car and took it for a ride."

"That is quite a dream. How many were in the car?"

"There were four in the car."

"The car represents ministry. The four represent reign or domin-ion. I think what God is saying is he is taking you for a ride beyond your control. There are others who are being trained in this too. That dream will unfold more for you as the future unfolds for you. Someday, you will understand it."

"Have you always been able to interpret dreams?"

"No. I do understand a few things, but that is about it," Jon said.

"I hope I catch up soon," Valerie said humbly.

"I hate to tell you this, but we are always growing and learning. It is just a part of life."

A few minutes passed.

Valerie asked, "What are you going to do with that ping-pong table you brought back?"

"That is for my basement. It is good to have more than one table when crowds come over."

"Do you play much?"

"No, but my sister and her husband love it. Valerie, do you want to stop to eat or drive straight through?"

"I'm not sure. I'm not hungry right now but might be later. Can we take it on the road with us?"

"Sure. We can go through and get Subway or something like that."

"I would like that. You and your friends were great hosts. You don't have to feed me like a queen all the time."

"Oh, darn."

"I guess it makes you eat like a king, doesn't it?"

"Sure, and I don't do that for myself as much as I should. I work some crazy hours sometimes. I eat on the run way too much."

"Maybe we should stop to eat. We both eat on the run a lot."

"Whatever makes you happy," Jon said.

"I have been struggling with what to do about my job at the *Dispatch*. I don't want to be sucked into a system that breeds decep-tion. I never thought that being back home would be a place I could be happy, but I am."

"Keep taking it to God in prayer. He will reveal himself to you in due time. Keep a humble spirit. I think that scripture is in First Peter five six," Jon said.

"Let me look. Yes, you are right. It is in First Peter five six. Verse seven goes on to say, 'Cast all your anxiety on him for he cares for you.' I needed that today. I have been feeling anxiety over these decisions, and I shouldn't be."

"I agree, but it is a process. It is like the wound we get for serving God. We have to let it go. God will use those things to grow us into his character."

"I am glad you brought that up. I was wounded by the way Damian treated me when I went to him for help. He blew me off. I called my pastors at my old church in Columbus. They never called me back. It made me feel like my money was good enough but my problem wasn't worthy for them to give me a few minutes or even pray for me. I was hurt by it all. I was thankful that you and Mason came along to bring a healthy distraction."

"I am sorry the body of Christ hurt you. It shouldn't be that way, but many times, it is the body who wounds its own. You have heard the saying that you hurt the ones you love. It happens in the church too. I am referring to the little *c*, not the big Church. The big Church is the true body of Christ, the remnant. It is not the local body or what we think of as what happens inside the building. We have gotten so far away from the true values of Christ. We have put buildings and titles above loving each other. All you needed was someone to show you God's love."

"That is what you did for me. I feel free and comfortable because it was God through you. I don't feel like you asked me out to have a romance."

"I didn't, but I do see a wonderful woman. If that is God's plan, I would be open to it."

"Me too. Once I figure out what God is telling me, I will be all right."

"You will."

"How do we get to center?"

"Pray and ask God to first align you where you need to be. Then ask him to bring his body to the rightful place. I see a shift coming. Well, it has already started. I think God is allowing our world to fall apart to get our attention. In my field, I see how tragedy changes people. At first, people panic, but most end up on their feet in a better place."

"I was thinking about that with the support group. The problems are varied. I was trying to judge who would come out better and who would just stay a victim of circumstances," Valerie said.

"You do know that character is not built in trauma, but it is revealed in those times. Character is built slowly over time. It is the little choices we make on a daily basis. Those who choose to cheat the system someday will find themselves not being able to cope or deal with life. I had a dream a couple years ago. I dreamed I had waited in line to go into a stadium. I had paid a large price for my ticket. When the gates opened, there were many who ran past me and jumped over the seats, taking front-row seating. I looked at the security who stood and let it happen. A first, nothing was done. After the show started, those in the front row-seats couldn't see anything. They were blinded by the lights. They would have been better off taking the seats they had paid for and waiting patiently. Many of them got up and left the stadium, for the seats they had paid for had been taken by others. They didn't get anything out of it. Those who try to take a shortcut from God's process will find that they too won't get anything out of jumping past the security or God's process."

"That is a great analogy."

"It isn't mine but God's. Want another one?"

"Sure."

"About ten years ago, I was in a church that was not where they should be, so I started praying. God gave me a few dreams. The first one was like an expressway with four lanes going in two different directions but divided by grass in between. I was standing talking to someone for a while. Two accidents happened. We continued talking. A third accident happened. We went to find the cause. A policeman was sending traffic going westbound on an eastbound lane, thus causing the head-on collisions. God gave me the interpretation. Many spiritual leaders are sending their sheep down paths of destruction. I can now walk into a church building and God will bring that dream up when things are not of him."

"How cool is that? You really are a gem of a guy."

"Humility is key. If I go off thinking it is about me, I am in the same trouble as the shepherds. At that point, I am more harm than good to the body. Me being a doctor has a great disadvantage."

"Like what?"

"I save people's lives. If I ever think I am it, I will fall. You have heard the higher you go the farther you fall. I see many in my profession who think they are it. We are human and make the same mistakes anyone else does. Our mistakes can cost a life. I went to medical school with a lady who no longer practices because of one such mistake. Anyone could have done it. She was sued and couldn't take the pressure from losing."

"What kind of doctor was she?"

"A heart surgeon. She was really good. She had a bad moment that cost her everything."

"Where is she now?"

"No one has heard from her in a couple years. We don't really know. It could happen to me too."

"The difference is your world is not built around you but is built around God. When tragedy would strike, you turn it over to God. You would pray and allow God to work it out. Do you think she cracked under the pressure?"

"We don't really know. She moved out of the area she was in, and for all intents and purposes she has disappeared," Jon said sadly.

They drove in silence for a long time. Valerie was deep in her thoughts.

"We are approaching Saginaw. It might be a good time to stop and eat. They have a few good places to eat at the next exit. Are you ready?"

"Good timing. I am hungry, and I have to empty my bladder again," Valerie said.

CHAPTER 25

It was three o'clock when Jon dropped Valerie off at Mercy Hospital's door. The flower/gift shop was right inside. She quickly ran in, buying flowers while Jon parked the van.

"There you are, beautiful." Jon said with a twinkle in his eye.

"Aren't you sweet. I got Dad some flowers and I bought some mints. Do you want one?"

"Do I need it?"

"No. It just helps to calm my nerves. I use the mints to distract me."

"Let's take the private elevator."

"I don't get this chance very often," Valerie said.

"Your dad is going to be fine. No matter what, he is in God's hands."

"I know. Praying today really helped me."

"It helped me too. I'm enjoying seeing into your heart. You were so transparent with me today. I saw a woman wanting God in control. I want to be there all I can for you."

"Thanks. You have been there already, and I know if I needed you in the future, you would be there. I can't say that about too many people."

"Mason..."

Valerie cut him off, "He was, but now he has an agenda."

"He really does have a good heart. I think he might have some insecurity issues from his father dying. Mason never dated."

"He can take them someplace else. I have enough on my plate. I need to be where things relax me. I am tightly wound already. You do what you have to get the story completed, and sometimes it is thirty-six to forty-eight hours before you get a break."

"I understand. Working at the hospital can be the same thing. We have two doctors, so we have to work out the hours."

"How have you gotten the two Saturdays off?"

"I only got this one off. I worked last week. It just worked out. You have to admit the hospital is not that big."

"True. The metro area hospitals are huge. Hey, we're here. Thanks for calling and getting his location."

"It is my pleasure," Jon said.

Jon let Valerie enter the room. Her dad had just been brought back from having a battery of tests done. He looked okay. One side of his face looked as if he had a stroke.

"Dad, what did they find out?"

"Nothing yet. Is that for me?"

"Oh yeah. I just about forgot the flowers are for you."

Valerie embraced her dad. He returned the hug.

"They are very nice. Your mother always like these kind of flowers. What are they?"

"The bouquet has daisy and mums and a few other flowers. I don't know what they are. I liked it too. It was nice fall colors. I was hoping you would enjoy it."

"Is Dr. Stephens taking good care of you, Jacob?" Jon asked.

"They have had me in tests all day. They promised me food for supper. I haven't eaten all day. I fell before breakfast, and I was in testing at lunch."

"Do you want anything specific? I can order it for you."

"Not really. I was hoping I would get those test results soon."

"Unless you need me, I am going to let the doctor finish what he started. You are in good hands. Valerie, I am going to go to the nurses' station and see what I can find out. I won't be too long."

"Thanks, Jon."

"I see you two are getting along well," Jacob said.

"He invited me to meet some friends of his up north. We got the call about you an hour after we had left to come back home. I am sorry I wasn't here quicker, Dad. I shouldn't have left without telling you where I was going."

"You worry too much. I will be fine. I am a tough old geezer."

"You have made it past the odds now. Maybe you're right."

Jon returned to the room. "Jacob, it was a mini stroke. It doesn't look like too much damaged happened. They are going to keep you for a few days."

"I thought it might have been. It could be worse."

"We are going to get you a diet that will help. This is a sign that the body is not doing well."

"You can tell Valerie what to cook for me. I haven't cooked a day in my life. I would have no idea where to start." Jacob smiled at Valerie.

"Yes, Dad."

"Jacob, if you don't mind, I am going to return Valerie to her home. I promised to have her home by suppertime."

"No. You two kids go and enjoy."

Valerie kissed her dad on the cheek before walking out of his room with Jon.

"Valerie, we will have to put him on blood thinners to prevent another stroke. It was a blood clot in the brain that created the problem. Dr. Stephens scheduled sonic wave treatments. They help break up the blood clots in the brain."

"When will that happen?"

"In a little bit. They are going to feed him first. Food is on the way up. It is important to break up the clot fast. They have the technician coming in now. He might need therapy for this, depending how well the sonic treatment does."

"Is that why you got me out of there?"

"Yes, it really is Dr. Stephens's call. Your dad might have not wanted to eat if we were there. After he eats, he will be tied up for a few hours. You can use that time for yourself."

"What are you going to do?" Valerie really didn't want him to drop her off.

"I have to get this table out and return the van. I then need to go see my sister. I don't want to put any pressure on you. By me leaving, you have the opportunity to do what you need to."

"I am going to miss you."

"I was hoping to hear you say that. Do you want to go with me to return the van?"

"Yes."

"Okay. I could use the extra hands in getting the table out. It's not heavy. Just bulky."

"Glad to do it. I was once a farmhand," she teased.

The time went by quickly. The table was placed in the basement. They enjoyed a couples of games. It was time to get the van back.

CHAPTER 26

Tuesday night came fast. The support group had a new lady leader. She had a timer and gave each person twelve minutes. They had to use every bit of the time allotted, even if they told jokes. She said that it forced people out of their shell. After the meeting, Valerie had gone to have coffee with a few from the group. They had gone to the only place around still open at ten p.m., the truck stop by the highway. Many exchanged phone numbers. Valerie found the stories exciting. Driving home, Valerie pondered what each one was experiencing. Mike and Sally lost their grandbaby. Now they were being forced to testify against their daughter. It was affecting everything they did. Recently Mike had lost his job working at the mill. Sally said she hadn't slept in months. They asked if anyone could give them money or food. Valerie gave them a fifty-dollar bill.

Angie and Arlie lost their three-year-old girl in a fire and their home. The community had been wonderful, but they couldn't seem to get it together. They now were bunking at a brother's house in his basement. The threat of the brother losing his home was getting closer and closer. They asked if anyone could take them in.

Teresa told more of her story in the smaller group. She said that she had been molested by her father since she was nine. She admitted to being loose and fancy free after that with the boys. She was raising two boys of her own without a father. She admitted that she had a problem with addictions. She gave up drugs, replacing them with alcohol. She had been given an eviction notice last week. She too had nowhere to go. She joined the group looking for answers.

Valerie went to bed. She lay for hours on her bed. How could she help them without getting pulled into their traps? How much of their stories could they have prevented? With most in the group, she saw a thread: they all were living in lack. She sat up in bed and turned the computer on. She typed in "poverty spirit." She found many authors offering information. She read for hours. Studying what the poverty mentality and spirit was, she knew it wasn't about not having enough. It carried through into every area of these people's life. It affected them emotionally, mentally, spiritually, physically, and financially. This was something she wanted to know more about. She wanted to teach them how to help themselves, not just eat for a day. I don't understand why I've been drawn in so far. Was it because they all, in their own way, had asked her for help? She lay down to go to sleep, but before she could let sleep come, she had to pray.

Lord, I need your wisdom, my compassion and my own dysfunction compels me to want to do something for each one of these people. I know that may not be the best choice for them. Speak to me through dreams or visions or your word. Give me a good night's sleep. I love you because you have shown me your deep love for me….

Sleep overtook Valerie.

ROSALYN ZOGRAFOS

CHAPTER 27

Elaine returned and removed her things from the house. The shock of the last few weeks' events were starting to wear off. She borrowed her dad's car. It had enough room to get her clothes. Before returning, she would stop and see Valerie. Elaine pulled up at 11:20 a.m. She found Valerie raking fall leaves. Valerie immediately stopped and invited her in. Over tea, the two talked.

"Elaine, I know this has to be very hard for you. What can I do to help?"

"Just listening to me is a great help. My parents just want it over. They don't want to ever hear me say Damian's name again. I can't believe I married a monster. I miss Kala. I haven't been able to sleep much. I sleep for an hour and wake up with nightmares. I keep seeing flashes of that night he moved us out. I never thought Damian

could have anything to do with Kala being taken until then. Was I so miserable to be married to that he had to just take off?"

"I doubt it had anything to do with you at all. Damian is a messed-up man. Things probably started with him as a child. Any man who would take their baby and have someone hide her until he could take her is sick."

"How do I prove it in the courts?"

"Elaine, I doubt it will be that hard after the national publicity your case had. They will want him evaluated to know what is going on with him. It could be a lot of things. Bipolar people do things like that from time to time. Did you ever notice major mood swings?"

"He was more self-absorbed than anything. Everything revolved around him."

"When he was in college, did he ever act strange?"

"He hung out with his guy friends more than with me."

"You had said you had been getting marriage help. Did it ever help?"

"No."

"Elaine, I have always wondered, why did Damian become a pastor?"

"I don't really know. He was so good at that financial company. I didn't know why he wanted to do this."

"Did you know the company was going belly up?"

"Not until Kala was taken and the FBI told me."

"Has the FBI been in contact with you recently?" Valerie asked.

"Not since they interviewed me. The media has been leaving me alone too. I doubt they know where I am."

"Your privacy is a good thing. You don't need them hounding you."

"Most of them aren't compassionate like you have been. NBC tore into me one day."

"I didn't hear about that."

"They drilled me up one side and down another. That was before Damian packed me up and left the house."

"How is the divorce coming?"

"My dad hired an attorney for me. We can't do much yet. It is on record at least."

"Someday, it will be over. You will find growth in all of this."

"I can't see it."

"It is because you are still in the middle of it all. When the pain is too great, that is all we see: pain."

"You have done well with your circumstances," Elaine said.

"I'm working through the pain. I started group therapy."

"Is it helping?"

"Well, Elaine, it's interesting. When you see other's problems, it makes your own look livable. It doesn't diminish the pain. It does make you see life from a new angle. I am glad I started. I have met a group of people who are teaching me about the other side of life," Valerie said.

"Maybe I should find one. How did you find it?"

"The hospital recommended it to me," Valerie said. She then realized that that was of no help. "Call the county and ask what they have available."

"I will do that when I return. I was thankful my dad loaned me his car. He wouldn't even let Mom drive it. It is a good car. It doesn't get the greatest of gas mileage." Elaine was babbling on as she walked out the back door and to the car. "My parents have been good to me. They are just so angry at Damian."

"They never fell in love with him. You did. It is hard for a parent to see their child hurt. I think it is harder for them then for us to see them hurt."

"I guess so. Listen, Valerie, I am so thankful you let me stop by. I have to go. I will keep in touch with you." She hugged Valerie. She saw a gift she had brought for Valerie on the car seat. She reached over the driver's seat and gave it to Valerie. "This is for you. You can open it later."

"Thank you."

"Open it when you feel alone," Elaine said.

"When you feel all alone, God is still there," Valerie said. "Thank you. So many times, that is how I do feel."

Valerie cleaned up the dishes. The cell phone rang. It was Melissa from the group, needing to vent. Things weren't looking good for her mother. Hospice had given her less than a week to live. Valerie invited her over to talk.

"Come on in," Valerie said.

Her eyes were red and swollen from crying. "I can't make it without my mom. She's been everything to me. She's always been there for me."

Valerie held her. "It's okay to get it out. You can't hold it in forever."

Valerie handed Melissa a tissue to wipe her eyes. She thought about how she would have felt at twenty-two if her mom had died from cancer. She wasn't much older, but the shock didn't drag on like cancer did. She was thankful for the way things had happened. God had known what she could take.

"Melissa, we are going to make it through our rough days. Better days are ahead."

"Your mom died. How do you do it?"

"I found God to be an excellent source of help. He listens, comforts me, and is bringing healing to my pain."

"I have heard about him, but I don't know him."

"Melissa, would you like to?"

"Is it hard?"

"No, honey. You just ask him to forgive you of your sins and let him into your heart. I will warn you, it won't always be an easy life, but you will always have hope. He will fill you with peace when it makes no sense. He will guide you through the storm to get safely to the other side," Valerie said gently.

"Can you help me with the prayer?" Melissa said.

"Sure. I will lead you in the sinner's prayer. Just repeat after me."

"I am so glad I called you and not one of the others from the group."

ROSALYN ZOGRAFOS

Valerie led her in a simple sinner's prayer. She had her ask Jesus into her heart. She renounced living for self.

"Valerie, will you go with me and ask my mom if she wants to accept Jesus too?"

"Yes. Let me grab a coat and a bottle of water."

"I'll drive. Then do you mind if I take you out for something to eat?"

"If it is good for you, then, no, I don't mind," Valerie said, grabbing the coat and the water and following Melissa out the back door and locking it as she left. "Your mom is still at home under hospice care?"

"She doesn't want to die in a hospital. She said that was cold. We have her set up in the living room with a hospital bed. They have her on some pretty heavy painkillers."

"I don't know anything about breast cancer. Is she in a lot of pain?"

"I don't know, she never says anything, but I have tried to encourage her by making her homemade cards."

"So you are crafty?"

"Not more than anyone else, but my mom loves it, so I do it for her. When I was young, she hung my Crayon pictures on the fridge and the walls. She made a big fuss over it. I don't want to regret not doing something for her."

"How is your dad handling all this?"

"He is angry and elusive."

"What does he do?"

"For a living, or how is he elusive?"

"I was wondering how he was elusive."

"He stays at work until it is time for bed. Sunday is the only day he is around. He takes me grocery shopping and anything else we need do," Melissa said with anger.

"You are angry at your dad for his response to all this."

"I guess I am. He makes it harder for me. Can't he see that?"

"He is trying to cope just like you are. Everyone deals with difficult things in their own way. Have you talked to him about how this makes you feel?"

"No. I would probably blow up at him."

"That might be okay, but you need let your dad know how you feel. Men don't deal directly with their emotions. We, however, are very emotional. How we feel is important to how we do things too. Give your dad a chance."

"I guess the next time we go shopping I can talk to him. I don't want to upset Mom."

"Does your mom know how you feel?"

"No."

"You might talk to your mom. She can guide you on how to talk to your dad. She'll know his patterns of communication better than anybody. Just talk to her gently about the subject. Melissa, it is already on her mind I bet anyway. If she knows she is dying, she knows you will be forced into more communication with your dad."

"That is wise counsel," Melissa said. "We are almost there. We live in the trailers less than a mile from here."

"Do you like it there?"

"It is all I know. My dad had a gambling problem, causing bad credit. The trailer was bought by my grandparents. They were afraid my family would end up on the streets. So it has been a cheap place to live. We pay lot rent and utilities."

"Does your dad still gamble?"

"He says no. He quit ten years ago. Right now, I sometimes wonder the hours he is gone."

"Does he drink?"

"Not at home," Melissa said.

"Does his job require him to be gone long hours?"

"He cleans carpets. He worked forty or so hours a week before Mom got sick."

"Oh." Valerie had assumed he worked something requiring long hours or was self-employed.

They found Mable sound asleep. Melissa tried to wake her, but she was out. So Melissa suggested they go eat.

CHAPTER 28

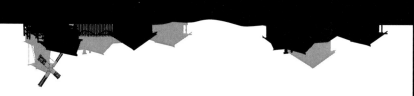

Valerie returned home from grocery shopping. Mason was parked in the driveway, waiting.

"Is everything okay?" she asked.

"I just came to talk to you. Do you mind if I come in?"

"For a little bit. I am headed out shortly."

"Valerie, I think you are making a mistake. A life with Jon will never amount to anything. He will always be on call and won't be there for you."

"That is my decision to make, not yours."

"The rumor around here is that things are heating up between you too. I heard you even took a trip with him."

"I am a big girl. Jon is not going to hurt me. I am not in any trouble here. I really do appreciate your protection, but it is not considered necessary."

"I could provide you with all the things you could ever want. I would be there for you. I won't be working twenty-four hours a day," Mason said.

"What do you have against Jon anyway, or is this just jealousy?" Valerie asked sternly.

"I don't think you will be happy. He will work too much."

"And you are telling me accountants work less hours than doctors?"

"For the most part they do."

"And what about tax season, when they work eighteen-hour days for two to three months?"

"That is just it. It is only temporary," Mason snapped.

"Mason, I am used to working crazy hours myself. I would never judge a husband on him working long hours, nor am I looking for a man who can give me the finer things in life. I was raised in a middle-class home. My needs were always met. I don't have a large list of wants. I want someone who believes in me and can feel what I am going through. If they work a few extra hours, that is okay too."

"You are impossible," he yelled.

"Why am I the impossible one? I have never led you on. I told you not to get any ideas about me."

"I love you, and you are not paying any attention to how I feel."

"Mason, I don't feel that way about you. I care about you but not in a romantic sense. I am sorry if I did anything to mislead you. From what I see, we would never be happy anyway. You make me feel uptight. Jon makes me feel free and happy."

"You never gave me a chance to make you happy," he snapped.

"Jon reached out to me. In the process, I fell in love with him." *There. She had said it, admitted it for the first time.*

"Does he know that?"

"Not yet, but I bet he will within twenty-four hours."

"What is that supposed to mean? You think I am going to go around blabbing what you feel?"

"I am not trying to make you mad, but I didn't tell you about the trip to see his friends. You had to find that out through gossip. For people to be talking about us means someone is gossiping. I didn't know how I felt until I just said it now. Jon and I have not talked like that before, just so you know. I would appreciate it not coming to him the way you are coming to me right now. Let me tell him how I feel when the time is right. Don't push the relationship any faster than it needs to go. I am happy to take it slow."

"That is what I am trying to get you to see, that he is not the right man for you."

"If he is not the right man, then neither are you. You don't have to worry. If it doesn't work between us, you and I won't be dating. Is that clear?"

"Valerie, I just think you are making a big mistake."

"Okay. The record is stated. I got it. Now is there anything else you want to talk to me about other than my choice of friends?"

"No."

"Well, have a nice day." Valerie walked him to the door and opened it, waiting for him to walk out.

Mason slammed the door shut, making comments under his breath.

Valerie just laughed.

How could he really think that after his behavior, I would date him? That was not the kind of man I would marry. He would be controlling her every move the rest of her life, which could end up short due to stress.

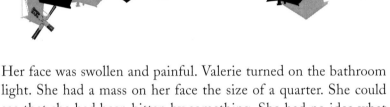

CHAPTER 29

Her face was swollen and painful. Valerie turned on the bathroom light. She had a mass on her face the size of a quarter. She could see that she had been bitten by something. She had no idea what to do with it. So she cleaned it with rubbing alcohol and put some antibiotic ointment on the spot. Maybe she had found a spider in the leaves she was raking earlier. If it didn't improve, she would call Jon to take a look at it. Valerie went back to the bedroom and opened her e-mails.

Elaine sent an e-mail: "I got home safe and sound. Thank you for listening to me. Love, Elaine."

She found one from a single mother telling the story of how her x-partner had abducted her daughter years ago and was still at large. The story was a tear-jerker. The woman told her of how she had lived with the man for three years. She had a good job as a

nurse. One day while she was working, the man disappeared with the baby. He left a note saying, "This is good-bye." She had no paperwork to track him down. She hadn't even listed him on the birth certificate. She asked if Valerie would help. So Valerie lay on her bed and thought about how she could help. Maybe Shelly could get permission to do a column. There might be plenty of other readers who shared these experiences.

"Shelly, I have an idea for a series. I have received several e-mails from parents telling their stories of abducted children. Find out if we can do a series on it. Valerie."

She forwarded the e-mail with the story. She had been pushing off reading many of the e-mails. Maybe that wasn't the right idea. She might have more stories like this one asking for help.

By two in the morning, she read each and every e-mail. She must have read over five hundred that night. Most were the common comments, but four were similar in content. "Dear Abbey" is syndicated. Maybe she could be too. She would be able to do that around the farm and not have to quit her job. The readers' responses to her were wonderful. Before turning out the lights for the night, she asked God for his wisdom and to open the door if this was truly from him.

She quickly fell asleep. At five the next morning, she was awakened with more pain. Her left jaw hurt from the spider bite. She was tired and wanted to sleep. She rolled over and tried to sleep on the right side. She fell back asleep until she again awoke on the left side at 6:20 a.m. At 8:00 a.m., she quit fighting the process and got up. Her face was red for a few inches around the bite. It looked like she had been bitten twice, but the second one wasn't as bad as the first. She sent Jon a text message for medical advice. He called her within five minutes.

"Are you okay?"

"I have a bite on my face that is swollen and all red," Valerie said.

"When I get done with rounds, I will be right over."

"House calls? You do them?"

"For you I do. For my mother I would. The rest of the world gets to see me at the hospital. Give me an hour and I will be right over," Jon said.

Valerie showered quickly, washing her hair. She added a little ball of gloss and ran her fingers through the hair strands. She partly dried her hair with a hair dryer. She left it damp so it would not dry it out. She pulled on a blue fleece sweater and a pair of jeans and face powder and a little mineral eye shadow with mascara. She looked refreshed, even though it had been a rough night.

She was going to make Jon breakfast. It was the least she could do. She had fresh oranges to make fresh orange juice and ingredients for a quiche. Eggs were plentiful on the farm. She added spinach, garlic, black Greek olives, and feta cheese. She hoped it would be tasty. While the quiche baked, she read the fresh e-mails. The first one she opened was from Shelly.

"I love the idea. I need to sell it. Give me a few days. Any more e-mails like that, send them to me. Hope all is well. I will call this afternoon. Shelly."

The group owning the *Dispatch* had several other papers. It wouldn't be that difficult to get this nationwide. One of Valerie's teachers in college said that journalism gave many opportunities, and if you didn't find what you were looking for, make it yourself. This would be an opportunity made by Valerie. If she could council all these woman around town for free, she might be able to help women on a national level. Women trusted her. She was compassionate and gave truth.

At a few minutes to nine, Jon knocked on the back door. Valerie didn't hear the car in the driveway. His winter vehicle, a Pathfinder, made a lot of noise on the gravel. She must have been too deep into thought to notice.

"Come in."

"I see you do have a boo-boo. It looks like a brown recluse bit you. Their bite leaves poison deep in the tissue, eating away at the muscle tissue. I want to get that out of there, but I don't want to do that here. Can you meet me at the hospital this afternoon?"

"Sure I can. What time?"

"After three. Something smells good."

"I made you breakfast."

"Aren't you a doll," he commented.

"You could use a breakfast this morning, right?"

"Sure could."

"Have a seat. Do you want coffee or tea too?"

"I will have some tea. Thank you."

"Jon, yesterday I had a visit from Mason. He—"

"I have already heard. I think you did a great job handling it."

"You heard about him coming here?"

"He told a mutual friend of ours and he called me. I was going to check up on you this morning anyway. I can see that Mason didn't do any real damage."

"No. I guess not. I laughed after he left. I really thought he was a nice guy."

"Are you making some new friends around town?"

"I have met some needy people through the group. Several called and wanted me to listen to them. I guess right now it is too early to tell who will be a friend and who always include trauma in their lifestyle. Some I think you could hand them a million dollars and have everything perfect and they would ruin it in a week. There are others in the group who I think are there for real help."

"Anytime you work with the public, you need to be wise. Both groups are out there. God is giving you more discernment I think," Jon said.

"He is giving me more of something. Hey, I had a great idea. I asked Shelly, my boss, if she would get me approved to do a syndicated column."

"Tell me more."

"I had a few e-mails asking for my help finding their abducted children. These woman are bearing their souls to me. They are looking for a place to help them get their story out. What better way than through print?"

"Maybe not a bad idea you have. You did an excellent job covering the baby abduction," Jon said.

"That is what hundreds of readers tell me. Telling me doesn't make me a paycheck now does it?"

"No. The idea you have would keep you local, wouldn't it?"

"You bet it would. All via the Internet."

"I like it," Jon said. "Your food is pretty good."

"Thank you. I was hoping the quiche would turn out. It sounded good."

"It is very good. Don't let that reputation get around town. The local restaurant will have competition."

"Or will you have competition?"

"Both," Jon teased.

They finished breakfast.

Jon lightly kissed her on the cheek and said, "I will see you this afternoon."

"You know, Jon, I did this on purpose."

"You silly girl." He knew better. He waved as he pulled out of the driveway.

Valerie cleaned the dishes, putting the leftovers away and finishing as her cell phone rang. It was Shelly.

"Valerie, I have a story right up your alley. A Shell gas station owner called reporting that seven people have come in over the last two days reporting giving a ride to a man all dressed in black. He tells them that Jesus is returning soon and then disappears."

"Where is it?"

"It is in Delaware, not too far from where you are."

"It's not that close," Valerie said.

"Oh, come on. It can't be but forty-five minutes, maybe fifty at the most. Tell me you will do the story. It should be a quick in and out."

"Okay. I will do it. I need to be back here at about three to have some minor surgery."

"What happened?"

"I have a spider bite," Valerie said, thinking that sounded really dumb, but she didn't take the time to explain it.

"I will e-mail the directions and the store's location to you. You should have it in less than five minutes. Thank you."

"You're welcome."

The story sounded exciting. Most of her coworkers weren't believers and would make a mockery of the truth. Valerie would be a good choice. She had time to get it done before going to the hospital later.

CHAPTER 30

It had been a long day. Valerie interviewed three of the people giving a ride to the man in black. All said exactly the same thing. A man was hitch hiking along Route 23 going north. They stopped and gave him a ride. He said he was going to Toledo. They would chit chat a little, and he would say, "Well, you know Jesus is returning very soon." Then he would be gone. No doors were opened. Their cars never stopped. He was just gone. Valerie tried to drive the stretch they all had picked him up in. She put fifty miles on the car driving in a circle. She never saw him, but she did believe the stories.

Surgery went well. It took less than two minutes to cut out the source of the problem. Jon gave her a sheet with instructions. He asked her to take it easy for the next day and to use a warm cloth on the wound to draw any infection out. He had given her a pack of gauze bandages to use and some ointment that would heal it quickly.

After surgery, she saw her dad. They were taking him back to the nursing home in the morning.

She lay down to get some early shuteye. The lights on the farm were all out except the large gas lights by the barn. A car drove up in the driveway. She heard the car door open and then shut. The next sound was a boom with glass shattering all over her floor. She jumped out of bed and found that a large rock had been tossed through her bedroom window. She ran to the window, but the car was too far away to correctly identify. Then she saw taillights.

Valerie dialed the sheriff's office from her cell phone laying on the bed. "This is Valerie Sharpe. Can you send a cruiser by the farm? Someone tossed a rock through my bedroom window." She gasped for breath. *What in the world? Breathe, Valerie. Breathe.*

"We will have an officer there soon. Are you okay?"

"I am fine." *I don't feel fine. Lord, I need your help. Who would want to scare me and why? Am I too close to the Kala's abductor or is this personal? Fear gripped Valerie. Am I in danger?*

She grabbed a robe and went downstairs. She knew better then to clean the mess up. She did, however, go out to the barn where her dad kept his tools and supplies. He might have a board to close the window up until she could get it replaced. She was fortunate. There was a board about the size she needed. She found a hammer and nails in his tool chest. As she was walking out of the barn, the deputy pulled in. He pointed his big spotlight attached to the car at the broken window.

"Miss, can you take me up there to see?"

"Sure. Follow me." Valerie took him in the front door, instead of walking back around to the kitchen.

"Have you had any threats?"

"No threats, but a local was pretty aggressive with me yesterday."

"We will take the name and check into that. First, I want to look at the evidence. I'll take a mold of the tire tracks. Did you get a car make and model?"

"No. All I saw where taillights leaving the end of the driveway. I could identify the style of lights maybe."

He followed her to her bedroom. "This took some force. I doubt a woman could have thrown this that far." He picked up the rock, turning it. There were no flat surfaces to get any fingerprints from.

"I doubt it too. It weighs, what, five pounds or more?" Valerie said.

"I would guess, Would you mind filling this out while I go get the tire tracks?"

"Not at all." Valerie thought she would be asked the questions, not handed his report. She filled in Mason's full name and cell phone number. She didn't know exactly where he lived.

Ten minutes passed, and Deputy Smith returned.

"Okay. I got it. Do you have the report filled out?"

"It is done, all that I know."

"You can come by in the morning and get the report. Here is the case number. I'm officer Johns." He handed her a little card with a ten-digit case number. "If you have any questions, my name and cell number are on the back of the card. Good night, miss," he said, as he walked out the door, shutting it behind him.

Valerie placed the board up against the window. It was as close to perfect as she could expect. It was an inch short of covering the window panel, but as long as the glass didn't break out, the hole would be covered. She hammered the nails into place. It worked. A little glass fell out as she nailed, but for the most part, it stayed intact. She took the hammer back to the barn and placed it back in the tool box. On her way back in, she grabbed the broom and a dustpan. She took a paper bag with her to put the glass in. She took the broom, dustpan, and bag of glass down to the kitchen and went back to bed. *I will finish cleaning up in the morning. What a night. I hope I can sleep after all that. Would Mason stoop that low? Damian is out of the area, so how could it be related to Kala?*

It was after eleven o'clock. She crawled into bed and found little pieces of glass in bed. The bed was three feet from the window. She should have expected that glass could have flown that distance. Tonight, she'd sleep in her parent's bed.

At seven o'clock the next morning, her cell phone was ringing. It was Jon.

"Are you okay?"

"Yes, I am fine. It was a wild night, but I made it through."

"What happened?"

"I had a rock thrown through my bedroom window after I had gone to bed."

"Did you file a report?"

"I did. I even boarded the window up."

"I will have a friend of mine come over and fix it. He owns a glass company not too far from here."

"That would be nice. Do I need to do anything?"

"I will call him after nine and have him call you. How is the face?"

"I haven't looked yet. It hurt some in the night, but not too bad."

"Did you take good care of it last night?"

"I tried. Maybe it needs your touch."

"I hope to see you today, Valerie. If you come by the hospital, call me. I have to finish rounds but wanted to check up on you."

"Thanks, Jon." Valerie rolled over in bed and went back to sleep.

At 8:15 a.m., she was awake. She took care of the wound and then turned the computer on. She expected at least a few responses to that morning's paper. She had more than she expected. It would take time to read them. She hunted for the e-mail from Shelly.

"Your story on the mysterious man in black was a crowd pleaser. Keep up the great work. PS, I think your syndicated idea might have found a home. It is going to vote at 1:00 p.m. today with the board of directors. Talk to you later. Shelly."

Excitement filled Valerie. This could be her answer to prayer.

CHAPTER 31

A few weeks passed. Still no sign of Damian. Elaine had not been able to serve divorce papers. She posted it in the newspaper for seven days. The court date was in three weeks. She was asking for full custody due to the circumstances. Her attorney had suggested that Damian might have a mental issue, causing him to behave strangely. Until he was found, it was all guesswork. If she had to, she would ask for a court-appointed evaluation. Elaine found a job as an advertising assistant. If she did well, she was open to being promoted to doing full advertising layouts, which she already knew how to do. Things were tight around town, but Elaine felt that God was providing for her needs. The job was perfect. It was close to her parents and offered some flexibility if she needed it. She had forty mandatory hours she had to work each week. She could work four ten-hour days or work six days a week. For any hours over forty, she

was paid overtime. She had to clear it with the advertising agent she was assisting before she took any time off. She worked for a fifty-five-year-old woman from England. Victoria had been easy to work with. Elaine worked extra hours with Victoria from her house. Victoria had the same computer setup at home, transferring files back and forth. One Saturday in November, Victoria had invited Elaine to come work for a few hours. When Elaine got there, cars were parked all up and down the street. She thought that strange.

She knocked on the door. Victoria let her in.

"Surprise," rang from twenty coworkers.

Elaine had forgotten it was her birthday.

"How did you know?"

"Personnel records, of course," Victoria said. "Come in and enjoy your birthday."

"With all the crap going on, I forgot all about it," Elaine said. Tears dripped off her face.

"Your parents didn't forget. They are here," Victoria said.

"Mom, Dad, I can't believe you never said anything to me. What a surprise."

Elaine's cells phone rang as she finished speaking.

"Yes, this is Elaine. You have him?" Elaine fell to the ground, tears running down her face. She breathed in deeply, held her hands over her mouth.

"Great! …Is my baby okay?" She let out all the air she had held in.

"Okay." Sweat appeared all over her face, goose bumps on her arms. Elaine looked at her mom then her dad while listening to the caller.

"Thank you."

"Hallelujah!" Elaine ran to her mom's arms. Excitement rang through her voice.

"What is it, baby?" Her mom asked.

Elaine spun around and grabbed her dad jumping up and down a few times.

"They found Damian and Kala! They are flying back in the morning. They want to take Kala to the hospital and have her checked. They were in a not-so-good area of the Dominican Republic. The FBI agent said he was arrested for something and the charges here came up." Elaine burst into tears. Pent-up emotion came up. Her purse went flying through the air in the excitement. She held nothing back. Nor did she care she was in the room with twenty people she barely knew, her baby was found.

"What a birthday present, honey," her dad said, crying boldly.

"Do you have to go after her?" her mom barely got out with her throat all choked up.

"Nooo. They said they would bring her back to the house when she's done at the hospital. They are taking Damian there too and don't want me there. I will have to trust that it will be okay." Elaine sat down on the couch. She was in shock; the fight to find Kala was over. "I still can't believe it, Kala is back!"

"At least you know she has been found. He can't get away with this any longer. Kala in the care of the FBI is a good thing," her mom said more calmly.

"I can't believe it." Elaine had begun to pace between her mom and dad. "I want to go there and see her now! I can't wait until morning. Kala, Kala, my baby, Kala." Sobbing Elaine wiped her eyes and face on the Kleenex Victoria handed her.

"You look a little pale," Victoria said.

"I bet I do. My head is spinning. I can't believe it. I should have asked the agent more questions. I am sorry if I am not in the moment of the party. My mind is on Kala right now."

"I guess I don't have to buy you that new car anymore to make your birthday a good one," her dad teased.

"Did you buy me a car?"

"I did. I bought you a Malibu. I hope you like it. It is being delivered to the house this afternoon."

"Thank you, Daddy. I won't have to walk to work anymore. I'll need it to take Kala to a daycare."

"It has a remote start to keep you warm in the cold days of winter coming up soon. Your mom and I wanted to make this special. We didn't want Damian's bad behavior to cloud your memories of turning twenty-seven."

"I have the best parents in the world. You taking me in is much more than I could have ever asked for. I did need a car. Thank you both. I love you." Tears flowed down her face.

"We love you too," her mom said as she embraced her daughter.

CHAPTER 32

The sun was shining. Elaine was excited. Kala would be home in a couple hours. She changed the spare room into a nursery. She had worked all night long with her parents' help. She finished showering when her cell phone rang. The call registered as out of the area.

"Hello. This is Elaine."

"Elaine, don't be alarmed, but Damian fled. He was in having tests. Somehow, he escaped. We have Kala and will be delivering her on time," Quad said.

"Thanks for telling me."

"If he contacts you, please call us. We doubt he will."

"What about Kala's safety?"

"We will have twenty-four-hour protection on your street and are tapping your phone lines, just so you know," Quad said.

"I just want to be safe."

"We are working on it," Quad said.

"Thank you."

"You are welcome. You will see Talbot in a little bit. Have a great day. The line went dead.

Elaine was shaken. Her parents left to go eat with friends before church. They felt like Elaine would need time alone with her baby. She paced the floors. She went from window to window. Her chest was tight, and her breathing was hard. She felt all the blood leave her upper body; she felt numb.

She needed to eat but couldn't. Her stomach was in knots. It had been more than twenty-four hours since she had eaten anything. She could feel low blood sugar dropping even more. Dizziness and brain fog hit her suddenly.

"I don't want to lose Kala again. What if Damian comes here and takes her in the middle of the night?" she said aloud.

Elaine made a cup of coffee. At least it would give her something to do. The coffee smelled good as it brewed. It stirred her appetite. She made toast. She sat and slowly ate the toast, drinking the coffee a little sip at a time.

Eating calmed her down a bit. Elaine knew that she needed to trust God. She knew some of the Word but never let the power of the cross come into her life. Sitting at the table, she quietly prayed. She asked God to do his will in her life. She asked him to teach her to pray. She sat in silence until the doorbell rang.

"Kala!" she screamed with excitement, "My precious baby, you're all right!"

Kala ran to her and jumped up in her arms.

"Come in," Elaine said, stepping back to let the agent in.

"Thank you. This is a nice home," Agent Talbot said.

"It is my parents' home. Would you like some coffee?" Elaine asked.

"I would, with cream." Talbot sat down on the bar stool.

Elaine poured coffee. She pulled the creamer out of the fridge and handed it to him, while she carried Kala in her arms.

"Did Kala check out okay?"

"She has an infection in her intestinal track. They gave me a prescription to give you. Instructions are on the bottle. They included a list of foods to avoid for the next week. Other than that, she is healthy."

"She looks thin." Tears kept rolling down Elaine's face.

"She's had diarrhea for the past few days. Finding her might have saved her life. I heard they were living in a hut without plumbing."

"Oh my!" She grabbed Kala and held her tighter than she had before.

"Momma," Kala said, as she hugged Elaine.

"Talbot, thank you for bringing her home. Is there any word on finding Damian?"

"I wish there was. Security cars will be outside your house by noon today. I will stay until then. We want Damian maybe more than you want to keep Kala safe."

"How could that be?" Elaine asked.

"We think he might have answers to another big case we are working on. I am not at liberty to tell you anything about the case. We know he didn't do it, but the financial men he was connected to did. Damian might know how to find them. They are the same group that snuck Kala out of your house. The only way Damian will talk is if he is afraid for his own life."

"What? Taking Kala isn't enough?"

"Technically, Kala is his daughter. The charge is conspiracy to kidnap."

"Are you telling me a judge might go easy on him?" Elaine asked with anger rising in her voice.

"It could happen, Elaine."

"I can't be concerned for what you do to Damian right now. If I am, I will get too upset, and that is not good for Kala. Can you tell me who he was with in the backwoods?"

"Do you really want to know?"

"Yes. I asked, didn't I?"

"Okay. We found him living with another woman."

"Was she American?"

"Yes. How they met we haven't figured out yet. He said she was the maid."

"What would he need a maid for in a place with no plumbing?"

"Exactly."

CHAPTER 33

Little Sandusky fire was blazing in the First Methodist Church, Sunday morning. Valerie had been called to go the thirty or so miles to get to the truth. People were gathered up and down the little street, watching the fire roar across the roof. It was just before noon when Valerie arrived. It was a cool fall day. Valerie assumed it might have been an electrical failure until she started asking questions of the bystanders.

"Sir, can you tell me what happened in there?" Valerie asked.

"We were listening to our pastor preach when all of a sudden lightning came down and struck the pulpit. The pulpit split in two, and then the fire started," the older man said.

"Can you tell me what time that happened?"

"Ten forty-five. Our service starts at ten a.m., so I would guess that it must have been about ten forty-five."

That was amazing. I had been called a few minutes after that to come get the report.

"Did you hear anything?"

"Of course. First, there was the sound of the lightning and then the sound of the wood being broken apart. It was scary," the older man said.

"Do you have any opinions of how it happened?" Valerie asked.

"I don't."

"Is it possible someone dropped a fireball on the roof of the church?"

"No. It was lightning," the man said assuredly.

"Thank you for your time."

Valerie found a young woman wiping her eyes. She walked over to question her.

"May I ask you a few questions about the fire?"

"I don't know what I can tell you, but go ahead," the young woman said.

"Do you know what happened here this morning to cause this fire?"

"I was hoping you were going to tell me," the young woman said.

"I am still trying to find out, but thank you."

Valerie knew the woman was too shook up to see clearly. She looked through the crowd to who she should ask next. She saw a middle-aged couple hugging each other.

"Excuse me, but would you mind answering a few questions for me?"

"We only got here a few minutes ago. That was my grandmother's church," the man said.

"I am so sorry for your loss." Valerie walked to the next person standing by them. "Sir, would you mind if I asked you a few questions?"

"I will tell ya what I know," he said with a Southern twang.

"Sir, were you in the church when the fire started?"

"I was, but I was sleepin'. I heard something that woke me. All of a sudden, there was fire coming out of the pulpit."

"Was the pulpit in one piece?"

"Well, no. It was shattered on the floor, and the fire was risin' from it."

"Sir, was there a hole in the roof?"

"Well, no. I guess not. The fire started at the pulpit."

"Have you been attending this church long?"

"All my life."

"How long has the pastor been preaching here?" she asked.

"About two years."

"Do the people like him?" Valerie asked.

"As far as I know they do. What? Ya think he had somethin' to do with the fire?"

"Sir, I'm just asking questions, but no, I don't think he had anything to do with the fire," Valerie assured the man. "Can you tell me what he was preaching about this morning?"

"I was asleep."

"Do you sleep through all the sermons?"

"Pretty much."

"Can you tell me which man is the preacher?"

"I don't see him out here right now. If I do, I will send him over to ya. I got to go. My grandbaby needs me."

Valerie looked for the grandchild. She didn't see any young ones around. The wind was blowing the smoke in her direction. She walked around to the other side of the building where several were gathered talking. She would not interrupt the conversation but waited for them to stop. She heard them talking about how the sudden sound scared them. None of them could understand what did happen. Valerie waited a long time, sitting on the lawn. The questions stirring inside of her left unanswered. *If it was God that struck the pulpit, why? Did the lightning represent judgment?*

At three o'clock, the Ohio fire marshal Steve Southern showed up. The fire extinguished, most onlookers returned home. Steve had told her he would talk to her when he finished his inspection of the site. So Valerie patiently waited. *Not what I had been planning to do this Sunday.*

As she waited, she asked God what was behind the fire. She didn't expect to hear an answer, at least not immediately. She had been learning that God did speak to her, just not in the speed she liked or as often as she would choose. However, she was teaching her spirit to be quiet and listen to his still, small voice. Had she never left Columbus, she would still be caught up in the hustle and bustle of life. The *Dispatch* was giving her enough stories to make money but not keeping her swamped. Shelly was selective on what she asked Valerie to do. All the stories had been closer to her than Columbus. Just after five, Steve finished his inspection of the burned church. He approached Valerie, trying to not startle her, as she looked like she had fallen asleep waiting.

"Ms. Sharpe, I am ready for you now," Steve said softly.

"Oh, good."

"Let's go get some coffee," Steve said.

"Would you like to drive together?" Valerie asked.

"My truck is a mess. I have reports from two other fires on the front seat. Do you mind driving?"

"Not at all. I think we have to go fifteen miles northeast from here to find a place."

"That will give me time to fill in a few blanks on the report. I can tell you I have never seen anything like it. There is no electrical damage, and the roof is not burned from the outside but the inside out. The pulpit is burned almost completely. There is no residue on any surfaces to indicate that it was started by man. This looks like an act of God."

"It couldn't have been accidental?"

"There is no candle wax or lighter fluid anywhere in the place. The roof has less than a one-inch hole broken through. The biggest damage is the stage. There are no signs at all of foul play," Steve said.

Valerie wondered if she should tell him about the sighting story she did. What could it hurt?

"Mr. Southern, I did a strange story a couple weeks ago, where seven people claimed to have given a ride to a hitchhiker on Route

Twenty-Three south of here. The man was dressed in all black clothes. He did a little bit of small talk with each person and then made a statement to each of them that "Jesus was returning soon." He then disappeared out of their cars. I did three personal interviews. I have many e-mails from others claiming to have met the man in the same way. Do you think that God is trying to get our attention?"

"I was never much of a believer in him, but the fire today sure has me thinking I was wrong. I don't know what all this means."

"I do believe in God. He rearranged my entire life in a few months. Maybe lightning struck to get the people's attention."

"I would say he got their attention today," Steve said with a puzzled look on his face.

"There are two places we can go. We have Hardee's or Bob Evans's."

"It doesn't really matter. I have had a busy day with fires today. Sitting down a little bit sounds great. You pick it," Steve said.

"Hardee's has pretty good coffee."

"Tell me, what you drew you into working for a paper?" Steve asked.

"I love getting to the bottom of the story. It is an adrenaline thing to me. I'm weaning off for a little bit. My parents were in a terrible car accident that took my mother's life. My dad is still incapacitated to this day. Since I left the city and came home, I have been learning to live without my drug."

"Writing?"

"Yes," she said as she nodded her head yes. "So what about you?"

"I was a fireman. They gave me the opportunity to improve, and I took it. The state of Ohio sent me to California to be trained for eighteen months, and here I am. It has it's days, let me tell you. The fires come all at once, like today. I was in Cleveland at two this morning and in Youngstown before I came here. So far, there are no more calls I have to run off to. It might be quiet for days before I get a call," Steve said.

"It sounds like our jobs have similar threads. You never know when you are working or have time off."

Valerie parked her Volvo. They went into Hardee's.

"You drove. I am buying. Whatever you want. I'm going to grab a sandwich. I'm very hungry," Steve said, as he pulled his wallet out.

Valerie stuck to the coffee. She had plans to meet with Jon when she finished. She called him and told him what she was up to. He would cook for her that night.

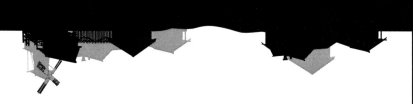

CHAPTER 34

Talbot had been commanded to go through and do another search for any information that could lead to where Damian would go. They had agents watching his father, whom they found in Utah. It was his father who had helped get Kala out of town. He met the men who had taken her, taking her on to the last legs of the trip to another world. Three million dollars was missing. Pete Wade, Damian's father, had been part of the scheme. It was a venture capital company swindled out of the money. He moved the money. No one knew where. There were five men involved with the scheme.

Talbot went to the house to do another search. No one had gone through the home with a fine-tooth comb. Talbot hoped he could find some evidence to point them in the right direction. Also on his list was to investigate the man whom Damian had met with the Sunday before Kala disappeared. The man too was involved in

investments, but not the same company. It was possible he'd transfer funds for the men.

It was Deputy Smith, a young man in his mid twenties, who had done the escort.

"So do you know Damian Wade?" Talbot asked.

"I never met him. He has been talked up around here, but I couldn't comment on it. I have not been a part of any of the calls so far. It is such a shame. He had the world by the tail if you ask me."

"Looks like greed took him down. Greed is behind many crimes we investigate at the bureau," Talbot said.

"I would think jealousy or rage would be first on the list," Smith said.

"Those are motives too. But with the FBI, more of them are rooted in greed. When the truth all comes out, greed is stuck in there somewhere. We cracked a large case recently of embezzlement and IRS fraud. It involved over twenty million dollars. The guy was good. He got away with his crime for twenty years. Now he is in prison for twenty years."

"We don't see things like that in the country," the young Officer Smith said.

"I would expect not. I am going to search that big desk left behind, hoping he left something for me to go on. Would you mind searching for anything in the closest? Call me if you find anything besides Elaine's clothes or Kala's," Talbot said.

He knew the guy didn't have much experience, but he needed his help. Time was crucial to getting to the bottom of the case. Every minute that passed gave Damian more time to escape from reach. With the millions of dollars at their disposal, they could be flown by private jets anywhere. Damian left the hospital with nothing but his clothes on. He wallet and cell phone had been taken when he was arrested. They hadn't, however, put him in a jail uniform yet. Kala and Damian were taken by ambulance to the hospital from the airport.

Talbot pulled out each drawer and found paperclips and rubber bands and a few empty files in the first three. He tried pulling out the big drawer on the left. Something was holding it back. He lay down on the carpet to see if he could see what was holding the drawer shut. He found an envelope stuck halfway in the drawer with part of it hanging out. He pulled the envelope out from the outside. He found it addressed to Damian Wade with no return address on the top left corner. He sealed the envelope in an evidence bag. On the floor by the desk was a cuff link. It looked to be real gold. It had been engraved on the inside with, "All my love, Elaine 2005." On the right corner of the desk, he found a spot of blood. He scraped it and placed it in the little Petri dish. He then placed the glass dish in a small bag. In the next drawer, he found two pictures with three men. One he assumed was Damian. The next picture was taken in an outback setting such as Alaska or Washington state. It was of two men whom he knew not to be Damian. Both men were taller and huskier with darker hair than Damian's. The men were holding four fish that they had caught. He turned the picture over, hoping to find names and dates. He found nothing. He bagged the two pictures and placed them with the rest of the evidence.

Talbot followed the hallway back to see if Deputy Smith had found anything. He was rummaging through many clothes and searching each piece.

"Here. Let me help you. I am surprised he left all this. Hey, look. I found a lighter with the initials KD. I wonder what he would have this for. They are not his initials." He bagged it and placed it in the big bag he had been placing the evidence in.

"I found a matchbook. It says, 'Freedom Girls,'" Smith said.

He handed the matchbook to Talbot. It had pictures drawn of mostly naked woman.

"Is there any place around here with a name like that?" Talbot asked.

"Not that I know of," Smith said.

"Let's finish this and check out the basement and the garage. I don't remember anyone ever looking in either place before."

"I haven't heard anyone talk of it," Smith said.

It was nine thirty in the morning when they finished. Talbot wanted to get in touch with Valerie. He could use the story as an excuse, but he hoped she would meet him for at least coffee. He dialed her number. She answered on the first ring.

"Hello. This is Valerie."

"Valerie, this is Bruce. I have more information on the baby case. Are you available to meet me tonight?"

"Can you give me thirty minutes?"

"Absolutely. Where would you like to meet?"

"Have you eaten?"

"No. I am starving," Talbot said.

"I have leftovers I'm bringing home from my boyfriend's. How about I meet you at my dad's place in thirty minutes? Jon made a great lamb stew. I will share it with you."

"That sounds excellent. Now your dad lives on County Road East, right?"

"No. He lives on Sandusky Pike Road. It runs parallel to County Road East. The number is 32567. It is the one with the big, red barn behind the blue-sided house. The gas light is on at the barn. You can see it for miles away. It is the only large farm on the left side of the road."

"Got it. See you in thirty minutes."

Talbot was disappointed. He was hoping for a chance with Valerie.

CHAPTER 35

Valerie finished her story in time to get it in Monday's morning paper. Talbot gave her permission to write the connection between the other case and Kala's disappearance. Talbot left last night, promising her first dibs on the info. Valerie anticipated that Shelly would be well pleased. The baby story was allowing Valerie to keep her salary for the time being. She used the money at first to pay her parents' bills, but they were caught up. She was saving the money. The time was perfect to be investing. With Ford shares down to .50 a share and others at an all-time low, she hoped that someday the money would grow, but rebuilding her relationship with her father was the first priority. He was doing better. He could walk with a walker. They were getting ready to release him from the nursing home soon.

Valerie felt fresh. She wanted to give the house a good cleaning from top to bottom before her dad came home. She ordered decora-

tions to be put up for his arrival. They would be there next week. She washed walls and floors, making sure every inch was clean.

At noon, Shelly called.

"Valerie, you have outdone yourself. My boss wants to know how you have been able to get the inside track. He is impressed."

"It must be a God thing. It comes right to me. Did he ever say if I could do the syndicated column?"

"He said you could, but he is working on the pay schedule. You won't be working for the *Dispatch* once that happens. So I am not pushing it yet. As long as this story is alive, you should stick with it. The syndicated column is a commission deal. You might not make the same money you do now."

"Shelly, I don't mind. It will give me freedom. This is working for now doing the story on Kala, but what happens when the story is closed?" Valerie asked.

"I hear you," Shelly said.

"What did Bob say about the church story?"

"He loved it. It has brought in all kinds of e-mails and calls. Most don't believe it could have happened like that. To each their own, I always say. Have you turned your computer on today?"

"Not yet. I'm cleaning the house. I wanted to be surprised later."

"I think you will be. You are building a reputation of telling only truth. That is causing an uproar with some. I'll bet your e-mail is loaded this morning with responses to your last two articles. That was excellent work, by the way," Shelly said.

"I appreciate the compliment."

"Valerie, I am going to be leaving for a two-week vacation. You will be dealing with Bob directly while I'm gone. I will be leaving on Friday this week. Promise you'll let things wait until I come back. Don't push him on the syndicated column. I can get you more money. You need to trust me on this one. I know things you don't. I will tell you when the time is right."

"Okay, Shelly. Where are you going?"

"A second honeymoon. My husband surprised me with tickets to Hawaii last week."

"I am so happy for you. You deserve it."

"Thank you. Most of your coworkers are jealous."

"That figures. They wouldn't know how to be kind to a spouse if they had to," Valerie said seriously.

"Maybe you are right. I was hurt by some of the comments they made. I think I should let it all go."

"I would. They couldn't have a long-term relationship if they wanted to," Valerie said.

"I am glad I called you today. You cheered me up. I have to deal with other employees, so I got to run. Thanks for the great work. You are a great employee."

"Bye, Shelly. Thank you."

She turned the computer on to see what the readers had to say. She had two hot stories in this edition. She found an e-mail from Bob, her boss's boss. She opened it. It had a contract attached. He was offering her the syndicated column at a $1,000 a printed entry. That seemed like great pay. She would be losing her insurance, 401K, and vacation package. She would no longer be an employee but an independent contractor. *Why had Shelly told her to do nothing? She would need to talk to her before she left.*

She started to blow it off. *No. Now was the time to call Shelly.*

She dialed the number. "Shelly, Valerie. I got the contract from Bob. He is offering me a thousand dollars per column."

"I know, but you can get expenses and more if you wait. Trust me. The bigger offer on the table is much greater than that. Bob is holding out on you, thinking he can keep part of the cut. I didn't want to tell you that. I don't want you having a problem while I am gone. Just tell Bob you are thinking about the offer. Let me call you back." Shelly hung up.

Maybe I should really think about it. Expenses could get pretty steep working on stories. I would no longer have thirty days of vacation or sick days or be paid to be a juror, I would only be paid to work on what they chose to print. That could be one out of four or five stories. I would no longer be given leads to write about. Shelly was right. I need to wait.

CHAPTER 36

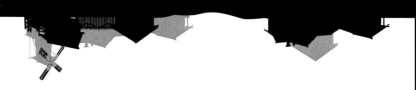

Jacob had been home a week. He was moving around quite well using a cane. That day of praying driving home from up north did amazing things. Valerie was much more humble about life. She quit her job at the Dispatch. She felt it was like a drinking problem to her; she was addicted to the drama. It was a high to work on a case and get down to the real facts. She still had the offer to accept or decline on the syndicated column. Shelly had told her to wait for a better offer.

"Dad, let's replace the kitchen and bath," Valerie said, handing him a cup of coffee.

"Your mom and I were planning on doing that next spring. I have twenty thousand dollars set aside for it."

"That should work out well with the bad economy."

"Did you pick a date for us to take that trip to Florida?" Jacob asked.

"I'm thinking February twenty-fourth."

"That sounds good."

"Dad, I'm meeting Jon for lunch. I have your food in the fridge. You can just warm it up when you are ready."

"Enjoy. Tell Jon I said hello."

Jon said he had something important to talk to her about. She didn't know what it could be, but the suspense was killing her. He had asked her to come to his place. That in itself was not normal. She arrived, and a catering truck was sitting in the driveway.

Jon ran to greet her before she could make it to the door. "I took the rest of the day off. I have something I want to pass by you."

"You're not cooking today?"

"No. I hired a past patient of mine to bring food in. Their food is excellent, better than mine."

"Can't be."

"You'll have to taste it and see." Jon took her by the hand and led her to the dining room. "Thank you," Jon said, as he handed the man an envelope with the pay for the food. "Sit down, my love." He pulled the chair back for her and then pushed it in for her.

"What has you all excited? I have never seen you like this," Valerie asked.

"I am going to start a practice. I want you to be my office manager and run the place. Valerie, I am not asking for your hand today, but I will be in the future. I want to spend the rest of my life with you. A private practice here will be less stressful than the hospital. We have no doctors outside of the hospital for twenty-five miles. What do you think?"

"Well, it does mean I can spend more time with you. I am happy when I spend time with you. I think it is great. Have you found a building yet?"

"I want to take you and show you one I found. I haven't signed the lease yet. It is three miles from here. I will be practicing three days a week. To start with, I will work at the hospital two days a week. As the practice takes off, I will leave the hospital. The hospital has agreed to give me benefits for two years. I never took my vacation time, so for the first six months, I will be paid the same. I found a bank in Marion to give me a loan to start the business."

"Is six months enough time to build the business?"

"Maybe not, but I wasn't expecting them to give me anything or offer me the two days a week. I have saved a lot of money the past several years. My house is paid for, and so are my cars. I don't need much money to live on."

"Did you need the loan from the bank?"

"Not really, but it made financial sense to keep the personal and business money separate. My dad offered to back me, and I declined. I want to do this on my own."

"When do you plan to get started?"

"I am going to open January second if I find a building to rent," Jon said.

"I am speechless. You have been working on this for a long time."

"Since I met you. When you came here and took the risk of leaving your comfort zone, it gave me courage to do what I really wanted to," Jon said. "Now I didn't know that you would be a part of it with me."

"I gave you courage?"

"Yes, my dear, you sure did. I saw you blossom into a beautiful flower once you became happy with the changes. You came here all uptight and not real happy. Now, I see that less stress and being home have done you well. I never wanted to follow in my dad's footsteps. I wanted to be a doctor helping those who needed it the most. If I wanted to chase money, I would have left my community, but I don't care about the money. I want to help people in need," Jon said proudly.

"I am in it with you. I have been saving my money. My dad reimbursed me for what I laid out for their bills. I was going to buy some stocks with it. I too have everything paid for."

"Good girl. At least I know how to pick a good one."

"Don't you mean I know how to pick a good one?" Valerie teased.

"I am very happy. I am sorry it was the accident and your mother's death that brought us together. I am falling deeply in love with you."

"Me too. No one holds a candle to you. I feel safe when I am with you. You also bring great joy to me."

"I am glad you finally told me."

"Why didn't you tell me how you felt about me before now?"

"I wanted you to be sure what you wanted. You had many opportunities for good men. Being married to a doctor has its pitfalls."

"I will take my chances. As long as I know you love me, I can make it though the hard times," Valerie said.

"Let us eat and we can go check that building out. I want you to be perfectly honest with me. If it doesn't look so good, we can get another one. The rent is cheap and it is the right size to start with."

"Tell me more about it," Valerie said as he dished the food from the aluminum pan onto her plate.

"It is twelve hundred square feet, and rent is five hundred and fifty dollars a month. The rent includes the water bill. This building doesn't have triple net, which is a big savings. Three tenants share the building: an insurance company and a dentist, and the other is the one we are looking at."

"I know that building. My dentist is in that building. It is clean and nice. Not exactly new, but for the money, it is a good value. I am excited. I would never think I would end up working for a doctor in a rural community."

"I never thought I would fall in love with a big-time journalist who would quit to be with me," Jon said.

"I still have the opportunity to do the syndicated column," Valerie said, looking for input.

"That is up to you. Don't do it for the money. Do it because it makes you happy. If we live life for that reason, we will make money as a byproduct."

"You are right. I read a book on management that said people who tried to go after making a million dollars never did. It was those who followed their dream who became the millionaires."

"That is my point. We will always have enough to meet our needs, but going after the big bucks might not make for a great marriage. I care more about us than money."

"Good. That is what my dad did too. I want that kind of relationship. I never thought my dad made much as a farmer. I found out that he made choices to do a second business to let my mom stay at home. He did well with the second business. Did I tell you dad is selling the farm?"

"No, you didn't. How do you feel about it?" Jon asked.

"It was his decision. It does release the pressure hiring help. I am thankful he did it. The farm wasn't making that much money for the trouble."

"Is he having any problems collecting his checks from the insurance company?"

"It was a pain to get it going. They wanted copies of his tax forms. They asked for all kinds of signatures."

"I knew that. I had to give a copy of the medical records twice. I am glad it got straightened out. So how have you been feeling?"

"I still miss Mom, I am working through all the emotions neglecting her brought. Having Dad home makes me more aware of her death. He talks a lot about her. We planned a trip to Florida I won from the *Dispatch* this morning. That brought him some real delight. We are going this February. I booked the trip for the middle of the month."

"That is a good time to go. Weather is terrible here, and Florida is pretty nice by then. I will miss you while you are gone," Jon said.

"We have trips we can take over the course of our lifetime."

"You bet, and we will. What kind of things do you like to do?"

"I like action, like skiing, water sports, hiking, and biking. I am not one to lay on the beach all day. That is too exhausting. I like to explore new places, and I love nature," Valerie said.

"What kind of weather do you prefer?"

"I like all kinds. When I was at college, we went to Colorado to go skiing. That was a blast. It was cold, but we dressed for it. After I graduated, a group went to Cancun for four days. I haven't taken too many trips other than that. I was too busy working. That all worked out now. I took my vacation recently. Had I not used it before I left, I wouldn't have been paid for it," Valerie said.

"Once you finish that perch, we can go," Jon said, as he watched her take a bite.

The caterer had brought in French-style green beans with garlic and almonds and coleslaw with corn muffins. The meal had been tasty.

"I have had enough to eat. I am ready now."

"Whatever you say," Jon teased.

He gathered up the dishes and placed them in the sink. He placed the leftovers back in the dishes and covered them with the cardboard lids. Valerie came in behind him and rinsed the plates and silverware off quickly and placing them in the dishwasher.

The office was small but clean. The landlord had it freshly painted white. It wasn't exactly what Valerie would have chosen, but it would be easy to resolve. There were three rooms and a bathroom besides the entry room, which would work out well as a waiting room. He could easily have two exam rooms and an office. None of the rooms were very large, but they would do. It was large enough to put an exam table and chair and cabinet in each room. The office would need to have a partition built and a desk and filing cabinets. The waiting area could fit three or four chairs and an end table. It would work.

"What do you think?" Jon asked.

"For the area, I think it will work great. Have you looked at the lease yet?"

"No. I am to get a copy after I call him back. I'll hire an attorney to look it over and get it back to me next week. So shall we go for it?"

"Sure."

Jon took the key back to the tenant he had gotten the key from. Valerie waited by the door for him.

"Have you thought about what you will charge?" Valerie asked.

"I am going to call around the areas like this, unless you want to do that for me. I have an appointment with the insurance company for malpractice. I was told it is seventy percent cheaper here than in the city."

"Is that because they get sued a lot less here?"

"I guess so," Jon said. "People in the country just don't think like that. No one here is looking for a handout like in the city."

"There is too much of that, I am afraid. Things needs to change."

"In time, they will. As America gets poorer, so will the welfare system," Jon said.

"Do you see much government help at the hospital?"

"Not like my friends see in the bigger cities. We see some, but not much. That helps keep our rates down too," Jon said.

"I don't know. My dad's medical bills were pretty high to me."

"Thirty percent less than a big city."

"Really?" Valerie asked.

"I bet so," Jon said. He squeezed her hand to let her know how much he loved her.

"I am just glad the car insurance paid the entire bill."

"Valerie, be glad your dad made it through. I have seen many in bad accidents like him who die. Your dad had a will to live."

"What about my mom? She died. Did that make her weak?" Valerie asked.

"The way the car hit your parent's car, your mom didn't have a chance. She died pretty quickly. I was at the hospital when she got there. There is no evidence she lived past the impact."

"Well, I am glad she didn't suffer."

"She was a mess. The doorframe penetrated her heart. She had glass embedded in her face and body. Did you ever go clean the car out?"

"I had the man at the storage yard give me the stuff. I couldn't look at it. They offered to do that, and I said yes. I heard the car has been sold and is now gone from the area."

"That happens to many cars in accidents. The insurance company gets more for a scrap car than fixing some. The junkyards piece them out, getting huge money for the parts. Have you bought another car to replace the one in the accident?"

"No. Dad wants to wait. With the economy taking a turn for the worse, he thinks he might get a better deal waiting. He is not sure what he wants now. He can't drive yet anyway. His leg is too stiff to move quickly from gas to brake."

"I am proud of how well you have taken care of him. He is a lucky father."

"I am a lucky daughter to have him survive. I could not face losing them both. Getting to know Dad has been wonderful. He is a kind and gentle man. He loved my mother dearly. Did I tell you about the letters I found?"

"From your dad to your mom?" Jon asked.

"Yes. Some were love poems and cards. It made it very clear to me how much he loved her. He still misses her. I can hear him cry at night sometimes."

"That is sweet."

"That is the kind of man I want to marry, which is what I see in you. I see the kindness and gentleness of my dad. You might be a doctor, but you show so much compassion to everyone. That is important to me."

"I am glad that is what you see and not my title. Being a doctor is a big responsibility. It is not about show but healing lives one life at a time," Jon said.

"You know, Jon, you need to come up with a motto for your new office. That statement would go well as a motto."

"We'll have to think about that and see if anything fits any better than that."

"I have gone to church with a couple who own a big print business in Columbus. Carmen worked for them until they fired her."

"She probably deserved it," Jon said.

"Who knows? I don't know what happened. I do know this couple does good work at fair prices. We used them at the *Dispatch* a few times. They were quick on top of being good."

"Can they do layouts for me? I am not an artist. I need someone to give me the idea, unless you can do it."

"I can work on it. I am not that good. I can get a basic idea that they can run with," Valerie said. She quietly thought about the subject. "Jon, what are your two favorite colors?"

"Blue and yellow," he said.

"That could work. I was thinking if you picked colors to represent your business and used them through the business, that would be good. I know it is country folk and they don't really care, but why not make it nice? It won't cost much more."

"Valerie, I am going to let you decide on those things. That is what an office manager does. I see the patients." He winked at her.

She liked the feel of working with Jon. He would be easy to please.

CHAPTER 37

"This is agent Talbot," Talbot said, as he took a call on his cell phone.

"Talbot, I need you to go to precinct twelve B and pick up Damian. The number is 614-555-1254. Detective Cabot is handling the case. Get a copy of the report. Fly him back to corporate. The reservation's made. Tickets are at the counter. Any questions?" Quad asked.

"How did we find him?"

"The locals picked him up for indecent exposure. I am not sure how much of a help he will be. He has some mental issues," Quad said.

"Am I safe?"

"I would guess you are, but be careful. Call me when you get in. I will send a car to pick you up. Good luck," Quad said before hanging up.

Damian had stuck around the Columbus area. Talbot called and got the address and headed straight there. It was about thirty minutes from where he was. He had gone shopping in Columbus while waiting for his next command. Talbot found the police station without any problems. Detective Cabot had left the building but left instructions and the file for him to take with him. A Ms. Henderson helped him secure Damian and make sure all the documents were in order for the transfer. Talbot handcuffed him to his right arm. The disadvantage was that it was a regular car, not a police car. He hoped for the best. He had Damian sit in the passenger seat, which meant he had a left hand to drive with.

"So, Damian, what made you stick around? I figured you would have taken off by now."

Damian was silent.

Talbot asked a few more questions only to get the same response. He drove to the airport the rest of the way in silence. Damian looked pretty rough. He hadn't showered or shaved in days. He was thinner than Talbot remembered. His face didn't have good color. His eyes looked empty. The flight went off without any delays. Upon landing, Talbot called the boss to have a car transport them to the local office. He figured Damian hadn't eaten in a while, but he could not get him to answer him. They had a specialist who could handle it. It wasn't what Talbot was asked to do. At 7:20 p.m., they arrived at the local office. Quad had Peters there as well as a psychologist to talk to Damian.

"Thank you, Talbot. I am going to give you the night off. You have done a fine job. I doubt we get anywhere with Damian right away from talking to the detective. Be back here at nine tomorrow. I will have you do some of the questioning then. Is that good for you?" Quad asked.

"Well yes, sir, that works great for me. Good night."

Talbot turned around and went to his own SUV. He hadn't expected the night off. Talbot called Valerie on his quick drive home.

"Valerie, Damian is safe and sound. They picked him up in Columbus today."

"What for?" Valerie asked.

"He had no clothes on. I picked him up. He wouldn't talk to me. I hope they have better luck with him than I did."

"What can they do?"

"I don't really know. That is their problem."

"I made the decision to leave the *Dispatch*. I accepted a job as office manager for a local doctor. Right now, it gives me time to spend with my dad and make some money."

"I am very happy for you. You were an excellent journalist. I am sure you will be just as good at whatever you choose to do. So I take it things did pan out for you and the doctor?"

"They did."

"I am really happy for you. I am going to go shower. It has been a very long day."

"Thanks for calling, Bruce. I will call Elaine and let her know about Damian."

"Thank you."

Talbot entered his condo and dumped everything at the door. He sat down on the white leather couch. Things had not turned out at all the way he had expected them to. He thought Damian had taken Kala for money reasons. From the turn of events, that probably wasn't accurate. He was clueless what they do with cases like that. Maybe that was why they sent him home. He would ask when it was all over with and find out what the bottom line was. Tonight, he was at peace. Kala had been found and returned to her mother. Elaine was safe now. He wished he had told Valerie he would make the call, but he knew Valerie would be the most sensitive to Elaine. He fell asleep on the couch. At one thirty, he woke up and went to his bed.

CHAPTER 38

"Elaine, this is Valerie. The struggle's over. Damian was arrested in Columbus today and flown to Oregon, I think. You can relax. The details will be given to you as they find them. I just wanted to call and tell you."

"Do you know any more about it?" Elaine paced the floor, letting out a sigh of relief.

"He was arrested for indecent exposure. They think something is wrong mentally. That is all I know. How are you doing through all this?"

"Better but not real good. Kala has been sick since she got home. I can't get her digestive tract to settle down. I am very stressed. I am facing the truth now. That is the good part," Elaine said.

"Elaine, after coming through some pretty dark days myself, I can tell you that God is the source of all life. Read Psalms. It will

give you a boost. I have to go for now. I am working on a new project. I will call you soon."

"Valerie, I couldn't have done it without you. Thank you."

"I will send you my bill," Valerie teased.

"That would be fine. Good night," Elaine said.

"Jon, do you mind if we take some time and pray for Elaine and Kala? Kala has intestinal issues since she was returned home," Valerie said.

"Of course not." Jon set the lease that he was reading down. "Father, you know all things. You created all things. It is in you and through you that all things exist. Valerie and I come to your throne to ask for you to heal Elaine from this trauma. Show yourself worthy to her in her dark hour. Allow her to see you for who you are, not for the way the enemy wants to portray the situation. Allow her to see the safety you allowed for her and Kala. Bring healing to Kala's intestinal tract. Wash away all the pain that has come through this, but bring fruit that can only come from you. Father, I also ask that you would lead and guide our steps as we prepare to move out to minister to those in need. Father, if this is not from you, then shut the doors. If opening the practice is from you, then meet each need. Allow humility to be foremost in our lives and our love for you be far surpassing the desires to do this. Protect your will for our life. Let us to not out step your will. Keep us pure and holy as we learn who each other are. Block us from moving into temptation in any way. Let greed not take us over. Give us compassion for the lost. Use this as a springboard for more to come to be used for you. All these things we ask in the name of Jesus."

"Oh, God, you have become so real to me through this hard time. I now see the depth of love you have for me. I want to pass that love on to the world one by one. As I see people hurt like Elaine, I want to comfort them with your love. I want to pass on the arms you used to bring me to this place today. As you wrapped me in your love and wiped the tears away, wipe away the tears Elaine has. Bring her joy for her sorrow. Replace light with what she has known to be dark in this hour. Open heaven's gate for her to a new place of understanding of you. Let her have a desire to give back as you gave to her. Put a spirit of forgiveness in her for the things that happened so she will be released to go on to the next phase of life. I also ask that in the right timing, you bring her godly friends to come around her and hold her arms up. We praise you, Jesus, for who you are and for the ways you love us; not just a surface love but deep enough to grow us into your character. I ask that your character would be manifested in all of us in these times of change, that we all would seek you first and not put what we think to be right in the first place but we would wait upon you. Even in this relationship with Jon, let me wait for you and your timing. Let me look to you, not down as you bring forth your will. Even in times of money not flowing, let us not grumble and complain but seek your face. Let us grow from the past but not live in it. As Jon already prayed, guide each step we make. Your Word says that you order the steps of the righteous. Allow us to be made righteous so our steps will always be ordered by you. Whatever we lack, Lord, fill us. What is not of you remove. Allow us to say no to sin and temptation quickly. Allow our ears to hear what your Spirit is saying, not what man is saying. Let us get the godly council we need daily from you. Let us not let the manna mold by not coming to you early in the day for your Word. Let us not put pressures of things that need to get done replace our time with you. Open our ears to hear. Let us sit and wait for you to speak to us. In Jesus's name," Valerie prayed. "Father, we seal this prayer. We thank you that from glory to glory you are changing us. Amen."

Jon opened his eyes and saw that Valerie had a glow about her. She looked angelic. He hated to break the mood to get into paperwork, so he didn't. He came closer to her and just held her.

After a few minutes, Valerie moved. "We should get back to business. We still have to finish the patient forms."

They had several models to choose from. Jon decided that he would charge according to income. He would not refuse treatment based on income. If he had to, he would barter with the farmers. It wouldn't lead to having a high income, but it would lead to happiness and a peaceful life. As long as Valerie was his helper and on the same page, they would make it. Valerie had chosen to do the syndicated column so they could have income coming in. She would work for Jon but not take pay. They both felt good about the decision. Many of the stories would come from the experiences and things seen at the doctor's office. It was a win-win situation.

CHAPTER 39

It was a bright, beautiful day on the farm. Jacob awakened early. His partner in the dairy business wanted to buy him out. He thought and thought about it and accepted the offer. He never saw Valerie so happy in all her life. He didn't need the house or the dairy business to tie him down. He could bank the money and travel. He would do it one step at a time. He knew that the man who bought the farm wanted the house too. In time, he would sell it. He would wait for Valerie to marry and get settled to drop that bomb. He would tell Valerie his decision. He planned on giving her money from the sale. She had earned it. She had given up her life to make sure he was taken care of. Now he was going to return the favor. Jacob was sitting in the rocking chair that his wife had loved so much when Valerie came walking down the steps.

"Good morning, sunshine. Did you get enough sleep?" Jacob asked.

"I did. Jon and I worked late into the night on the paperwork to get the practice set up. We read through the lease and created documents for the patients when they first come. We put together a mission statement and a motto. I designed a layout to take to the printer today," Valerie said.

"Well, honey, you sure look happy. That brings me great joy. I was hoping we could talk for a bit this morning."

"Sure, Dad. What is on your mind?"

"Sit down. Valerie, I called my partner and told him that I would sell my shares in the dairy this morning."

"Okay, Dad. If that is what you want. What do you plan to do?"

"Retire early and travel a little," Jacob said, watching her reaction closely.

"Are you going to travel by yourself?"

"Yes. At first. I am sure I will meet nice people along the way. I am going to give you some of the money from the sale of the dairy. It is to repay you for what you lost taking care of me."

"Dad, I didn't lose anything. You paid me back for what I paid on your bills already."

"Honey, you lost the place you were going to buy and you had to lose some income along the way. I want to do this. I have more than enough with the disability income and what I am going to keep from the sale of the business. Please let me do this. It will help you while you are in transition."

"Well, okay, Dad. If that is what you really want. I didn't tell you, but I am going to be working with Jon at the doctor's office for free. I accepted the contract with the syndicated column."

"I expected you would. I also think in time you and Jon will marry. I can funnel money through the sale of the business directly to you right now with tax breaks for both of us. If I wait until I die, it will cost you more. This is good for both of us."

"Dad, what are you going to do with the house, sell it?"

"In time, yes. I was going to wait until you and Jon get settled to sell it," Jacob said.

"Okay."

"That is it. I expected you to give me a hard time," Jacob said.

"Dad, I knew it was coming. The house holds too many memories for you to stay here. It was the only house you and Mom ever lived in. I really do understand why you want to leave and move on to a new place in your life. I might do the same thing. I think it is good for you. I am in full support of your decision. Dad, I might be able to find a place to rent around the area if you want to leave quicker."

"No. I will wait for your life to come together before I go."

"Dad, I will miss you if you leave. You have taught me so much in the last few months."

"Honey, it was God who taught you. I just loved you," Jacob said with tears rolling down his face.

"Dad, I don't know how I missed that when I was young. I never knew how much you loved me," Valerie said.

"I had a hard time expressing my feelings. I let your mom handle those kind of things. I don't have her to coddle me anymore," Jacob said as he grabbed Valerie and took her into a long hug. "Honey, the way you look at Jon is the same way your mom looked at me. I think Jon is similar to me. He might not know how to express how he feels, but I can tell he is deeply in love with you."

"I know, Dad. I am finding that out. I think he knew from the beginning that I was to be his wife, but he needed to wait for God to change me. Jon is a patient and loving man. I am very grateful that God placed him in my life. I will never be over Mom being gone, but in a way, Jon has replaced that void in me. I know I am loved and cherished in a deep way. I think it was through Jon's love that I really saw how much God loved me. God let me do my thing until I got to the end of my rope. He then reeled me in and cleaned me up. Jon never pushed me. He waited for me to see it myself. He is a true gentleman," Valerie said.

"Valerie, I watched him take care of me in the hospital. He is a true and genuine great man of God. He is silent about his beliefs, but it shows in the way he lives his life. When I was in a coma, he prayed each day over me. When I woke up, he stopped. We never talked about it, but I am sure it was his prayers that got me back on my feet," Jacob said.

"He prayed over you?"

"He did, and it worked. He imparted faith for me to recover while I was out of it. My spirit grew. He spoke of my recovery daily. I have faint memories, but they are still there."

"I didn't know any of that. Wow!"

"He has my trust. I know he would never hurt my little girl," Jacob said.

Tears rolled down Valerie's face as she thought of the love Jon poured into her dad. *Maybe dad was right and it was Jon who was used to bring about all the change in both their lives. If God could use him to change their lives, he could do it for the entire community. The practice was just the start. I know in my heart that we will be a part of starting an organic church in the area. God is preparing the ground and laying the foundation now.*

"Dad, I am going to make you breakfast and get going. I have to file paperwork for the practice and drop off the signed lease. I am headed to Columbus. Is there anything you want me to do for you while I am there or do you want to go too?" Valerie asked as she walked toward the kitchen.

"No, honey. You go ahead. I have some things I need to do here too. I will be fine. Thank you for asking."

Jacob watched her pull the pans out.

She grabbed bread and whisked some milk in with eggs to make French toast. She learned all that from her mom. Through Valerie, she would live on.

"Your cooking is getting as good as your mom's," Jacob commented.

"I guess it takes practice. I want to know how to cook before I get married. I don't want to disappoint Jon in any way."

"I doubt you will. You're a good kid," Jacob teased her.

"I am not a kid anymore. I'm about to become a partner in a medical practice. Can you believe it, Dad?"

"You are going to be his partner?"

"Yes a thirty-five percent partner. He said it would pay me in the long run since he might not have any money for a while. We made the choice to treat patients even on a low income. We won't turn anyone away."

"Are you investing anything upfront?"

"Besides my time, no. He got a loan from a bank. I think he said it was PNC. He will sign the loan in three days. He wants to keep personal money separate from business money. He should be okay, Dad. He has everything paid off. So it is not a big deal if he doesn't bring a lot in quickly. The rent is cheap, and he will be still working a couple days at Mercy for a while," Valerie said.

"Have you talked about money if you get married?"

"No. We are just dating right now, Dad. We don't want to rush anything too fast. I don't want to assume anything. I think working with him will help me to get to know him better faster. I will see everything: how he treats people, his books, his good days and bad. We agreed to put the business first for now. After six months, we will look at where we want to go. So that will be about June. It will take time to plan a wedding."

"You have a level head. I am glad to hear that. I know things will work out in time."

"Me too, Dad. We all know it will. The more I know about him now and vice versa, the easier the adjustment will be when we marry. I think the way it is working out is perfect."

"Me too, honey. I am so proud of you. You let go of what held you back, and now you are really happy," Jacob said.

"That is true. Had Mom not died and you been in the hospital, none of this would have happened. Had I made the choice to stay at the paper, I wouldn't be here now. Jon really does make me happy. I never told you about the guy I was dating in Columbus. I threw a big party for his thirtieth birthday. That was the night I got the call on the accident. I lost him that night to my girlfriend.

The two started something that night that ended our relationships. That really hurt me at the beginning. God asked me to offer it up as a living sacrifice, and I did. When I let it go, then God was able to open my eyes to see what he had for me. I have found that God's plan trumps ours."

"You are becoming a wise woman. Your mother would be very proud of you," Jacob said.

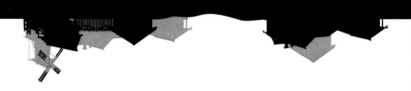

CHAPTER 40

Valerie dropped the signed lease off to the landlord. She was very nice, a fiftyish Jewish woman, Leila. Jon said that paying the rent was Valerie's job. He wanted her to meet Leila and ask whatever questions were necessary to get the ball rolling. Valerie headed to the print shop. She made an appointment with the couple who owned it. Kit and Irene Joseph were standing at the door, facing Valerie as she walked in. They were talking to a woman. Oh my. It is Carmen.

"Hi, Carmen," Valerie said.

"I was just leaving. I'll call you guys later. Bye," Carmen said to Kit and Irene.

"I didn't mean to chase her off," Valerie said.

"She came to ask for her job back," Kit said.

"Oh," Valerie responded.

"Let's go in the office. We won't be disturbed there. We appreciate the opportunity to earn your business," Irene said.

"I want to use someone I trust. It is a ride, but I have other things I need to handle here anyway. Here is what I put together. Do you think you can do anything with it?" Valerie open the portfolio revealing the inside contents.

"I love it!" Kit said.

"You're a natural," Irene said.

"Thank you. God gave it to me as I slept one night. He's been doing that a lot. He gives me the answer, sometimes before the question comes up. It is really cool," Valerie said.

"Sounds like you have done a lot of growing since you left," Irene said.

"I have. Things were wild at first, but now I see that God was always in control from the beginning. I am learning how to surrender my will to him. So far so good. He hasn't asked me to do anything radical yet."

"I would say that he did. You quit your job at the *Dispatch* and will be walking on faith. You forgave a woman who backstabbed you," Irene said.

"That is true. I wish Carmen well. She actually did me a favor. It was hard to see at the beginning. Now I see that it was right on track. I had to trust God, not man, for my needs to be met," Valerie stated.

"That is a big lesson I need to learn," Kit said.

"I haven't gotten there yet," Irene said.

They worked out a deal for five thousand fliers, business cards, printed receipts, and the customer disclosure statements. They agreed to give her a 25 percent discount for being a church member.

Valerie was off to see Elaine. She called on the way. Elaine said the FBI had called and she would fill her in when she got there. Worthington wasn't that far from the print shop. She had gotten on the expressway and lost track of time when she saw the exit where she needed to get off. Valerie was feeling the presence of God. She felt that God had used her to draw Kit and Irene into something deeper. The residue was still lingering in the air. It was a feeling that Valerie liked.

Her GPS led her to the door of Elaine's parents. She found two extra cars in the street. She wondered who was there. She would find out soon. Elaine answered the door. Bruce Talbot was sitting on the couch with a cup of coffee. He stood up and walked toward Valerie, shaking her hand.

"Good to see you again," Bruce said.

"You too," Valerie said.

"Come in and have a seat. Mom is in the kitchen, making us a snack. Bruce was giving me the details of the situation with Damian," Elaine said.

"Do you mind me being here?" Valerie asked.

"No," both said in unison.

"I was telling her we did a complete evaluation on Damian. We found that he has some malnutrition issues that are adding to the problem, but we found him to be schizophrenic. We have him on Haldol. We don't expect an immediate recovery but hope that little by little, he comes back around," Bruce said.

"So that is why he did all this?" Valerie asked.

"Yes."

"What about the local men?" Valerie asked.

"We have arrested them. They did it for the money. They took Kala and met Damian's dad, who might have mental issues as well. We have not found Pete, Damian's dad, or the stolen money. We figured he would come back and get Damian, but he didn't. We think he made it out of the country."

"Bruce, you know I don't work for the paper anymore. I won't be writing the story, per se," Valerie said.

"It is a real shame. You did such an awesome job with it. You were fair to all sides," Talbot said.

"So what will they do with Damian? He won't do jail time, will he?" Valerie asked.

"We will be bringing him back to Ohio in a month. Ohio, however, has no long-term facilities to get mental help. We will be placing him in a group home for six months, assigning him a case manager who will make all the arrangements," Talbot said.

"What about Kala?"

"He won't have unprotected visitation. An adult will be with her at all times. The FBI will not be prosecuting him on any charges. We won't be the ones to make some of those decisions. It will be processed more than likely through the courts."

"What can Elaine do in the meantime?"

"She can file for social security for Kala. Damian is not able to support his child at this point," Talbot said.

"I mean what can she do legally?"

"She made the choice to finalize the divorce. The judge will determine the rest," Talbot said.

"Elaine, are you okay with all this?" Valerie asked.

"It sure explains his behavior over the last few years. He made me feel like I was losing it, not him," Elaine said.

"If you need my help, call me," Valerie said.

"You have been a great friend. My parents said they would help me get through this legally. I want to get out and enjoy the daisies though," Elaine said.

"You got it," Valerie said.

She knew that it would all work out. Elaine felt safe now.